MAY   2002

Strawman's Hammock

ALSO BY DARRYL WIMBERLEY

Dead Man's Bay

A Rock and a Hard Place

Strawman's Hammock

DARRYL WIMBERLEY

Thomas Dunne Books
St. Martin's Minotaur
☏ New York

THOMAS DUNNE BOOKS.
An imprint of St. Martin's Press.

www.minotaurbooks.com

Library of Congress Cataloging-in-Publication Data

Wimberley, Darryl.
    Strawman's hammock / Darryl Wimberley.—1st ed.
        p.   cm.
    ISBN 0-312-27187-5
        1. Police—Florida—Fiction.   2. Political campaigns—
Fiction.   3. Florida—Fiction.   I. Title.

PS3573.I47844 S77   2001
813'.54—dc21

                                                     2001041817

First Edition: November 2001

10 9 8 7 6 5 4 3 2 1

Acknowledgments

It is a pleasure to be able to thank some of the many folks who helped me write this book. Russell Mobley is an unselfish source for fact and procedure, as are the ladies and gentlemen at the Live Oak office for the Florida Department of Law Enforcement. Thanks also go to Lieutenant Buddy Williams of Live Oak's municipal force and to Sheriff Dwayne Walker from Lafayette County. A little further down the road I found great support from Dr. Michael Warren and Dr. Anthony Falsetti at the University of Florida's Human Identification Lab. Thanks go, once again, to my classmates Rowdy and No-Neck and, with love and affection, to my wife, Doris, daughter, Morgan, and son, Jack.

And thanks, finally and always, to my readers.

Strawman's Hammock

One

Northern Florida. Near the coast, the Gulf side. The first frost of the year bit deeply for those unaccustomed. A leaden sky hung low and bruised, like a boxer's ribs. A pleasant aroma of coffee mingled with the resins of conifers and cypress that arbored the campsite. That, and the sweet smell of blood. The deer, a Virginia whitetail, hung by his hind feet from a pair of four-by posts in front of the shack that constituted the Loyds' camphouse. A pair of tenacula pierced the buck's Achilles tendons to support that weight, jerry-rigged hooks anchored head-high in their wooden frame. A nice six-point rack raked the sand below into unintelligible grafitti. Saul's dreams writ large on the forest floor.

A deep ravine carved up the buck's crotch, through his belly and broken ribs to the throat. The guts were being removed, the source of bacteria and the organs most likely to spoil the meat if inexpertly handled. A five-gallon pickle bucket placed below caught the slippery mess of integument that ran with the deer's disembowelment, a rude catch basin for the blood and leavings that would be buried far from camp both to avoid the recent and unwelcome attention of coyotes imported into the wood and waterlands of northern Florida, and to refuse encouragement to the insects always ready, even in this autumnal chill, to feed.

A compact man in his fifties butchered the deer with a gray Case hunting knife honed with years of sandstone and skinning, and soaked with blood filling his hand. Linton Loyd exuded an unquestioned authority in this setting, holding forth like a surgeon on the correct procedure for skinning wildlife to a bullpen of subordinates hatted in baseball caps. Bring along plenty of fresh water to wash the carcass. Avoid puncturing the bladder. Protect the meat. Linton liked talking. He liked having folks listen.

Barrett Raines huddled against a bone-cold wind, pulling a frayed billcap tightly onto a broad head, sipping coffee from a porcelain mug chipped so as to abrade his lip with every swig. He was removed from the evisceration of the deer and distant from the surgeon's circle, the only man of any color other than white among the dozen or so who mingled in jeans and jackets and Red Wing boots around the carcass and campfire.

He had not slept well. The Dream, again, had come to inflict what his wife dubbed "the wearies." "Daddy's got the wearies," was all that Laura Anne would say, when the boys, sensing their father's melancholy, and seeing the sap of energy from his otherwise ursine frame, would inquire. She did not want to tell them about The Dream. Neither did their father.

It was always the same. He was returned to childhood in a twilight between memory and nightmare, a boy barely nine years old. The dream would start with some innocent activity, chasing a tire, making a fort. And then for no apparent reason he was running, running, running—

Through the dark mouth of a shotgun shack and into a closet. The door slammed. He was trapped. It was a

2

small closet, filled with laundry. Jeans and gingham and flannel. It was odd, because daytime memories recalled that hollow space as a haven, a retreat from the man outside who, drinking hard, raised his fist against his wife and sons. The flannel was recalled fondly in the light of day.

But not at night. In Barrett's dream the closet was a place folded onto itself, a place where your chest constricted as in cardiac arrest. The closet was not in fact a space at all but a cloying hand pressed velvet and dark over your face and you could not, could not breathe.

He would suck for all he was worth against that press of dark but there would be no air. The nightmare played out in suffocation, Barrett struggling to find breath, terrified, his heart hammering—

Help!

He would try to scream but no sound would come. The only sounds to be heard were outside the closet, in the bedroom. *"Don't, please,"* a woman's voice.

"Don't do it, Randall!"

The slap of leather on an arm. Then perhaps a buckle across bruised flesh. A fist. A woman's scream. He had heard the belt before. Heard the unmistakable reunion of knuckle on bone. But it was not the sounds that evoked The Dream and the suffocation so vividly.

It was the smells.

The most vivid sensation in his nightmare was olfactory. He could smell fear in the dirty clothes tossed onto the floor of the closet. Fear in blue jeans. Terror in flannel. He would fight to find air in a pair of socks and smell his mother. And then—another smell. Smelled before felt or seen. A length of hardwood. Something hard and round. Perfectly lathed and balanced. It came to his hand.

"Fuckin' bitch!"

A sudden, slender line of light as the door began to

3

open, just the merest thread of illumination, the door opening—

That's where it ended, always, and Barrett would wake in his bed choking for air. Sometimes Laura Anne would bring him a paper bag from the kitchen.

"Just pull it tight," she would say. "Breathe in easy. Out slow. Come on, baby. You know what to do."

It was a nightmare that, as most, stopped short of revelation. Once awake, Barrett seldom returned to sleep. He would go to the living room, usually, try to set the fan on the air conditioner to run continuously, some soothing sound to take away the sound of fists and the nightmare smell of flannel and something else, always something else—that stayed in dreams.

Just out of reach.

The Dream had come last night. In his bunk. He had no idea what triggered that midnight horror. Laura Anne was not there, in this camp of hunters, to help him breathe, so he crept from his rude crib like a shamed child and slipped outside. The frosty air helped. It filled his lungs with icy air. And then he waited for dawn to come, which it did. Along with the wearies.

Time to shake off the night, Barrett told himself. Problems enough in daylight.

He glanced to the gallows that held the deer. Linton was bloodied to the elbow in his work, but the lecture, Barrett could see, would finish soon. He sampled his morning java at a remove from Linton Loyd and his cabal of killers, but Barrett knew them well.

Raines had, in fact, known most of the men here since childhood. Most of them were on Linton's private land by invitation. These hunters, unlike Linton, were not in the big money. Rolly Slade, for example, a local mechanic self-sustained for forty years repairing everything from lawn mowers to jet skis, was now facing bankruptcy. "I'm owna sell ever'thing I can," Rolly confided, "and then

4

shut down. Cut my losses." Sharold Lawson was in similar straits, forced to sell his tobacco allotment and dairy. Some even said he was carving up his riverfront property into lots for auction. How would he get by? Lawson shrugged. "Out for hire, I guess. Paper mill in Perry, maybe. Or maybe the prison."

The prison. At a time when companies like Dell and ADM and Motorola were recruiting wage earners from all over the nation, the Mayo Correctional Facility was the employer of choice in Lafayette County. They didn't tell you when they came selling prisons that the term "minimum security" was not a commitment to a permanent status, but a way to counter local opposition to "the facility's" initial construction. A jail's transition from minimum, to medium, to maximum security was not so much a slippery slope as a greased track. Within four years of its construction the prison was harboring violent felons, a change in status made with no compunction to seek approval from the local and law-abiding population. Guards initially employed to secure a population of drunken drivers and petty thieves now risked exposure to shivs, ice picks, and AIDS. All in return for regular wages, health insurance, and the chance at a state pension.

Not every man or woman was driven to such a pass, of course. Take Thurman Shaw, for instance, hanging there on Linton's elbow like a dying calf in a hailstorm. You'd never guess by looking that Thurman had made himself a pile of money standing in courthouses all the way from Cedar Keys to Perry. A hell of a lawyer, a small, fiesty advocate, with a comb of red hair like a rooster.

Barrett would never forget the homicide that put his own brother in Thurman's hands. That case had driven Raines off his beloved Deacon Beach and north to Tallahassee and the Florida Department of Law Enforcement. Barrett didn't see much of Thurman while working in the sunshine state's moss-shaded capitol but a requested transfer to the FDLE's field office in Live Oak had brought Raines closer to the home and family he desperately missed—closer to his wife and boys, closer to the beach, closer to folks like Thurman Shaw. Closer, as well, to Linton Loyd.

Loyd got the deer with a single shot, admirers reported. Just after first light. A hundred yards with iron sights. Right behind the shoulder. Linton slashed the deer's throat, on the spot, opening the carotids for a quick bleed before slinging the kill over his shoulder and then onto the hood of his Cherokee, a trophy to be seen and envied by luckless hunters puncutating the sandy, rutted roads that snaked back to Linton's camp.

The county's game warden had already inspected the deer. Lieutenant Jarold Pearson went on to make his rounds, checking the licenses of the gathered hunters and ensuring that their armory of shotguns and rifles did not exceed the state's five-shell limit. It was not until these neccessary tasks were completed that the warden strolled over to join Barrett at the fire-blacked pot. Jarold was a shade taller than Barrett, but lean as a rail, with a weather-tanned face beneath hair white as salt. His skull was unusually shaped, narrowed savagely at the temples as if pulled at birth with an overeager forceps.

Growing up, Jarold had endured any number of taunts because of his appearance, because of that unnaturally narrowed cranium and those close-set eyes. It didn't help that he grew up in a county and culture where any noted difference was subject to instant ridicule. *Grouper Head*, he was called. *Squash. Fish.* Barrett was ashamed to admit that he had, on one occasion, joined the mob to torment Jarold Pearson.

Barrett and Jarold used to ride the same bus to school every morning. Though Deacon Beach's high school had been integrated in the sixties, Barrett was the only African American boy in his freshman class. The only black kid of his age on the bus. When Barrett first rode the bus he was ostracized in much the same way as was Jarold Pearson. The comments would come behind his back or barely concealed. *Goddamn nigger. Jungle bunny.* Things like that.

It never quite stopped, but by the time Barrett was a senior, a basketball player and headed for valedictory honors in his class, he had earned, at no small price, the acceptance if not the respect of the sons and daughters of the Confederacy. But he never forgot what it was like to hear a slur cast in his direction. The pain in the gut. The sudden anger. And the absolute helplessness to respond. If you punched a kid in the mouth for calling you nigger, *you* were the one who received the most serious punishment. Sticks and stones may break your bones, the teachers chanted it like a mantra. Words can never hurt. But Barrett knew better.

The boys and girls who threw racial javelins at Barrett were the worst sort of cowards. They threw with impunity. They taunted knowing that Bear would be punished if he fought back. So why, oh why, after living through that experience, had Barrett one morning joined the mob to spear the boy with the misshaped skull?

It happened on the bus. Jarold always rode up front. Always had a book in his hand, Barrett recalled. Always the biography of some famous man: Lincoln, Washington, Lindbergh. The biographies were identically covered and stacked together on a pair of shelves in the school's badly stocked library. Jarold read from one every morning on the way to school.

Flounder face.

Roland Reed, a kid with money, already set on law school, threw that jibe as he bounded up the stairs of the bus. A caw of laughter answered Roland's insult. Barrett could remember feeling uncomfortable with that first laughter. But then Roland leaned over—

"What about it, Barrett? You think his mama got laid sideways?"

And he joined in. He could have responded in any number of ways, he the only kid of color on the bus. Barrett could have said, wished a thousand times that he had simply said something like "Knock it off, Roland." Or better, "He's not any uglier than you, white boy."

Any response in Jarold's defense would have been noble and right. But on this singular occasion Barrett joined the mob.

"Naw, she got laid all right," the words came from his mouth. "But when she birthed him she turned to look, took a fright, and rolled over on his head."

Peals of laughter split the bus. Barrett saw Jarold's close-set ears go scarlet.

Then he closed the book.

He turned around in his seat and singled out Barrett Raines with that narrow stare.

"You say somethin' to me?"

Jarold Pearson had replied to insult. That had not happened before. To anyone.

"You heard me," Barrett brazened it out. A thousand times he wished he had taken that chance to apologize.

"Sorry, Jarold, I was being a jerk . . ." "Jarold, I don't know what made me say that . . ."

Some kind of apology. Some acceptance of responsibility.

But he didn't.

"Fish head," Roland taunted again.

Barrett could still remember the unwavering examination of Jarold's tightly squeezed eyes.

A fight was imminent. Everyone knew it. But then the bus driver, searching his wide mirror for the sudden commotion, barked from the front of the bus, "You boys best leave Jarold alone. Less you wanta walk to school."

"Take him, Barrett." Roland nudged Barrett hard in

the ribs. "Hit him once in the nose. I bet his head splits like a pear."

But Barrett's own ears were now flushed with blood. And for the first time he could remember, Barrett was deeply and incontrovertibly ashamed of himself.

"Go pound your pud, Roland." He shrugged off Roland's guiding hand. Fresh laughter echoed in the bus's sheet-metal shell, and Reed retreated in confusion, not used to being the object of derision himself.

Jarold was already back to his book, turning a page, slowly, inside its gray cover. It wasn't too long after that incident that Jarold's father was sent to prison for killing his mother. Barrett made an effort to find Jarold in the hall, to approach him.

"Sorry 'bout your mama," he offered, and received no reply.

Within the year Barrett's own father was killed. Fortunately for Barrett's mother, the sheriff ruled self-defense on the spot. Mama Raines was not even arrested. You might imagine that a bond of sorts would then develop between the two boys. Both Jarold and Barrett, after all, had a parent who died violently, endured abusive fathers, rode the same bus to school. And they both grew to become men who enforced the law. But in twenty years, Barrett probably had not spent twenty minutes in conversation with Jarold Pearson. He still felt bad about that time on the bus.

"Morning, Bear."

Barrett roused himself with a shake.

"Jarold. How's things at FFWCC?"

Jarold offered an embarrassed chuckle in reply. The agency for years known simply as Florida Fish & Game was lumberingly renamed the "Florida Fish and Wildlife Conservation Commission." The warden had a revised seal embossed with the new name pinned neatly to his light tan shirt. That shirt, topped with an olive-green jacket, seemed insubstantial in the morning's chill, but Jarold did not appear uncomfortable. He nodded at the hanging carcass.

"First kill of the season?"

"I believe so," Barrett replied. "This club, anyway."

Jarold opened a pouch on his belt to pull out a knife.

It was a Boy Scout knife. The warden went through a corkscrew and toothpick before settling on an awl.

"I hate these clubs."

The candor took Barrett by surprise.

"Used to," Jarold said, cleaning a cuticle meticulously, "you could buy a shotgun for fifty dollars from a Sears catalog, get yourself some shells, and go anywhere in these woods, anywhere at all, and hunt to your heart's content.

"Long as you were a good steward no one cared. Do anything you want out here, long as you respected the animals. Not a penny out of your pocket.

"Now look. Linton and the paper mill and everyboy else has chopped up their land into leases. Now to even see a deer you got to buy a lease. And you cain't get on a lease unless you get in a club. And not just anybody gets asked, Barrett. You know that."

Barrett knew only too well.

"Used to, a man with a box of Number Ones and some skill could feed his family off these woods. But now—now, hell, you got to be rich just to come out here."

Barrett watched as Linton Loyd kneeled to warm his hands in the fetid vapor that geysered from the gut bucket.

"It's cold," he remarked.

"As a well-digger's ass," Jarold agreed.

The climate often turned bitter in northern Florida, but seldom this early in the season. It was not unheard of to have hurricanes in November, the sullen, persistent heat of Gulf waters encountering the capricious influences of *la niña* and a dipping jet stream. This morning, however, a stiff breeze and forty degrees felt Arctic.

"Well. Guess I better be movin'," the warden declared abruptly, pouring his coffee onto the fire in a careful stream, like a small boy pissing on hot coals.

"Nice seeing you, Jarold."

The warden only nodded in reply. Barrett followed his solitary retreat. Linton had his buck gutted by now. The bladder had been removed without a single drop of urine contaminating the carcass. The skinning would come next. Linton would assign another hunter that task, returning himself only to dismember the choicest pieces of the buck's meat from its entaglement of bone and sinew. "Here," he nodded to his sullen son, and strolled past the bunkhouse to wash up.

The Loyds' bunkhouse was no more than a pair of thirty-foot construction trailers slapped together, the interior walls ripped out to allow a woodstove, tiers of beds, an overstuffed couch, and a card table. An open shed set some distance from the trailer provided a new luxury, a cold-water shower and washstand where Linton, bloodied to the elbows, now washed his hands with soap and sink cleaner. There was no latrine. You needed to shit, you walked off to the woods and found yourself a stump unencumbered with scorpions or patient spiders. You forgot your toilet paper, you made do with moss or something similar.

There was a kind of verandah added on to the camphouse, an unfinished porch fashioned with plywood and mounted on cement blocks looking out over the firepit to the gallows or cruciform beyond. It was only after Linton had washed that he came to the campfire and the black man drinking coffee. "Morning, Bear. Been out yet?"

Barrett Raines might fairly be described as a bear, with a great lump of neck and shoulder squeezed into a frame a shade shorter than a coffin. But it was the habit of sweetening his coffee with honey, locals knew, that gave Barrett his sobriquet. He was at it now, squeezing honey from a Pooh Bear decanter into his lacerated mug.

"Not yet." Bear replied to Linton's question honestly enough, but the smile he offered was disingenuous. Barrett did not for a moment believe that the invitation to hunt with this members-only club was a simple gesture of sociability. There were no overt indicators to arouse suspicion of any other purpose, of course. Bunch of boys out to hunt. But Barrett could not forget that he was the only black man ever to set a foot that wasn't running on Linton Loyd's well-stocked grounds, let alone sit down with paying members at the massa's camp.

Barrett knew, as did everyone who came out here, that an invitation from Mr. Loyd never came without some expectation of reciprocity, some quid pro quo. Even the sickly son, Gary, the whelp who would one day inherit a fortune made on fertilizer and agricultural equipment, begged his daddy's permission before coming to camp. The father's largesse never came unless strings were attached. There was a nice ball of twine rolled up by now, taking in everything from stocks and bonds to holdings in timber and tobacco. And other things.

Linton Loyd was well fixed by the time he was forty, but he didn't flaunt his money. Not by any means. When not hunting or fishing he was most often seen in shirts and slacks from Sears, Roebuck. He was a compact man, shorter by a couple of hands than Barrett, and tightly wrapped. A streak of pewter ran off-center through raven hair still thick and worn long over a large dome of a forehead. His face was cut deeply into seams and lines that one might romantically assume to have derived from labor outdoors instead of from intrigues conducted behind a custom-built, cherrywood desk. Linton Loyd betrayed few emotions, except an abiding and furious prerogative over his son. He drank, but moderately.

Linton loved to hunt. He loved the spoils that came with hunting: the hides and heads, racks of antlers. The walls of Linton's study were littered with the photographs of slain animals. But whatever other passions the Loyd patriarch nurtured were kept private.

Linton's son, Gary Loyd, was a good bit younger than Bear, taller than his father. Probably not yet thirty. He had not been so fortunate as to inherit Linton's thatch of hair, and partly in consequence spent too much time trying to wind stray survivors over what was a prematurely balding pate. The boy had, as they say, a reputation, having plowed quite a row for himself over a three-county region. And Gary never hesitated to drop his father's name—another bone that stuck in the sheriff's craw. But Barrett had been largely absent from the region during Gary's hell-raising years and, since he was older, had virtually no memory of the man from school. Their orbits simply did not intersect. That was not quite the case, however, with Gary's elder brother.

Athletic competition provided the one arena in which a poor black boy and a rich white one might meet. Barrett was once opposite Gary's older brother, Linton Jr., on a basketball court. He was the only black kid and the only freshman playing for Deacon Beach's high school team. Junior was a senior, playing guard. Barrett didn't remember too much of that elder brother. A good ball handler. Unselfish. Had, even as a youth, the beginnings of that trademark Milky Way streaking an otherwise glorious clutch of hair. Junior was killed in a boating accident. The family had always kept silent regarding the details. Drinking, it was said, however ambiguously, was involved.

A small place like Deacon Beach, everybody kept up with everybody, and everybody's business besides. When Barrett was a youngster that was almost universally the case. But he returned an adult to his boyhood haunts to see folks taking refuge inside air-conditioned modular homes. Porches and verandahs, once the ubiquitous meeting places of family and neighbors, the forums for argument, discussion, or simple recollection, were displaced now by dish antennas and TVs. Friends, kinfolks even, who used to be thick as thieves grew into jobs and habits that never seemed to touch. It was astounding to Barrett how people living in a place so small and intimate managed to be so distant from their neighbors. Ten miles might as well be a hundred. It was a change in the region that he did not like.

On the other hand, some things Bear would have liked to see changed remained stubbornly the same. Deacon Beach and the county beyond was still not a region where a black man—or a Latin man, or an Asian man, for that matter—was accepted as equal. You still had to know your place here. And if you got respect, you had to earn it at twice the price paid by the sorriest cracker living.

Barrett had paid that coin firsthand. If it had not been for Ramona Walker, he'd never have gotten his first job as a beat cop on the Beach. Even in the eighties, with a college degree and an honorable discharge from the reserve commission that had sent Bear rolling with artillery into a storming desert, he was not good enough to be considered for hire by Deacon Beach's all-white council. White men did not want a black man in blues.

Seven years later Barrett found himself one of only four black men interviewed by the Florida Department of Law Enforcement. He got that job and made it stick. He was by now a well-known and respected lawman throughout the Third Judicial District, as well as on the Beach, but Linton Loyd had remained completely unimpressed. Their paths crossed often enough, at Rotary Club meetings, on football fields, or in the county's consolidated gymnasium. Even Barrett's recent transfer to the nearby field office in Live Oak, practically next door to the Loyd fiefdom, failed to evoke from Mr. Loyd the modest reception typically extended to homegrown boys done good.

So when the invitation came to join Linton Loyd at his deer camp for the benefit of venison and good company, Barrett had been, to put it lightly, on guard.

Something was expected. What would it be?

Linton stabbed his long knife absently into the sand—the preferred way to clean a blade, to keep it from rusting.

"Question for you, Bear."

"Certainly."

"Want you to think about something for me. No need to answer just yet."

Bear blew softly over the rim of his cup. "What is it, Linton?"

"You know Lou Sessions and me don't always see eye to eye."

This was an understatement. Lou Sessions was the county's sheriff, the unchallenged authority in his jurisdiction. Lou Sessions hated Linton's guts. Linton held Lou in something much lower than contempt. The beginnings of the conflict were personal. Something to do with the fact that Gary Loyd had gotten the sheriff's daughter pregnant and then refused to marry her. Linton backed up his son. Didn't help that he also pronounced the girl a whore.

"Don't see how I can help you with the sheriff, Linton."

"Not just me involved, Bear. He's bad for the county. Why, we got meth labs and marijuana growin' all over these woods!"

That much was true.

"But Lou, hell, he don't even want to look. Won't let *you* people look, and that's a fact. You know that, Bear. Hell, ever'body in the county knows it."

Even allowing for personal bias, Linton's assessment of the sheriff's performance was not far off the mark. Lou

Sessions was embarrassed early in his tenure when an FDLE probe uncovered a drug-dealing deputy in Lou's employ. The incident almost cost Sheriff Sessions his second election. He was now in his fourth term and so hostile to FDLE, or for that matter to the DEA, ATF, INS, or any other outside agency, that by now the sheriff was widely suspected of being guilty of something more than incompetence.

"I can't get between you and Lou." Bear stated that fact firmly. "And I can tell you there's nothing like probable cause to make the FDLE go after the man. We are out of that loop, and you know it, Linton. You got a problem, best I can tell you is—go to Tallahassee."

"I'm thinkin' closer to home," Linton replied. "We got an election comin' up, you know. Next year. Qualify by July fifteenth. I'm thinkin' of backin' a candidate against Lou Sessions. I got the money behind me. I can get the votes. And I got a man in mind."

"A candidate?" Barrett was mildly surprised. He had never known the Loyds to be involved in any honest contest.

"A name, at least," Linton affirmed. "I'd be interested in your opinion."

"Not sure I'd be the best to judge."

"No one better. He's a good lawman. Solid record. Broad experience. And he's trusted. Ever' swinging dick in this county trusts the man. *I* trust him, and I got to tell you, Bear, there ain't many I trust."

"So who is he?"

"He's you, Bear."

The words took a moment to sink in.

"You think—you're thinking I should run? Against Lou Sessions?"

"I think lots of things. I think you want to be closer to Laura Anne and the boys. I think you'd like a way to be near to your home and people. I think you'd like to be the best damn criminal investigator in the state, too. And so I think if you chew it over, you'll see the best way to do all that is to be the sheriff."

To be sheriff! It was sinking in. To be the head lawman in his hometown! His home county! To be able to rise with Laura Anne in the morning, see the boys off to school, and still get to work before eight o'clock. To end those endless commutes, canceled dinner dates, lost ball games and Sunday socials. To be able to throw Ben and Tyndall a ball every day after work, or go fishing. Sit beside them at homework. Hear their after-school tales! To be able to earn a living and be at home! That alone was worth considering. As for the other—

"It's a natural progression for you, Bear. Either you go on to a federal agency and kiss off ever having a family life or you come home, as sheriff, and make your career right here where you belong.

"You'll be the man, Bear. You can set your own course. Call your own shots. You can be the lawman you always wanted to be and have a life at home to boot."

"Provided I could get elected."

"Not a thing to keep you from it," Linton assured him. "Not unless you got some deep, dark secret I don't know about. *Is* there anything like that, Bear? Any Lewinskis in your closet?"

"Nothing but clothes," Barrett replied.

Not in his daytime closet, anyway. Not in any closet he could recall.

"But that doesn't mean I could beat Lou Sessions."

"Let me back you, you can beat the goddamn pope."

But what would be the cost, Barrett wondered? What would be expected in return?

"Let me think about it."

"Surely," Linton smiled, just as happy, apparently, as if Barrett had accepted outright. "You do that, Bear. You think it over. And when you get done thinkin' you come to me."

Two

Assuming you could find your way, Hezikiah Jackson's cypress shack perched raw and primitive on loblolly stumps in the middle of Strawman's Hammock. The Hammock, so named for its captured wetland and for the millenia of straw deposited by the last yellowheart pines to survive the timber barons, probably occupied no more than a thousand acres. Even an uneducated arborist could see the difference in the forest here. The loblolly or yellowheart pine was easily distinguished from the uniformly tall and narrow conifers hybridized to build houses or feed pulpwood mills. The trees in Strawman's Hammock had survived for more, in some cases much more, than a hundred years. Their limbs—unlike the slash pine that grew close to tall, slender trunks in uniform rows over endless tracts of company land—spread out widely from thick, heavily barked trunks in stands of trees arranged only by the random deposit of conifers.

Resin seeped from those ancient trunks like maple syrup. The pinecones were large. They reminded you, when opened, of pineapples. Even the straw was different from the straw of slash pines, bursting from pods of pinecones in circles or starbursts of heavy needles, a rambunctious and native parallel to its polite and manufactured cousin.

The hammock itself had so far remained unspoiled only because a private landowner refused over the years to sell his acreage to St. Regis, or Buckeye, or any of the other pulpwood mills coveting the acreage. It was rumored that this would soon change, that a probated will would see the land awarded to heirs only too happy to plant the land in regular rows of domestic pine and exploit its value on the market. When that happened Hezikiah Jackson would be forced from the land whose usufruct she had enjoyed, some said, for more than ninety years.

Hezikiah's homestead squatted deep inside a tract whose boundary was no more than five miles as a crow would fly from Loyd Linton's comparatively modern hunting grounds. But unless you were a crow that wouldn't help you. A single, twisted sandy rut of road wound a serpentine path along the periphery of the Hammock, but did not penetrate to the hammock's interior. Contemporary hunters lazy with their deer blinds and truck-mounted towers seldom hunted on foot anymore, and so seldom ventured anywhere into Strawman's Hammock.

You had to have a good reason to come here. A better reason yet to risk the snake bites, quicksand, and man-traps that threatened pilgrims wending their treacherous way to Hezikiah's stark homestead. Locals said the place was haunted, the ghost of a slain Creek or Seminole chieftan, Billy Bowlegs, say, or Osceola remaining to torture the souls of Spaniards or U.S. calvary. Hezikiah's shack was situated on what had surely been the mound of some ancient Indian or marauding community. When rain was plentiful you could see, exposed from the sand, arrowheads or occasionally the rusted crest of alien armory.

A clearwater spring fed a limestone aquifer that extended east and away from the mound's ancient site. Hezikiah drew water cold as ice from that underground cistern with a hand-jacked pump. Even her dwelling was anachronistic, a completely unvarnished throwback to the days when cypress-shingled roofs, shotgun halls, and outdoor privets were the common denominator of regional architecture. The shack leaned dangerously to one side now, which suited Hezikiah fine, her bed now canted on an upslope grade. Good for the rhombisis, she'd say, and the sinuses.

Let ever'thang stretch and drain.

The single and characteristic breezeway that split the shack in half gave access on the one side to a pair of rooms, one of which housed a single, molding trunk and an unmade poster-bed, the other room doubling as kitchen and what Hezikiah described as "a settin' place."

A man was sat down there, now, in the sitting place, his knotted arms anchored akimbo with leather straps to the rests of a home-crafted chair. The chair was made of cypress, its joined limbs bent when green to take the shape, its leather-lashed armrests now arresting a Latin man, brown and sunbeaten and bathed in sweat before the ancient crone who limped in from her kitchen.

The settin' room was completely unsegregated from the kitchen. The Latin American strapped to her childhood furniture could see clearly the cornucopia of herbs and medicinals that Hezikiah had collected over nearly a century of shamanlike administration. Shelves of dog fennel and deer tongue dried open to the air while alongside were arranged murky Bell jars filled to the brim with the heads of moccassins and bullfrogs, the gizzards of chickens.

The hearts, locals whispered, of babies miscarried from their mama's wombs.

The migrant and Latin workers recently come to the northwestern isolates of Florida called her a *curandero*, which for these Spanish-speaking newcomers connoted something more than a medicine woman. Something only slightly less remarkable than a witch.

"Done got yo'sef a nasty 'fliction."

Hezikiah spat some variety of tobacco through one of the many long creases that separated her floorboards.

The man sweated exposed on the precipice of her chair.

She turned absently to gather a rolling pin under the rank pit of one arm. A rolling pin. A hardwood cylinder fashioned to roll freely between lathed handles. She might have been making biscuits. That thought must have occurred.

"Gonna make me some hoecakes after," she declared. "You want some? Be good. Hoecake and mayhaw jelly. Pussome lead back in yo' pencil."

His Spanish was slurred in reply. "(Mother of Jesus, protect me from this crazy woman. Make her hand quick. Heal me.)"

She inspects him briefly.

"Same girl?"

The man nods silent assent to her reproach. And then—

"(I kill her! I cut her fucking heart! Slit her guts!)"

Hezikiah offers an uncomprehending smile to that threat. She sees before her a strong man, strong as a bull, barrel chested, thick forearms. A twist of muscle knots along the trapezoids that anchor his neck and shoulders.

"Better start usin' some kinda protection," she counsels. And then she comes to him. Drags with a bare foot a stool before him, a milkstool, its cool, metal plane only slightly lower than the Mexican worker's exposed crotch.

"Wont some more whiskey?"

"Sí," he nods. "Andele! Andele!"

She scoops up a jug from the floor with sudden dexterity. Offers it to him. He slurps the hooch down. Her nostrils flare to see his throat constrict with his stomach. He has an erection fully risen now.

"Ain't you somethin'?" She murmurs admiration.

She takes the jug away, reaches for the rolling pin.

"Next time use some protection," she offers once more, pulling him hard and flat along the stool's cool, metal pan.

"Will this . . . ? Be bad?" he gargles the question in English.

She smiles. Reaches up to slip her unwashed rainment free. A bony shoulder thrusts from beneath that flimsy shroud. Then the remains of a breast, a dug dried hard and gnarled as a raisin.

"Take it."

Her eyes shine wet and bright.

"See who lets go first."

A silver knife on a silver belly opened a black mullet stem to stern. A tall, vital woman cleaned the fish, raking its innards into a slop-sink braced with two-bys on a wide porch. A flight of gulls fluttered white as ashes across the face of a setting sun that settled into the Gulf of Mexico. She was bent at the waist, this woman at work, her bare back rippling sinuously with activity. The chill that surprised folks on the first of November had reverted by week's end to temperatures fueled by the Gulf of Mexico.

It was a sultry afternoon, an Indian summer's day shot with humidity. Her skin caught the setting sun in a sheen of perspiration. Locals speculated too often regarding the etiology of that skin, its remarkable tone and color, rich as it was, a deep milk chocolate. The skin of a Nubian. Her hair was full of body, hard to tame. Black as a crow's. A short row of metal tines pulled back those wiry strands like a handful of hemp to reveal a proud face. It was a tourist's gift, the barrette, a comb of copper set in lapis lazuli.

23

The mullet went immediately to ice in a tub filled with fish. You wanted mullet to stay sweet, you'd better not let him warm. Laura Anne hefted her aluminum tub onto a wide hip and banged through the steward's door that led to the kitchen behind. Other restaurateurs would keep the mullet untaken by customers and refrigerate it for two, three more days or longer in an effort to avoid a loss of inventory and profit, but Laura Anne would rather buy sparingly and tell a customer, "Sorry, folks, we're out," than to give them a mullet gone stale.

That kind of integrity, of course, was one of the several things that made folks drive to the coast from Lake City and Tallahasee or further to dine on hardwood plates at Laura Anne's restaurant.

The restaurant seated perhaps thirty tables around a central island and bar. A large, naked-beam interior was cooled with paddle fans and ten tons of air conditioning. Diners inside looked onto a wraparound verandah and patio that faced west to the Gulf of Mexico. The place was called, simply, "Ramona's." That designation derived from the diner's first owner. Ramona Walker was a white woman, a staunch friend to Laura Anne and her husband, and also the victim of a brutal homicide. Laura Anne's husband caught Ramona's killer. Laura Anne rebuilt Ramona's restaurant.

But in her own image.

The patio beyond the verandah was added, along with a wide, shaded boardwalk that extended out over the water. There were some changes inside, too. African American and Cajun recipes were added to the menu. Grits and crackers and jumbalai went well with seafood and steak. Bacon bits and green onions tasted good in hush puppies. But the biggest change in the restaurant was its personality. Ramona was a flirt, gregarious, voluptuous, and vulgar. Laura Anne was reserved, polite, and refined. Folks wondered how she'd get along with customers used to Ramona's ready and provocative wit. What would Laura Anne bring that was distinctively hers to this place of community, this family-wide dining-in?

What she brought was a piano.

One of the first things Laura Anne hauled to the restaurant was her own, hard-earned instrument. It was a grand piano won just shy of Laura Anne's twenty-first birthday in a competition sponsored at Emory University. Her formal background was in music education, and after Laura Anne's family, the piano was still her first love. At first she reserved the instrument exclusively for herself, pausing from labor in the kitchen to simply relax or, occasionally, to entertain customers, opening the Steinway's sounding board to the Gulf Coast to sounds never heard or imagined by the sunburned locals on Deacon Beach.

These were erratic, solitary engagements. But then a pair of graduate students from the music department at Florida State came to Ramona's looking for summer employment. There was the grand piano. Of course *they* might play, Laura Anne allowed. She had taught piano for years. She knew that this young man and woman would treat her instrument with respect. And so two job-seeking students became the first waiter and waitress to sit at Laura Anne's coveted Steinway.

Later that summer three more students came.

Word got out that there was a place tucked away on a strip of coastline an hour from Tallahassee where you could eat and, with luck, hear a concert at the same time. Performances became numerous, if irregular. Locals were not, in truth, too much impressed with this change in ambiance, though they tolerated it well enough, knowing that Laura Anne loved her music, but for students seeking a summer gig, or for music aficionadoes seeking exotic fare, the combination of seaside food and uncertain concertos proved irresistible.

Cellists and violinists brought their instruments to play

alone or to accompany Laura Anne's aproned pianists. Chamber music began to compete with country & western for the locals' attention. There was still no schedule for these performances, of course, which brought an element of randomness or chance that outsiders found charming. The students, at first, simply performed during breaks from work, when the tables were bussed and the customers tended. Sometimes Laura Anne would join in. Only in recent months had something like scheduled performances taken its place on the menu beside mullet and red fish and the catch of the day. The musicians on these occasions did not wear aprons.

Ramona's was by now a resting place for professional instrumentalists. Concert pianists, lured by a helping of snapper and hush puppies, would consent after eating to provide an apertif of Rachmaninoff or Debussy. The restaurant once solely known for its excellent cuisine and service began to be lauded as a watering hole for a whole variety of performers, who passed the word, "If you're ever in Florida . . ."

Customers came from miles around to sample the food and to enjoy concertos beside the water. But they came *back* because of Laura Anne herself, to see the tall, athletic figure, the raven hair caught in its copper comb, the golden skin of a remarkable woman who served swamp cabbage and Mozart with equal alacrity.

She was—a smile eased Barrett Raines's tired and preoccupied face—the most beautiful and accomplished wife a man could ever hope to have.

Bear was waiting just inside the restaurant's front entrance, a foyer linked to a door salvaged on one of Ramona's saltwater adventures. WAIT TO BE SEATED—that directive was embossed on a laminated sign wired with Twist-Ems to a copper chain and anchored into a pulpit. Barrett waited patiently. He did not exempt himself from Laura Anne's discipline. One of the employees was having fun at the piano. Show tunes. Bear thought he recognized something from *Chorus Line*. In a little less than ten minutes he faced a hostess over the pulpit.

A young woman. Newcomer.

"Be one this evening, sir?"

"I'm hoping two." What Barrett intended as a humorous rejoinder came out sharp.

The hostess winced.

"Would that be a table, sir? Or would you prefer to wait at the bar?"

"Sorry. Bar'll be fine. Can you get Laura Anne a message for me?"

"Ms. Raines is in the kitchen, sir. It might be a while."

"No hurry. Just tell her Bear's here."

" 'Bear,' sir?" She seemed alarmed now.

"It's all right," Barrett reassured the new employee with a smile. "She knows me."

A few minutes later Laura Anne Raines joined her husband sans apron at a table near the bar.

"Word has it you're a little uptight."

"Sorry. Didn't sleep well."

"Ah. The wearies?"

He nodded.

"Baby. You never liked camping."

She kissed him lightly. The spices she used to conjure her kitchen wonders lingered on her skin, in her hair. The smell.

"Mmmm. Makes a man hungry."

"Try the snapper."

"Wasn't thinking on food."

"You bad boy." She nudged her bare foot against the instep of his shoe.

"When you getting home?" he asked.

"Oh, Bear, it won't be 'til late."

"Thelma with the boys?"

"Mmmhmm."

Thelma was related to Laura Anne. An aunt by marriage, childless. She had become indispensable. Laura Anne had tried, at first, when Bear was assigned in Tallahassee, to go it alone, juggling the twins and the restaurant by herself. School days she generally tried to take a break from three to five, to pick up the boys, get Ben and Tyndall settled with homework and good habits. But a restaurant, as anyone who's run one knows, is damn near a day-long job. Laura Anne had to rush every morning to get her ten-year-olds off to school and still make it to "the store" in time to prepare lunch. A dash from work to pick up the boys at three, then back again by four to deal with everything from cranky cooks and irresponsible waitstaff to salesmen from Sysco and Alliant. Not to mention air conditioning, plumbing, linen supply—everything necessary to make things right for the evening diners who were Laura Anne's bread and butter. It turned out to be a round-the-clock responsibility, which meant that someone had to be on tap to feed, comfort, and when necessary, cajole Ben and Tyndall.

Barrett would love to have that job. His separation from his family while in Tallahassee drove him into a deep depression. He vowed never to accept that kind of isolation from Laura Anne and his sons again, even if it meant leaving law enforcement. *The* reason he had requested a transer from FDLE headquarters in Tallahassee to a field office in Suwannee County was so that he could be with his family during the week. Be a husband. Be a father.

Things had improved. Live Oak was, nominally, closer to Deacon Beach than was Tallahassee. Still—Bear's hour-long commute got him out of the house before the boys were fully awake, and rarely got him home before seven in the evening. Any arrest, snafu, gripe, or phone call could cancel a commitment to a school play or a ball game. A rare evening alone with Laura Anne. But the biggest problem that remained was how to tend the boys during afternoon and evening hours when both parents were away from home. There was nothing like day care in Deacon Beach.

Barrett solved the problem. He bought a thirty-foot push-out trailer from a dealer in Valdosta, set that fifth-wheeler up with its own septic tank, phone, and power hookup on the backside of Laura Anne's perennially productive garden, and gave Thelma the keys. It was a good arrangement. Aunt Thelma, for the first time in her life, had a place of her own. The trailer together with a modest salary compensated Laura Anne's kin for looking after the boys from three in the afternoon until their parent's return.

"Haven't forgot the party, have you?"

"No, ma'am," Barrett shook his head. Ben and Tyndall were counting the days until the celebration of their eleventh birthday. A big day for fifth graders. A day for family and friends. "I got Tyndall a football, and Benjamin the newest *Harry Potter.*"

"Barrett. You keep that up, Tyndall won't be reading at all."

"Just kidding, baby. Actually I got 'em both a ball and books. Same book, mind you. I don't want them fighting."

"Wise man," Laura Anne smiled. And then, more cautiously, "I invited Cory and Corrina. Hope you don't mind."

"No," Bear replied quickly. He knew he ought not to mind. Cory and Corrina were girls a little over a year apart, both younger than Ben and Tyndall. They were sired, if not fathered, by Barrett's elder brother. The girls were orphans now, living in Dowling Park—one of the best facilities for that purpose, thank God, in the state.

Barrett provided part of the cost for the girls' care. It

was not a sufficient emollient for the guilt of declining to raise the children himself, but Barrett knew that Cory and Corrina, through no fault of their own, needed structure and supervision that Barrett and Laura Anne could not provide.

Or would not, Bear amended silently.

That's where the guilt came from.

"One party won't make 'em family," he warned.

"But leaving Cory and Corrina out, Bear—that would be cruel."

"Yes." He shook his head. "Do I need to get 'em?"

"Preacher will," Laura Anne said. "He's over on visitation that morning. Offered to bring the girls by. I can have Thelma take them back afterwards."

Barrett grunted. "Hell of a lot of logistics for a birthday party."

She sighed. "It does seem like you have to think ahead for everything."

And how much easier things would be, Barrett reflected as Laura Anne ordered snapper and steaks, *if I got elected sheriff.*

The sheriff's office at the county seat in Mayo was twenty-five minutes from Barrett's Jim Walter home, a straight shot over a single strip of blacktop. Twenty-five minutes to commute. Even with the inevitable emergencies and unexpected interruptions that punctuated a lawman's life, Barrett's hours would be more regular as sheriff than they'd ever been in Bear's law enforcement career. And he would have much more time at home. For the first time in four years he could half-ass count on being there at Tyndall's Little League games, or at Ben's piano recitals. Even more, he'd be well and truly back in the county of his childhood years, near to friends.

And he'd be the boss. County sheriffs were by statute the chief law-enforcement officers in the state of Florida. In theory, the State Attorney General could fire a sitting sheriff, but absent massive proof of incompetence, prejudice, or criminal activity, that would never happen. Barrett, in fact, had no firsthand knowledge of a sheriff ever losing his job other than through election.

The election, however, was its own downside. Job security was important. It would be hard to sell Laura Anne on the idea of an occupation that depended on the whim of white folks' votes. A black man had never been elected sheriff in Lafayette County. A black man had never been elected to *any* office in Lafayette County. That was where Linton Loyd became very important. Barrett was certain he'd need Linton Loyd's backing to win an election; what bothered him more was that he'd need Linton's help to *stay* elected.

"Got an idea," he opened.

"You usually do."

"For a job."

"So do I," she surprised him.

"Come again?" Barrett delayed his own proposition.

Laura Anne leaned forward. "I got an offer today. Informal. Some folks from Atlanta. They asked if I'd consider selling the restaurant."

Barrett sat back in his chair.

"But—you're doin' so good, hon. *We're* doin' so good!"

"Their opening offer was four hundred thousand dollars, Bear."

Four *hundred* thousand—?

". . . But after taxes, you'd be skinned," he finally replied. "I mean, it *sounds* like a lot of money, but we got to plan on living for another twenty, thirty years at least. At least, I *hope*."

She smiled, "I know. I know. Still—you know what my margin of profit is here, Bear? Not profits. Just the margin."

"No."

"Something like eleven percent," she replied. "That's

eleven pennies on every dollar earned. We sell Ramona's for four hundred thousand, I figure we'll wind up with a little over three hundred thousand cash. You take *that* money, put it in something sensible, maybe a mutual fund, you can make, what? Thirty thousand a year? Sometimes forty? That's without a lick of work. And that's based on their opening offer. They'll pay more."

"How much more?"

"Doesn't it make sense to find out?"

"I s'pose." A flutter invaded Bear's stomach.

Laura Anne leaned forward eagerly. "They're not just talking about a restaurant, Bear. These are businessmen. They see this whole area, the whole Beach, as a retreat for musicians and music lovers from all over. A community of jazz and classical and pop. Kind of like a Bourbon Street by the sea."

"It's a nice dream."

"They ain't talkin' dreams." She resorted to vernacular when roused. "And I think I'm worth a lot more than four hundred thousand dollars!"

" 'Course you are, hon. I didn't mean that."

"Then what did you mean?" she replied sharply.

Customers glanced in their direction. Barrett lowered his voice.

"What would you do afterwards?" Barrett said. "I mean, if you gave up the business? While we're throwing darts at the stock market. What would you want to be doing then?"

She stiffened. "What I always wanted to do."

Barrett remained silent. He knew that Laura Anne's abiding passion was to educate kids in the joys of music. She loved nothing better than to be in a room with children and instruments. Laura Anne had never been happier than during the years she taught at the local high school. And Barrett knew that it was *his* move to Tallahassee that had cost Laura Anne her hard-earned position.

"I'm going to be teaching the next couple of weeks." Laura Anne withdrew, tucking her long legs beneath her chair. "Substituting. But that girl they hired from Orlando? She's quitting. I'm not surprised. This isn't the big city, and this girl isn't used to our kind of life."

"So the school's gonna need another teacher?"

"A teacher and a band director." She nodded. "But if I'm going to apply I have to do it quick."

"Lord, Lord." He took a sip of iced tea. "Give up the restaurant? Bank our future on NASDAQ and Mr. Dow? That's a lot to think about."

"Don't worry," she softened. "At least we'll both have a steady job."

Barrett had just about decided at that moment that this was not the occasion to tell his wife he was thinking of running for sheriff when Rolly Slade came lumbering up to the table, the baseball cap testifying loyalty to FSU firmly in place on his mat of uncombed hair.

"Bear. Laura Anne."

"Why, hello, Rolly." Laura Anne smiled as if Slade's interruption were a looked-for benediction.

"Wanted you to know 'bout my dog." Rolly plunged straight ahead.

"Your dog?" Barrett responded politely.

"My rottweiler."

Barrett was familiar with Rolly's dog. He was also familiar with the manner in which Slade treated his animal.

"Just got 'im where I wanted 'im," Rolly complained. "There to guard the shop and awl."

The shop where he repaired lawn mowers and chain saws and such. Any number of complaints had been lodged against the beast that charged at customers from his now-chained restraint. Before the chain, Rolly used a rope to restrain his mascot. It broke. One of Rolly's kin, fortunately for the proprietor, was the subject of the assault that followed. Terry Slade barely made it back to his pickup before his uncle's rottweiler broke through the window on the shotgun side. Just drove right through, a couple of hundred pounds of head and fangs. Terry stomped the accelerator through the floor. Good thing, too, people said, or Rolly's dog would have taken off his head.

"What's happened now, Rolly?"

"Stole 'im is what. I come home from Linton's camp, sunnuvabitch is gone. My chain? Cut slap in two."

"You call it in to the sheriff?"

"What? Lou?" Rolly looked around as though to spit. "Oh, Sheriff Sessions's too busy for the likes 'o me. Why, he's out catchin' the big crooks. The ones cookin' drugs and sellin' pot all over the county? He's got no time for a man's dog."

Neither, Barrett reflected, did the FDLE. But perhaps this was the time to begin behaving as a man running for office.

"Tell you what, Rolly. Give me a description. I get to work tomorrow I'll put out a fax to Sheriff Wilson in Suwannee County and copy Lou. See if we can get some folks looking."

" 'Preciate that, Bear."

"Glad to help."

"Laura Anne." Rolly tipped the bib of his cap and left without another word.

Laura Anne turned her attention back to her husband.

"You didn't tell me you were going to *Linton's* camp?"

"At least you know why it wasn't relaxing."

"Don't softshoe me, Barrett Raines. What'd he want you out there for? Couldn't have been hunting."

"Tell you later," Bear replied.

A place this small, he thought, it was impossible to keep a secret.

That, at least, is what Agent Raines believed to be true at the time.

Three

The field office for the Florida Department of Law Enforcement, Third Judicial Circuit, is housed in the unlikely architecture of a juke joint once owned by Papa Smiley, one of the most endearing and crooked characters in Suwannee County. Papa opened a kind of combination bar, barbecue, and disco on the site that now promised law and order. He was an enormous man, never wore anything but overalls, no shirt, no underwear, his gut distended as with a hernia. He lumbered from side to side like a drunken sailor, in workboots that he wore without socks. Hard to imagine a creature like Papa doin' the Hustle, but legend had it the man could dance like John Goddamn Travolta.

The dance hall, however, was only a front for Papa's riskier and more profitable enterprises. You used to see everything from stolen cars to cocaine bartered outside Papa's establishment, while inside teenagers and older singles drank beer and whiskey for fifty cents, sucking on baby ribs and dancing all the while beneath the town's first coordinated light show. Pickup trucks and fast cars used to spread in groves beneath the oak trees that sheltered the one-story disco. It was, for a time, a popular place.

Then Papa himself went bankrupt, after getting arrested on various counts of trafficking, possession, and larceny. Which left the town richer in piety, but poorer in conversation. The one-story, completely unremarkable structure that survived Papa's incarceration was put up for auction. No one had much use for a used disco stripped of its liquor license. The FDLE got the place on the cheap. Nothing betrayed the building's serious purpose. The barbecue pit that remained out back might have signaled that this was the home to some family-based business. A plumber's office, say, or insurance agency.

Even the riverbed stones piled thin up the walls like you'd see in some other state—Colorado, say, or Pennsylvania—were not enough to catch the eye of a casual traveler wheeling down Highway 129 on the way to the town's only Wal-Mart. The town was called Live Oak, appropriately enough. Live Oak trees thrived in Suwannee County, one giant step inland from Lafayette, separated and landlocked by the Suwannee River. Barrett could normally leave home at a quarter to seven and safely get to his office on time, but this morning he had been forced to leave Deacon Beach an hour earlier, because on this particular morning there was an eight o'clock meeting to which Bear could not be tardy.

The session to come promised some acrimony. Cricket Bonet, Barrett's one-time partner, had been temporarily assigned to the Live Oak office from the violent crimes squad in Tallahassee. Barrett was glad to have the Crazy Canuck, or any competent agent, for any duration. The third district was responsible for an immense expanse of territory, six large counties stretching from Dixie County in the southmost part of the jurisdiction a hundred miles north to Hamilton County and the Georgia line. Cricket was in charge of a presentation this morning that would outline special areas of concern identified by the FDLE. Each county's sheriff was to attend the briefing. Some came willingly. Others not.

Suwannee County's sheriff, fortunately, got along well with everybody. Buddy Wilson was elected to sheriff while still a lieutenant in Live Oak's municipal PD. One of the youngest sheriffs in the state, Buddy was also one of the most cooperative with outside agencies. As did most sheriffs, Wilson appreciated the forensic and technical support always offered poorer districts by the FDLE, but he was even more willing than most to recruit field agents in innovative programs designed for rural law enforcement.

At Buddy's request Cricket had already visited the local high school to institute a program designed to prevent violence among teens. Everyone knew that the Columbine High School that was the site of a teen slaughter was in an upscale suburb of Denver, but statistically, random killings committed by young people *in schools* were more likely to occur in rural environs than in New York's Harlem or the barrios of Los Angeles.

Cricket Bonet's goal was straightforward. To curb violent behavior among teenage boys and girls, he wanted to make violence uncool for kids in school. To that end Bonet convinced schools to allow their teenage students to identify their own problems and flashpoints, and to arbitrate in situations where their peers experienced anger, frustration, or persecution.

Early identification of conflict was crucial to this process; aggrieved parties or sullen castaways would not always volunteer to bring a problem before a student committee. Student arbitrators were required to take an active role, identifying the boy too terrified to admit that he was being bullied in the locker room, or the overweight girl too ashamed to complain that her obesity had become a target for torment.

Once identified, the relevant parties were required to come before the student committee where an airing of grievance could safely occur. Sometimes an open exchange between antagonists was enough. But whether the precipitating incident was a fistfight or an unintended slur, the agreed mantra for settling all conflicts between students was simple: Use words!

Without Sheriff Wilson's help, Cricket never would have been able to persuade Suwannee County's School Board to give its teens authority to arbitrate disputes. Buddy threw his weight behind Agent Bonet's proposal, knowing that any mechanism venting anger and fear inside a high school made its own and the outside community a safer place. He represented about the best you could ask for in a sheriff.

Lou Sessions offered the other opportunity. Behavior at school, so far as Lou was concerned, was the teachers' responsibility. What they did at home was up to the parents. Everyone else was an interloper. And he didn't want interlopers anywhere. If there was a drug operation cooking in the county, he'd handle it. No FDLE. No DEA, thank you. Cars being stolen? Trucks? Just stay where you are, Agent Raines. I don't need no Tallahassee lassies poking around my county. How about a corrupt cop in your department? Well, Lou had already been through that wringer. But the lesson he learned from the experience was to keep dirty linen well hid.

Sheriff Sessions would be in attendance this morning, an officer of the court to whom Barrett Raines was, by law, subordinate. This was the man who hated Linton Loyd's guts, the man Linton wanted to depose from office. Their meeting, Barrett knew, would be fraught with more than the usual number of complications.

You get to the briefing room at Live Oak's field office by walking in from the pleasant shade of ancient oaks to find a front door naked to a blacktop street and a blistering sun where you push a buzzer to enter a foyer cramped with three folding chairs and the most recent arrivals from FedEx or UPS. You take maybe two steps to reach a formica-topped counter, show your identification and a broad smile to Bonny, take a sharp left to round the counter, the first right down a narrow, plaque-lined hall and then straight back to a room shaped like a cigar box, chilled to freezing, furnished cheap, and paneled with acoustic tile. It was amusing to recall that this had once been a dance floor. There were still dances, of a sort, going on.

Buddy Wilson and Lou Sessions were seated side by side. It would be hard to imagine a starker contrast. Buddy was clean-shaven with a complexion smooth as a freshman. Crisply pressed tans; polished brass. Lou wore Tony Lima boots, kept his trousers for a week, and had a lunar face pitted as if with meteorites. His arms joined his shoulder at an odd angle, did Lou's. He was fairly tall, but with a prematurely stooped posture and hair gone gray, pressed at the temple from the weight of his sweat-stained Stetson. This was Lafayette County's sheriff.

Besides Buddy and Lou there were three other sheriffs in attendance. The sheriff from Dixie County was absent, hospitalized for his second bypass operation. A deputy unfamiliar to Barrett stood in for Sheriff Folsom. They had one distinguished visitor: Barrett's boss, Captain Henry Altmiller, was down from Tallahassee for the meeting, ramrod straight, as usual, wearing a stiff, white-collared shirt and tie, a pin always on the lapel of his suit, attentive to the proceedings but discreetly seated in the rear. Captain Altmiller was a legend to most FDLE agents, well respected, sometimes feared, but the captain was smart enough to know that his reputation at the department didn't count for jack with these gathered sheriffs.

So Captain Altmiller remained in the background and

41

Bear's former partner, Agent Cricket Bonet, took center stage, his giant frame threatening to bend beneath the room's depressed ceiling, his preternaturally red hair and pale skin glowing beneath flourescent lights whose ballasts hummed like a nest of hornets.

You could still hear, in words like "hoose" or "aboot," the influence of Bonet's French Canadian origins. You could hear some South Side Chicago, too, were your ear carefully tuned. And Cricket could come up with a great rendition of Houston cops, into which patois he frequently reverted when breaking the ice with southern-raised lawmen.

"So bein' raised French and Catholic I was confused when I got down here—" Cricket smiled wryly. "—about lots of things. I thought calaboose, for instance, must be some kinda local vegetable. And the first midshift in Houston I spent all night looking for an 'armed' suspect name of 'Adillo.' . . ."

A polite chuckle from the gathered lawmen. Cricket smiled.

"But I think it was in matters of theology that I really felt out of depth. I mean, you've got more churches down here. You've got Church of God, Church of Christ, Assembly of God, Assembly of Jesus, Assembly of Registered Holy Rollers. You got Mount Zion, Mount Ephesus, Mount Bethany—and I swear there ain't a mountain for a thousand miles.

"And every mainstream church is 'First.' You ever notice that? First Baptist, First Methodist, First Presbyterian . . . damnation, are there any Second Churches down here? Or Thirds?"

Another chuckle. More spontaneous.

Hell's bells, Barrett thought. *Cricket's the man should run for sheriff.*

"One other thing," Agent Bonet continued brightly,

"before we get to our business. Y'all may be able to help me on this one—I still don't know if I've got it straight. Maybe you can tell me: What's the difference between Northern Baptists and Southern Baptists? Any ideas?"

No one was biting, of course. But you could see the lawmen wondering what this Crazy Canuck was going to come up with.

" 'Cause the way I understand it—" Cricket smiled. "—the Northern Baptists say there ain't no hell. But the Southern Baptists say, 'The hell they ain't!' "

With that last icebreaker the lawmen began to relax. And suddenly the affable Cricket Bonet became all business.

"Gentlemen. Got a couple of problems we need your help with this morning."

A Powerpoint display replaced the chalkboards and felt-tip pens that used to be de rigeur for such gatherings. Cricket's laptop fed the monitor that glowed now in a suddenly darkened room. A few sheriffs pulled out ballpoints and spiral pads. Not Lou Sessions.

"First item will not require much more on your part than a call to Tallahassee. You may know that we have a division now devoted full-time to computer fraud, hacking, and so on. Well, the Internet is now being used to distribute child pornography in quantities the state deems epidemic. Children are being recruited; in some cases their pictures are taken without permission and scanned in to match up with salacious material. If you see a site yourself or hear of one through a civilian, just call the computer crimes center at 850-410-7000. We've got some folks there can trace the cookies to their source.

"That's all we need from you on our first problem. Second will require more work. The Immigrant and Natural folks have been receiving reports of civil rights violations among a population relatively new to northwestern Florida. I'm sure you've noticed that your white kids and black kids don't crop the tobacco or haul the watermelons the way they used to."

Everyone knew that young people could no longer be persuaded or threatened to do the menial labor that children, even in the recent past, were expected to complete as a matter of course. Most of the gathered lawmen *had* labored in the grow-crops common in the region. Tobacco was the big one in the past, the big money maker. A common lament among contemporary farmers was the flight of kids from those dwindling fields. But Barrett had harvested the sandy lugs of tobacco, he had puked his guts after a day in the sun and heat and nicotine. And the day he got an education he never went back. No one with a choice in the matter worked twelve or fourteen or sixteen hours in misery for the five or six or seven dollars a day that were at one time the region's piecemeal wage.

"So what we have now," Cricket went on, "is what we've had in California and Texas for a long time: a population of Spanish-speaking itinerants. Migrant workers who speak little or no English and are willing to work for piece wages.

"Now, the way the law reads, you can't enforce a minimum wage for piecework. If a man freely contracts to crop a row of tobacco for a dollar, that's legal. If he agrees to take off a stick of tobacco for two cents a stick, that's legal.

"Same thing with straw. You may not know it, gentlemen, but the ordinary pine needles that fall freely from pine trees all over your counties is now the fastest-growing agricultural product in this district. Plain old pine straw. Straw on the ground. A farmer gets maybe seventy or eighty dollars an acre, sometimes more, for every hundred acres of pines that are raked. That's money free and clear without lifting a hand. The man who buys that straw and bales it then sells it—for road construction, to the state, and especially to nurseries. You can take a twenty-pound bale of straw that costs less than a dollar to buy, bale, and transport, and sell it for two, two and a half dollars.

"The margin of profit is high because the cost of labor is low. Very low. Now—it's legal to *freely* contract for piece-work. If a Mexican worker agrees to load a bale for a quarter or fifty cents, that's his business. But we're hearing that the owners of these companies are getting kick-backs from Mexican foremen who gyp their workers in return for payoffs and rigged contracts."

Lou Sessions cleared his throat. "Let 'em quit. Let 'em work for somebody else."

"Well, that's one problem, Sheriff," Cricket replied patiently. "There isn't anyone else to work for. You either work for the jefes approved by the local businessmen, or you don't work at all. That's the first problem.

"Second problem—it's against the law. You can't blackmail workers or extort them in this or any other state. What complicates enforcement, of course, and this is where the INS needs our help, is that most of these workers are undocumented. They're coming across the river in Texas in droves, shoved into trucks and brought here more or less as a captive labor pool. Many, maybe most of the people you see working in those rows and rows of pine trees from Cross City to damn near Georgia are here illegally."

"What choice do the strawmen have?" another sheriff spoke up. "Hell, they cain't get the kids to do the work. They can't get a black man to bale their straw. Not for any wage. Seems to me the Mexicans are saving our bacon."

"They are," Cricket agreed. "And in return for that they deserve the simple protection afforded every worker under the law. Even undocumented workers, gentlemen, are protected by the law."

45

"So what do you need, Agent Bonet?" Buddy Wilson spoke up. "What can we do?"

"First of all, talk to your local businessmen. Just explain to them that rigged or extorted contracts have become a concern for law enforcement. Give them a chance to straighten things out on their own."

"And if they don't?" Lou grumbled. "Am I s'posed to be some kind of labor negotiator?"

"No, sir," Cricket replied firmly. "You are to enforce the law. Best thing, if you find evidence or accusations of threats against workers, would be to contact the state's attorney here in Live Oak. But you're not going to hear anything, I can tell you right now, unless you take time to get to know the migrants under your jurisdiction. Get a handle on where they make their camps. Most importantly, get their confidence so that *they* can come to *you* to report the kinds of infractions we're talking about. If you need help in this regard, or if you are unclear what the law requires, please do not hesitate to call me. I'll assist you any way I can."

"What about the illegals? Say we find 'em, we identify 'em. What do you expect us to do about that?"

"The INS right now simply would like to know how big the problem is. We have heard, for instance, that there are whole families of workers virtually imprisoned in deer camps out toward the coast, most of 'em on private land. Maybe even on the paper mill's acreage, who knows? But we need to know the conditions in those camps. We need to get a rough idea of the numbers of families out there and find out whether they are camped voluntarily or under duress.

"I want to make clear that the state's objective is not to find a way to kick a whole bunch of workers out of your counties, gentlemen. Our objective is simply to uphold the laws protecting these migrants and their families and, to the extent possible, make sure that they are not being extorted or blackmailed into accepting slave wages for their labor. That's the deal. That's what we're about. Any questions?"

A few questions followed concerning procedure and jurisdiction. The sheriffs, ever wary of their turf, did not want their borders opened to INS agents or the FDLE. Cricket explained patiently that he had been sent to the region precisely to give the lawmen first crack at the problem.

"Nobody wants to come in here and do your job," Cricket reassured the elected lawmen. But then he added, "However, this is a job that needs to get done."

The meeting broke up without pyrotechnics. Barrett extended his hand to meet Captain Altmiller's.

"Bear. How you like it down here?"

"Closer to home, Captain."

"A politician's reply," Altmiller retorted.

The hell? Did the Old Man suspect?

Cricket Bonet barged over to end that speculation.

"Hullo, partner!"

"Cricket. Good job. You see him up there, Captain? Another month he'll have 'em eating out of his hand."

Cricket beamed. "And they don't, they can kiss my—"

"No," Altmiller warned. "Not here."

"Let me take us someplace else, then," Barrett offered. "They got a cheap steak at the Dixie Grill. You can fill me in on wha's happenin' in the big city."

The three agents were almost out the door when a rasping challenge came from behind.

"Agent Raines."

Barrett stopped and turned to face Sheriff Lou Sessions.

The sheriff's pitted face was mobile.

"I hear you're gettin' tired of Live Oak, Barrett. Lookin' for a change of scenery."

"Funny." Bear offered a smile. "I was just telling my boss I like it right where I am."

"Way I hear it, you have aspirations for *my* job," Lou grated.

"Pardon me," Altmiller interrupted and extended his hand. "Henry Altmiller. Don't believe we've met, Sheriff."

"Never had the need." Lou shook the offered hand peremptorily.

"Well, you'll be reassured on our first meeting to hear that Agent Raines went to quite a bit of trouble to be assigned to the third district. From all reports he has no intention of leaving."

"That a fact."

"If I am incorrect, I'm sure Agent Raines will tell me. Barrett?"

Well, Bear thought. This was a hell of fix. Fucked if you do, fucked if you don't. Barrett almost took the politician's way out. Almost.

"What the sheriff probably heard, Captain, is that I was approached by some folks to run for sheriff in his county. That's next July, I believe, just to qualify. We're barely into November. As of now, I haven't even decided whether to follow up on the conversation."

"Well. There you are." Altmiller smiled congenially. "Seems fairly straightforward to me, Sheriff."

"We'll see." When Lou straightened, his shoulders pulled in oddly, like a marionette's. "And by the way, Barrett . . ."

One last, parting shot from the county lawman.

"I'm gonna find Rolly Slade's goddamn dog."

The sheriff stalked the five yards to his cruiser and left gravel spinning as he gunned the Crown Victoria out onto a blacktop city street.

Altmiller remained silent. So did Cricket. Barrett felt a tide of blood rising beneath his face.

Cricket spoke up to break the silence. "I can understand a man constipating over an election. But a god-damn *dog*?"

The dog was hungry. It had been three days without food. The water bucket was always filled; the rottweiler stood in a pool of its own piss. But a thick chain restrained him from the only source of food inside these corrugated walls. The food was strapped to the pine studs that were the shack's interior skeleton.

When the sun heated the tin that pressed against the woman's flanks she would arch away, the muscles in her belly contracting with the screams, curses, or impreca-tions that the dog, of course, could not understand and no one else would hear.

It was dim inside the shack, even in bright sunlight. Slits of light on beams moted with dust traveled across the interior, like cruel hour hands marking the terrified moments from morning to pitch-black dark. How many nights had it been? How many days? Hung on a wall with the dog howling at her, foam covering the pink of his gums, running over his bared fangs. Lunging at her from a fragile tether of chain. And then the man would come.

"(Mary, Mother of God.)" The prayers came erratically in a vulgar Spanish. "(Protect me, Mother. In my hour of need. Forgive my sins!)"

She was young, only nineteen, a firmly bosomed girl from Brownsville, a migrant girl from South Texas. If she had only stayed in the field.

But it had been so hard! The heat! The labor! Who could blame her for trying something else?

Her prayer disintegrated into a gargled scream. She had to hang for a minute, just a minute, even though the joints of her shoulders were near to dislocation. The straps that tied her wrists to the shack's vertical studs would not keep a determined hostage forever, so there were cuffs, metal bracelets anchored to the pine posts.

Her feet were cuffed, too, in the posture of Jesus. Christ on a cross. Her own crucifix remained, a cheap thing drenched with sweat between her taut breasts. Her clothes were taken but the cross remained.

He had her pulled off the floor. She could feel herself suffocate. But by stretching her legs to the dirt-packed floor she could put some weight on her feet and feel air expand her chest. She would stay in that posture until the heated tin that pressed against her back and flank could no longer be borne. The dog howled and she screamed in reply.

Footsteps silenced the dog first. Then the girl. She heard the fumbled key. The padlock. The door. Sunlight barged in to the shack's interior. The dog threw himself at the intruder.

"Fuck you."

The chain jerked the dog a foot short of a man in gloves and overalls. The man set a pail wrapped in burlap and a pair of bolt-cutters carefully onto the dirt floor. He noted the dog's water. Still a half bucket. The bucket was strapped to the side of the shed and filled from a connecting length of PVC that ran in from the handpump outside. It was the only way to manage the water, of course. He couldn't trust the dog.

"How 'bout you? You need water?"

He strolled over to the girl.

"No! No, please! Let me go. I beg! I will not tell anyone!"

He offered a bottle of Perrier. "Take it."

She took the water from the bottle's offered nipple like a foal sucking from its mama.

"That's enough." He threw the bottle toward the dog, who tore the plastic containers to pieces. Then he pulled a knife from his pocket.

She screamed.

"No, no. That's not how it's gonna be."

He took off a glove to open the knife's blade, then donned the glove and withdrew to cut the strand that bound the burlap sack.

The sack dropped to reveal a pickle bucket. He hefted the bucket. Strode purposefully to take a position just to one side of his chained trophy.

"*No!*"

He hoisted the bucket above her head. Tipped it. Blood splashed scarlet off her skull.

"*Nooo!*"

It ran off her matted hair. It coursed over her shoulders—

"*Please!*"

Down her back. Between her breasts.

The dog's rabid howl stopped short as he lunged for the target just across the dirt-packed floor. Only the chain was there to jerk him short.

The girl was choking, too. She had swallowed some blood.

The man paused to let her get her air before taking something else from his windbreaker. It might not be obvious from first appearances that the well-machined lump emerging from that nylon pocket was a camera.

"Get her, boy."

"*No!*"

She thrashed against the wall. For a moment he was concerned that the tin might actually break free. She would be exposed, then. Open to the outside world. But it was too late to worry about that. The dog lunged again and again, jerked short each time by the chain, his ass skidding across the pawed dirt. Her smell maddened the animal. Her stink.

He framed a shot carefully. Actuated the camera's lens.

"It won't be long," he promised, backing outside. A box of sunlight silhouetted him briefly at the door. Just an outline in black, like a stick man scissored from tar paper. The door closed, the silhouette vanished, a padlock snicked home.

There were no lines of light on the floor or walls now. Only the animal's and the girl's labored breath filled the interior. Nothing else. The girl sobbed, then, quietly.

Had he gone? Had she survived the ordeal?

But a groan of metal and a square of new light appeared. A window. The dog's chain snaked beneath the wood-shuttered window through a cutout at the bottom of the tin wall to anchor on a post set outside the shack. That had been purposeful. So that he could cut the dog's chain safely, from outside.

He fitted the bolt-cutter's jaws over a link of tempered steel.

"What—? What are you doing?"

He could hear her inquiry floating from the interior, weak in the heavy air. He strained over the cutter's long handles. The jaws snapped suddenly, like a turtle.

"Sic 'em," he commanded loudly.

The steel links chased away. The chain rattled wildly. The mastiff inside bounded like Grendel to take the meat hanging bloody and helpless on the opposite wall.

The camera captured frame after frame from the vantage of the shack's shuttered window. It was important, the photographer told himself, for people to see. To set an example. When it was all over he tasted copper in his mouth. A lethargy fell. As if he needed a nap.

He always expected it to be better than this. It never was. He straightened stiffly. It had taken longer than he planned; the sun was already sneaking below the pines. He was pocketing his camera when some shadow cast swiftly from behind; the change in light alerted him, some fleeting interruption of the failing sun.

He traded the camera for a handgun. Stepped around to the front of the shack. Nothing moving. No one in sight. But he knew who it was who had cast the shadow, the wraith hidden now in an impenetrable shield of vine and briars and pine. How much had the interloper seen? Or heard? That was a problem he would need to solve. He returned to the shack's shuttered window for a final view. The dog was still busy. He'd like to stay and watch that. But already it was getting hard to see inside the rustic chamber. And there was another pair of eyes, he was sure, who longed to see his handiwork. Should he remain? Kill two birds, as it were, with one stone?

He looked west. The sun was well below the pines now. He'd better leave. It was a long and circuitous walk to his vehicle, and it was not safe to be alone in Strawman's Hammock after dark. Not with the bogey man about.

Four

Lou Sessions worked out of an office contiguous with the county's jail in a three-story building rigged for the purpose. It used to be a firehouse, this building. The rising doors that once portaled a pair of fire engines were converted, now, to harbor the country's cruisers and to provide a sally port to the jail.

Barrett Raines pulled his unmarked Impala into a visitor's slot before the facility's side-street entry. A wooden door, peeling paint, beckoned from just off a weed-splintered sidewalk. He rapped on the locked door of the jail and waited just long enough to start to sweat when he saw a deputy peer out through a cracked pane of glass and the barrier of a window unit whose compressor, cutting in and out, begged along with Agent Raines for attention.

Barrett heard a key turn in its lock.

"What you got, Chief?" A deputy unfamiliar to Barrett opened the door with his foot, his hand ladled over a Glock that Barrett noted was unstrapped in its holster.

"Word with the sheriff, please." Barrett displayed identification. "Agent Raines."

"Oh, yeah," The deputy caught the door with his gun hand. "Come on back."

Barrett followed the younger man past a pair of high-ceilinged rooms littered with unused desks and chairs. Barrett saw an Olympic bar loaded with rusted weight and left to bend on a cheap bench and narrow rack. A Coke machine promised relief from that recreation. The deputy's fist flashed out to bang the coin return, but without a pause in stride turned Barrett into a narrow hallway that dropped down a half-step into what might fairly be described as a bunker.

A series of four wide, short hallways converged to provide a jerry-rigged office space. Everything Barrett could see was gotten secondhand or improvised. A mailbox converted with a pair of welded plates and a padlock served as an evidence bin. A sofa rescued from Goodwill was pulled up alongside. A pair of deputies were processing what looked like traffic tickets in folding chairs that slipped under metal desks salvaged (Bear had been told) from Eglin Air Force Base.

"Get some funds for remodeling, we'll move upstairs," the deputy explained. "Most of us look for that to happen in our next life."

Barrett smiled. The Third Judicial District was characterized by counties chronically short of resources. There simply was never enough money for law enforcement, or for schools. For anything.

"Wait here." The deputy deposited Barrett in a crowded hallway rigged as office space.

Hell of a place to work. Bear gathered his impressions privately: A damp cement floor spidered with fractures. A box fan. A pair of computers glowed on a laminated desk. A dispatcher's radio buzzed static from its own niche opposite. Barrett spotted a pair of mobiles deposited casually beside the deskbound wireless, their charging plates exposed for insertion into a cruiser's rejuvenator. A VCR propped atop a barstool on the far side of the radio, its too-short cord swaying upward from the stool's advantage to reach a TV wall-mounted below a ceiling Barrett guessed to be at least eleven feet high. On its screen an unrecognized starlet squawked to Regis Philbin regarding her latest tabloid ambush, while down the hall Barrett could hear, if not see, an investigator responding by phone to what Bear guessed was a reported burglary. It was hard to hear anything clearly. In addition to the investigator, the dispatcher, the roughhouse greetings of passing deputies, and the talk show's endless chatter, Bear could make out the nasal drone of a meterologist.

A cold front was expected, apparently. And rain.

There was exposed wiring up and down the hall and the twin computers required three-plug adaptors to draw current from outlets at least forty years old. A grid of text on the monitor nearest Barrett caught his attention, a shift schedule, looked like, while on the neighboring desktop a screen saver rotated from sylvan forest scenes to beachside bikinis. Barrett was wondering why Lou would risk a display of calendar girls in a workplace so vulnerable to charges of sexual harrassment until it occurred to him that there were no women down here. In fact there were no women in uniform anywhere. The secretaries and dispatchers, all women, were segregated in a single, carpeted office at street level.

Well. That was one way to avoid friction.

"Agent Raines."

Barrett turned to see Lou Sessions leaning on the wall. "Lou."

"I don't have an appointment wrote down for us."

"No." Barrett smiled. "I just thought it'd be a good idea to talk."

The deputy smirked. Lou cut him off with a glance, the cratered face briefly mobile.

"Come on back," he said.

Lou Sessions's office was only marginally an improvement over the warren inhabited by his subordinates. A coffee maker was mounted on a pair of milk crates. Barrett could see a narrow door behind Lou's chipped desk that he suspected led to a private restroom. The state flag of Florida competed with an FSU pennant on one corner of his desk. There was no indicator of national loyalty.

Some office. Barrett glanced about.

"It ain't yours yet," Lou growled from a lean-back roll-around repaired with duct tape.

Barrett faced him squarely.

"If I decide I want your job, Lou, you'll be the first to know."

"No. Linton Loyd'll be first to know."

"I'm not about to get in a pissing contest with you and Linton, Sheriff. Far as I'm concerned *you* are the authority in this county and it's my job to listen to what you have to say."

Lou inclined his head to one side with that declaration.

"Shit," he said after a long moment. "You want some coffee?"

"No, thanks."

"Just tryin' to be polite."

"I know you are, Sheriff."

"Well, then. That be all?"

"One thing. This problem with our out-of-state workers."

"You mean our Messicans."

"Well, Latin Americans, at least."

"Bullshit. Are you running for office?"

"Thought we settled that," Barrett replied stiffly.

"Then call 'em what they are. They ain't Cuban, they ain't Puerto Rican. They're Messicans. They come over the river in Texas, haul their ass here. You know that. I know that."

"Fair enough."

"Plain talk, Bear. It's easiest understood."

"Well, then, Lou, you got to let me be blunt."

" 'Bout time."

"I'd like to look around some of the camps in the county. See if I can get to know some of these people. See if there's anything we need to be concerned about."

"How you gonna talk to 'em? Sign language?"

"Yo hablo español," Barrett replied. *"Poquito,* anyway."

"I'll be damn."

Barrett shrugged. "Spent some time in Texas is all."

"And you can parlay with these people?"

"Not as well as Laura Anne. She speaks well. But if I can find 'em, I can get along. Well enough, I hope, to find out if they're being blackmailed or extorted."

"They're not gonna open up to you on that. They do, they'll wind up with their throats slit or their trucks burned or their wives hauled off."

Barrett leaned forward.

"You know that for a fact, Sheriff?"

"Just imaginin' is all." Lou shrugged. "Hell, ain't it what those people always do?"

Barrett settled back.

"Lou, did you ever consider making these newcomers your allies?"

"Allies? How you figure?"

Barrett frowned. "Haven't you ever looked at these people as a potentially valuable set of eyes and ears? They're working all over the county. They see everything. But nobody sees them. They're invisible."

"Invisible?"

"You know what I mean. I've seen men get out of their trucks and piss beside the road in full view of a family of Mexicans and not give a damn."

"No law says you cain't piss on the road."

"You know my point, Lou. No one *cares* what these people see. Everyone assumes they won't go to the law, that they're so afraid of losing their jobs or being deported or whatever that they're never going to be a witness to anything."

"So far they haven't."

"Then it can't hurt for me to talk to some of 'em, can it?"

The duct-taped chair squeaked as Lou leaned back.

"It was decent of you to come in here," he finally said.

"It's your county, Sheriff. I'm just a visitor."

"You wasn't always," Lou rejoined, and the hostility that had just cooled flared again.

Barrett set his jaw tight.

Lou rocked in his chair a moment longer. Judging the effect. Finally: "You wanta look around the woods, Bear, look all you want. Be my guest. But there's camps back there nobody's seen. And I'll be damned if I can spare a man to show you."

"I've got somebody, thank you." Barrett rose from his hard chair.

"Be nice if he was a officer of the court." Lou found a toothpick on his desk.

Barrett nodded.

"He is."

"Thought we'd go in by water." Jarold Pearson's squashed skull turreted side to side. "Most of the camps you're gonna want to see are close to the coast. 'Sides, it's more fun to take a boat."

They were in Jarold's four-wheeler, or rather, the Commission's, an olive-green Chevy Tahoe fixed with the agency's seal, a V-8, and a boat hitch. Barrett expected to see an airboat trailered behind. The shallow waters near the coast from Deacon Beach to Dead Man's Bay were extremely hazardous to normally hulled watercraft. An oyster mound or cypress knee could rip through any hull, and props were ruined daily. But you could take a Hartzel propeller and a Lycoming engine, mount it above a long, wide-bottomed hull, and skip over those obstacles at fifty bone-jarring miles an hour. You could sail over grass or marsh, too. However, since most drug runners and poachers used boats, Barrett had never been convinced that this was a significant advantage.

On the other hand, Bear could cite some definite disadvantages for the airboat. The things were prohibitively expensive to operate and maintain. If taxpayers only knew. The airboat had a very limited range. And they were loud. Very loud.

Reciprocating aircraft engines designed in the '40s were not built with noise abatement in mind. Local fishermen hated them, and from the lawman's perspective they were not well suited to any operation where a stealthy approach or reconnoiter was required. You just sure as hell were not going to sneak up on anybody with a six-foot prop and a hundred and eighty horses of aircraft engine.

Which may have been the chief reason that Jarold Pearson preferred his own, customized alternative. Barrett was familiar with the newly painted bright-green craft that towed behind the warden's Tahoe; the bird dog was a working boat designed especially for fishing mullet. Bird dogs were especially effective in shallow water, but were outlawed along with certain dimensions of gill nets when changes in state law made their operation illegal. Barrett had spent one afternoon of his life throwing nets off a bird dog. That was plenty.

"The hell did you get that thing?" Barrett jerked a thumb rearward.

Jarold smiled.

"Confiscated. Fixed her up myself."

The boat had an unusual design. Fairly broad abeam, the hull only pulled six inches or so of water, even heavily loaded. There was no prop to stern, or even rudder. Instead, a waterwell mounted just forward of amidships served as transom for an outboard motor that would power and turn a prop just below the waterline. Those unique characteristics combined to produce a craft that was rugged, shallow drafting, and extremely maneuverable.

"Turn on a dime?" Barrett inquired.

"You bet." Jarold smiled proudly. "And give you nine cents change. And then I made my own modification. I swapped out the old Mercury that came with the boat and put in a water jet."

Barrett immediately saw the advantages. With a water jet there was no prop to foul, no blade to become tangled in grass or bent on debris. Instead the engine used impellers to suck up ambient saltwater that was then hosed sternward at terrific pressure. It was a simple system, reliable, easy to operate.

And fast as hell.

"I can make sixty miles an hour over six inches of water without pushing." Jarold eyed his creation briefly in the rearview. "And I can turn three times inside any airboat at full throttle."

But the biggest advantage for law enforcers related to stealth. The jet engine was, in comparison to an airboat, baffled and quiet. You could actually approach a suspect without advertising your presence eight miles in advance.

"Everybody out here's got a gun," Jarold remarked. "You sure as hell want to see him before he sees you."

Jarold's observation reminded Barrett how the role of the game warden had changed over the years, how the stewards of forests and wetlands had extended their role to other areas of law enforcement. Even experienced outdoorsmen misconstrued the warden's authority, greatly overestimating it in some cases, radically underestimating it in others.

A game warden did not, for instance, and contrary to popular opinion, have greater authority to search and seize than other law enforcers. A warden had to have probable cause to look into a footlocker in the bed of a truck, or into the cabin of a boat, just as did a city cop or FBI agent. The difference was that courts routinely allowed game wardens much greater latitude in deciding what probable cause *was* than the latitude allowed a state trooper or city detective. After all, a warden could not reasonably be required to wait for a warrant before searching a man's truck for deer shot out of season, or be forced to wait for a judge to say, yes, you can open Mr. Buchanan's duffel bag to see if he's bagged a dove or six more than his limit.

A Florida highway patrolman could stop you for driving drunk as a hoot owl, but without a warrant or plain-sight evidence he couldn't look to find the cocaine in your trunk. A game warden, in some circumstances, could.

Barrett had stopped a '68 Olds, on one occasion, near Jacksonville. The Olds fit the description of a vehicle recently involved in the shotgun homicide of a convenience store owner.

But a general description of a car did not give Barrett the right to search the vehicle or its driver. Bear knew that. So did the driver. And the driver could have rolled on down the road but for a game warden who came easing onto the shoulder beside Barrett's cruiser in an olive-green truck.

"Morning, gentlemen. I been listenin' to my radio," the warden spoke up for the benefit of the trooper and local sheriff. "What we got here?"

"Just a routine stop," Barrett had replied. "Looks like he's about ready to go."

"Well, I smell somethin'," the warden declared, and nodded to the car's backseat.

"That a rod 'n reel, sir?"

The driver stared straight ahead.

"My brother's."

The warden strolled back to the rear of the car. Bent deeply over the badly rusted trunk.

"I smell fish in here. Gettin' pretty ripe, seems like. You been fishin', sir?"

"No," the driver denied it.

"Got a fishing license, sir?"

"No, I don't."

"Well, there's definitely something fishy, here. I think I better look."

"You son of a bitch," the driver came boiling out of his car, but he couldn't keep that warden from opening the trunk of that '68 Olds.

There it was, a shotgun and a bag filled with cash. The driver was eventually convicted of armed robbery and second-degree murder. The warden's search was allowed, therefore the fruits of that search, however unrelated, were also allowed. Who, after all, could argue with a game warden's sense of smell?

Many folks, even experienced hunters, assumed that wardens could only enforce laws related to Fish & Game on lands that were hunted or fished. Nothing could be further from the truth. Jarold Pearson could enforce *any* state law on *any* private or state-controlled land.

A warden was not a Barney Fife looking out for Bambi. He was a professional lawman working in a sophisticated system with the same responsibilites and duties as any trooper, sheriff, or agent from the Florida Department of Law Enforcement. He was the perfect man to show Barrett Raines the camps and hideaways hiding the county's newest and most persecuted population from the protection of the law.

Bear and Jarold put in at the public boat ramp in Steinhatchee. There was no crystal strand along this beachhead. No sand, in fact, at all. You could not even see the Gulf, only great swathes of water that cut through the grass and zigzagged away from the slips of boats berthing near the ramp, aisles of water that trekked through antedeluvian carpets to some place where water and horizon met an uncertain boundary. The air was heavy here, a thick and fecund atmosphere conjured from decaying organic matter and saltwater heated over vast areas to settle in mists above ferns and conifers that crowded the ramp right up to the water's edge.

"Hard to believe we're three weeks from Thanksgiving," Jarold remarked.

A breeze rose warmly. The grass undulated below flights of pelicans and cormorants.

It was, truly, Barrett decided, a magical place.

What would it take to spoil it? Already you could see the mix of old poverty and nouveau riche that peopled the area. Rusted-out washing machines and dilapidated trailers mixed company with the trophy homes of out-of-towners. A grid of streets formed the township proper. Those homes seemed to belong here, their corrugated roofs and screened porches not much changed from the homes of fishermen who had lived for generations on this enchanted littoral.

A few businesses thrived, holding stubbornly onto strips of land up and down from where Barrett and Jarold launched their boat. Roy Buchanan, for one, still had his restaurant here, the only restaurant besides Ramona's for miles up and down the coast. The hurricane in '89 had destroyed his original business. Barrett could remember looking through the cracks in Roy's first cypress floor to feed mullet or carp with crumbs from the biscuits that used to come with swamp cabbage and snapper.

The place was sealed in, now, in the standard construction of studs and sheetrock and central air. Soon after the hurricane a man from Georgia came in to rebuild a pier and dockworks down the canal from Roy's. A two-masted sloop rode the low tide near a dry dock newly built alongside. You could buy ice and bait and tackle in a half-dozen other places. Some entrepreneur even started a Blockbuster.

"Cain't be anybody local," Jarold remarked and nudged the ignition.

A boil of bubbles broke to stern. The bird dog swelled up from the water like the sudden rise of an elevator. Barrett grabbed a gunwale on instinct. He had never been totally at home on the water.

"We're fine," Jarold reassured, taking a line to starboard of the nearest buoy and onto a lane of water warm as jade.

"Never get tired of coming down here." Barrett did not have to shout to be heard.

"Well, the first place you're gonna see," Jarold replied with some pride, "is mine."

Jarold followed the wavering coastline less than ten minutes before a tributary invisible to Barrett put him hard to port where a shanty rose on stilts not a hundred yards from the coast.

"My little hideaway," Jarold said proudly.

It was just a box on stilts. Tin roof and screened-in windows.

"I cook on propane." Jarold cut the bird dog's engine as he glided toward a crude pier buffered with a re-treaded tire. "And shit in an outhouse. It's primitive, but hey—it's mine. Grab our water jug, would you?"

Barrett picked up a canteen and stepped from the boat onto damp land. Jarold whipped a quick slipknot around a cypress stump.

"Got my Jeep up front. From here we drive."

Within minutes Barrett found himself in a vintage Willys Jeep following tracks fainter than deer signs that ran through bogs and lowlands to intersect tracts of pine trees set in identical rows stretching, apparently, forever.

"How do you keep from getting lost in here?" Barrett asked.

"I still do, sometimes. What amazes me is how these newcomers find their way."

The first migrant camp they visited consisted of three families camped in a square shack insulated with newspaper. What Barrett wanted most was to gain the migrant workers' confidence. Most folks south of the border were afraid of anyone in uniform, especially uniforms with sidearms. Barrett left his nine-millimeter in Jarold's Jeep and made sure that he was seen to be unarmed. He took a long time to explain that the armed warden at his side was here to enforce laws related to fish and game.

"(He's not INS,)" Bear assured in Spanish the wizened elder, who stared suspiciously from the shade of a water oak. "(He is a constable in charge to make sure that hunters and fisherman do not break the law.)"

"(We only fish for food,)" a younger man protested.

"*Sí, señor.*" Barrett smiled warmly. "*No es un problema. No problema.*"

A gaggle of children clung to their mothers' skirts as the conversation jerked haltingly forward. Barrett realized quickly that his Spanish, while sufficient for polite conversation, was nowhere near fluent enough when he had to inquire about blackmail or extortion.

"(How do you live?)" he tried that tack. "(How do you earn money?)"

The elder man shrugged.

"(We wait for El Toro,)" he said.

"The Bull?" Barrett replied in English and saw that this much, at least, the older man understood.

"(He is the jefe, señor.)"

"*Yanqui?*"

"No, no." The old man shook his head. "(Mexicano. He finds us work.)"

"(What kind of work?)"

A self-deprecating shrug of the shoulders. Eyes that suddenly shift and lose contact.

"(All kinds.)"

"(All kinds. Yes. Like in the straw, señor? Does the Bull get you work baling straw?)"

"(We just fish,)" a younger man broke in. "(We fish and we wait for work. That's all.)"

"(That's fine.)" Barrett nodded. *Muy bien.* (If you need help with anything—a doctor, maybe? For the children? You can call this number.)"

Barrett gave the elder his card.

"(My name is Bear,)" he said. And, still smiling, "(I am a good match for Señor Bull!)"

The gathered workers laughed nervously. But Barrett noticed as he swung into Jarold's Jeep that their patriarch tucked his card carefully into a dirty shirt pocket.

"Who the hell is this Bull?" he asked when Jarold had them safely around a sandy bend.

Jarold shook his narrow head.

"Some kind of go-between, maybe?"

"Maybe," Barrett nodded. "But you notice they weren't about to give us anything but his street name."

They made perhaps a half-dozen camps that day. The stories were all about the same. Workers waiting for work.

Waiting for salvation. Waiting for Godot. Only one camp seemed regularly employed. When Barrett asked if the contract came through El Toro, the younger Latin denied it so furiously that Bear knew it was true.

Clearly, Señor the Bull was someone well known to the migrants in these isolated camps. Barrett made a note to call the county clinic, see if they couldn't get somebody out to check up on the children. A sort of depression had set in, which he did not expect. These desperate residents, their hollow homes carved in the woods, stirred memories Barrett would just as soon forget.

Barrett knew what it was like to be raised in a shack. He knew what it was like to wake up in the night sweating hot, or shaking cold, depending on the season. Barrett knew what a piss bowl was, and a thunder jug. But that beat the hell out of running to an outhouse where the first thing you did before you squatted was to rattle the box with a stick to scare off the snakes. Barrett Raines had lived as these people had lived. He was surprised and ashamed, therefore, to find himself resenting these poor people for making him remember.

It was late afternoon by the time Barrett and Jarold Jeeped back along the sinuous sandy roads that would take them to the warden's seaside residence and alternate transportation. Jarold had become positively garrulous in the course of the day's work, explaining to Barrett the labyrinthine roads that spidered all over the flatwoods, giving him details of the region's camps and the easiest ways to reach them.

They were in the middle of one of these explications when the game warden shivered his Jeep to a sudden stop.

"The hell?" Barrett stiff-armed the dash.

"Sorry." Jarold was out of the still-running Willys and

squatting on the road before Bear could get out of his seat belt.

"Got something?" Barrett caught up to the warden.

Jarold nodded. "See for yourself."

They were tire tracks. Some vehicle, very wide, had left the sand road for offroad pursuits, apparently. Grass and vines, pressed at some point into ruts, already rebounded.

"Some four-wheeler?" Barrett offered.

"Yeah."

"See this all the time, don't you? Somebody wanting to go offroad?"

"Not this particular somebody."

"What do you mean?"

"You spent some time in the military, didn't you, Bear? Army was it?"

"It was."

"Take another look at those tracks. Take a good look."

Barrett kneeled to the soft earth to see a stretch of sand crumpled indistinctly into two widely spaced ruts.

"Big tire print," Bear grunted.

Something familiar there. In that print.

"Heavy, but not a truck," Jarold pointed out. "You see that? Got the wheelbase of a damn tractor, but it ain't no tractor. Damn sure ain't no Jeep."

"Be damned," Barrett exclaimed. "I know what is. Sure I do."

It was a Humvee. The all-purpose vehicle introduced to Americans in CNN footage of the Gulf War was now available to civilians. You could get plush seats, digital sound, and A/C in your customized Macho Machine. For a price, of course. Humvees were astronomically expensive. In fact, there were only two Humvees to Barrett's knowledge in his six-county district. One belonged to a car collector in Madison. And the other—

Belonged to Linton Loyd's only and sullen son.

Barrett stood.

"Think this goes anywhere?"

Jarold turned back to his own offroad accommodation. "Let's just see."

The limbs of trees slapped their needles onto the windshield of Pearson's Jeep as the warden and the FDLE investigator left the safe, sandy boulevard to follow the fading, wide-tracked trail offroad.

There was a change in topography, Barrett noted. The trees, for one thing, no longer stood in rows. The pines were taller, thicker, their limbs stretched out in elegant panoplies showered with starbursts of needles and pods of cones.

"Yellowheart pine." Jarold anticipated Bear's question. "Last natural stand I know of, around here. God knows how they got missed."

There was straw everywhere underfoot, fallen in ages of accumulated carpet. Made Barrett want to leave the Jeep and walk barefoot. But then the trail dipped abruptly and with the slap of limbs on the windshield the Jeep foundered axle-deep in something not quite like mud.

"Oh, shit." Bear reached for his seat belt.

"I got it." Jarold swapped cogs and the four-cylinder Jeep reversed field.

Four wheels spun for traction. A rooster tail of mud.

"Give her a chance." Jarold remained calm.

The Jeep lurched free of the bog.

Barrett allowed a pony keg of air to exhale from his lungs.

"Be a good idea to keep an eye out for quicksand," Jarold commented drily as he detoured around the bed.

Barrett could no longer make out even the trace of a trail, but Jarold pushed on, pausing briefly at intervals to inspect the torn bark on a water oak, or point to a broken vine of wild grapes.

Suddenly, abruptly, the canopy of pine gave way to an

open, ruddy sky. Jarold slammed on the brakes and skidded to a sliding halt before a smooth, freshwater pond.

Barrett released his seat belt.

"Where the hell exactly are we?"

"I'd guess one and a half, maybe two miles off the sand road. Not too far from the coast."

"There a name for this place?"

"Mmmhmm." Jarold nodded. "Strawman's Hammock."

Barrett paused. He had heard of the Hammock. There were all sorts of stories. Ghosts, bogey men. Witches.

You don't behave, young'un, I'm agonna take you down to the Hammock, leave your black ass onna stump!

Barrett followed Jarold's lead to debark from the Jeep.

"Looks like it'd be a hunter's paradise," he remarked.

"No," the warden disagreed shortly.

"No? Why not?"

" 'Cause hunters have got lazy, Bear. They won't get off the road fifty yards if they can help it. And nobody stalks game on foot anymore. Not even bowhunters. They just get in their blinds or up a tree and wait for it."

"If you leased this land somebody'd hunt it. They'd put in roads. And blinds."

Jarold nodded. "Paper mill in Perry wants to do just that. They been tryin' to buy this land, what I understand, for months. But there's some legal problem with title, or squatter's rights. I don't know the details."

Barrett gazed over the pond.

"Maybe our man just came in to fish."

"He'd've had to know there was a pond," Jarold pointed out. "Outside aerial photography, I don't know how he'd find this one."

"Accident, maybe." Barrett slapped a gnat off his face. "Or maybe he was just exploring."

Jarold remained quiet.

"Something botherin' you, Jarold?"

"This ain't the first fellah took a sudden interest in

exploring Strawman's Hammock. I was driving out this way a month, maybe a month and a half ago, on the Suwannee side, and I saw where maybe four or five vehicles had pulled off the road and into these woods. I followed the tracks right to this pond, pretty sure it was this pond. If it is, there's a shack on the other side. Some old cracker shack."

"Sounds like a place for hunters to me."

The warden shook his narrow head. "Nuh uh. You find hunters camping, you're gonna see things. There's gonna be a latrine. Someplace to bury the skinnings. Usually toilet paper or beer cans—they never clean up right.

"But this place looked scrubbed. I didn't see a soda can or a campfire, much less any sign of field dressing. But I did find a condom."

"Condom?" Barrett fell in beside Pearson as the warden stepped out to follow the water's edge. "Long way to come for poontang."

"Long way for anyone," Jarold agreed without looking back. "And there must've been three . . . four vehicles come in here. I thought, well . . . if you wanted to have a party . . . be hard to find a place much more out of the way than this."

"Probably." Barrett found he had to stretch to keep up with the game warden. "But Jarold . . . you don't mind . . . I'm mostly interested in Mexicans."

Again without breaking stride or looking back, Jarold pulled what looked like a credit card from the breast pocket of his olive green and handed it back.

"It's a phone card," the warden tossed over his shoulder. "The migrants, they all get 'em. To call back home, I guess. Or Texas."

Barrett took the card. "You found this at the shack?"

"Ways off from it. On the way back to the county road."

It was a Sprint calling card. Barrett pocketed the item.

"We should be able to see who made the purchase. See

where they called. But unless the place is being used now—"

"Oh, it's being used," Jarold said. "I'm just about positive of that. I just don't know for— Hold up. Hold!"

Barrett stumbled to a stop.

"You hear that?"

The wind in the pines moaned. But then Barrett did hear it. Something beneath the wind. A long, mournful wail.

"Come on." Jarold broke into a jog.

They had to break through another cordon of pine and vines to find a rusting, tin-paneled shack lying just behind the pond, shrouded in the shadows cast by a sun that settled below the treeline. All metal, to appearances. Not a scrap of wood showing. Some sort of animal bayed from inside. A hound?

"Is that PVC?"

Barrett edged to one side to see a white length of pipe running from the house to a handheld pump.

The dog was barking now, snarling, furious.

"He smells us." Jarold pulled the safety strap off the hammer of his .357. "You armed, sir?"

A sudden, professional detachment.

"Yes." Barrett slipped his Glock from its holster.

"All right, let's just do this by the numbers—*Hello!*" Jarold called. *"Anybody in there?"*

The hound or mastiff or whatever it was bayed in reply. Nothing else.

"This is Lieutenant Pearson, Fish and Game. If you are inside, please come out with your hands on your head. Come out now, please."

The breeze shifted in response. An awful putrid odor carried to the two lawmen.

Barrett had smelled that smell before.

And then something inside the shack smashed into the

74

wall. The shack shook with the impact like a cube of jelly.

"Jesus." Barrett jumped, startled.

Jarold remained steady as a rock.

The animal charged again into the interior wall and the shack shivered again. A shingle broke off the roof and fell as slowly as a snowflake to the sand beneath.

"I see a shutter above the PVC line. Do you, sir?"

"I do," Barrett nodded. "Window."

"Roger. Looks like there's a steel slipbolt holding it. I'm going to try and open 'er. Give us a look inside."

"Be careful," Barrett advised.

"Yes, sir." Jarold nodded, swapping from a Weaver's stance to a single arm. The warden held his weapon like a flashlight, straight ahead in one hand, easing to one side of the shuttered window.

The dog or whatever it was howled as though he was being branded. Then the howl disintegrated at the warden's approach into a high-pitched whimper.

"I'm opening up." Jarold shot the bolt—

And a hundred and twenty pounds of dog burst through the shack's solitary window like a tiger through a hoop of fire. Jarold swiveled his weapon to take the rottweiler—

But Barrett was in the line of fire!

"Shoot, Bear!"

Barrett emptied the clip of his weapon into the center of the dark blur of foam and fangs bearing down. The dog leaped.

Nine shots. Quick as he could pull.

The dog fell in a heap to one side. Bear could smell the rank of his breath.

"God!"

He clutched his stomach.

Jarold kept his weapon free.

"You all right?"

"Yeah . . . yeah . . . Jesus."

Jarold stepped up calmly and put a round at the occipital of the animal's skull.

The fluid in Barrett's ears compressed with the added concussion. His knees were weak as he nodded to the shack.

"What . . . what we got inside?"

"Haven't exactly had time to look." The warden seemed insulted.

"Sorry," Bear apologized. "Why don't we check it out together?"

They kept their weapons extended as they approached the shack. There could be another animal posing a threat inside. Conceivably an assailant. That smell, Barrett knew, was not altogether the dog's.

Barrett kicked the door open. Flies buzzed like bees inside. Light filled the room brown and amber and slow as syrup. Portions of a carcass, could have been more than one, emerged into view. It was all over the floor. At first Bear thought the scraps of meat he saw were come from a deer, the smell and recent disembowelment he had witnessed being so familiar. But then he saw something that made him know this was not the case.

"Oh, Lord. Up there. On the wall."

Pine studs formed a skeleton to support the shack's metal skin. A pair of arms hung from that wooden anatomy, arms ripped from their shoulders. Lots of bone showing. Lots of meat stripped off or rotting. The hands remained untouched in their steel cuffs. You could still see the fingernail polish. Down below—the feet. Nothing else. Whatever remained was scattered in shreds over the floor.

"Make a hole!"

A plague of flies chased Barrett outside. Jarold Pearson emerged moments later. The warden passed the rim of his Stetson over his forehead.

"Well," he said, studying Barrett. "I guess we better call the sheriff."

It took an hour and a half to get Sheriff Sessions to the scene. The Jeep's radio had not proved reliable, forcing Jarold to borrow Barrett's cell phone. "It's all right." Barrett handed the phone over graciously. "Happens to us all the time." The sheriff would have to be shown the way in, of course, which meant that the warden had to meet Lou Sessions at some mutually known location and then guide him into Strawman's Hammock.

"How 'bout Linton Loyd's deer camp?" Jarold spoke into the phone and Barrett quickly sliced his hand across his throat.

"Belay that suggestion," Jarold recanted. "I can do better than the Loyd camp. Tell you what. Just go to the boat ramp at Roy's. . . . Roy's, that's right. I'll meet you there. . . . What's that?"

Barrett saw Jarold nod to the sheriff's rejoinder.

"Yes, sir. . . . Right, Sheriff. . . . No, he's here, you wanta talk to him?"

Jarold extended the phone. "Sheriff like to speak with you, Bear."

Barrett took the cell phone. "Agent Raines."

"Goddammit, what are you doin' investigatin' homicides in my county?"

"I wasn't, Lou. I was checking out the migrants' camps. This thing here came because of the warden's sharp eyes, and I think we oughta be glad he's got 'em. Otherwise I don't know how long it'd have been 'til—"

"Kiss my ass, Bear. People don't die in my county without me knowin' about it."

"Didn't imply that they could, Sheriff. But what would you have us do? Walk away?"

"Goddamn right! Walk away is *exactly* what you should of done."

"There could have been a victim still alive in there, Sheriff!" Barrett stared into the receiver of his phone. "There could have been a perpetrator, for God's sake."

"There could have been lots of things. You should have called."

"I did call, Sheriff. I proceeded under exigent circumstances—"

"Exigent, my ass!"

Barrett took a deep breath. "You're gonna need some forensics out here."

"I don't need you to tell me what I need."

"Do you even care what you've *got*, Lou? Because I can tell you, you've got what appears to be an elaborately staged homicide. You've got a dead dog that I'm betting belongs to Rolly Slade. You've got blood and guts all over the shack, I'm guessing at least a week old. Now I can get you an FDLE mobile out here with a team to grid this whole thing off and sift the goddamn sand. Why the hell wouldn't that assistance be interesting to you, Sheriff?"

"If I need assistance, I'll ask for it."

"At least let me call it in. Have 'em put a unit and team on standby."

"You don't do a *goddamn* thing 'til I get out there, you got it, Agent? You sit on your goddamn hands."

"I will so note in my report," Barrett grated.

"Fuck you, Raines."

"Also noted. And by the way, Lou, I *will* write a complete and detailed report. And if you want to find fault with anything that I or the warden have done here, you can take it up with somebody who gives a shit."

Barrett killed the call and snapped the phone's thin receiver shut.

"The hell was that?" Jarold asked.

"Man worried about his job," Barrett said. "You go ahead. I'll do what I can to secure the scene."

"Awright. One thing."

"Yes." Barrett waited.

"Why'd you wave me off Linton's camp?"

"Avoiding problems," Barrett replied. "After all, we've found tracks that put Linton's son at least near the scene and in the approximate time frame of the killing. So what would you do if you ran into Gary at his daddy's camp? He'd want to know, Linton certainly would demand to know, what you're doing meeting Lou out there. And there's the other thing—between Lou and Linton."

"They hate each other." Jarold nodded. "I knew that. I just jumped the gun."

"Don't kick yourself in the ass over it," Barrett assured him. "You've done good out here, Jarold. Damn good. If it weren't for you this homicide might never have been discovered—a fact I will note in my report."

The warden offered his embarrassed chuckle to that compliment.

"Jarold, there's one other thing. It's the wrong time to bring this up, but there's no good time. Something between you and me I want to apologize for. It happened a long time ago, when we were kids."

"On the bus." Jarold nodded.

Jesus. Barrett's heart fluttered. *He hasn't forgotten.*

"Well, I don't know why I joined in with those boys to call you names and generally behave like a jackass, but I am ashamed of it. I was wrong and I want to apologize."

Jarold stared at the ground a moment.

"Long damn time to wait," he said.

Barrett swallowed. "Yes, it is."

Jarold took his eyes off the ground. "Past is past."

"It isn't always," Barrett said. "I know."

Jarold scuffed his boot across the Jeep's tire.

"I better go after the sheriff. We don't wanna be stuck in this place after dark."

It wasn't the best of exchanges, but it would have to do.

"Right, then. And thanks for the help, Jarold."

"Welcome," the warden replied and swung into his Jeep. Barrett waited for the Willys to clear the pond before he returned to his cell phone. Lou certainly couldn't keep him from reporting a homicide to his Live Oak office. And if one of Bear's peers at the field office just happened to assume that a mobile unit would be needed, or maybe even call to Tallahassee to get a team ready, why—

There was nothing Lou could do about that.

"FDLE." Bonny's voice answered thin and far away.

"Hey, Bonny. Bear here. Has Cricket left yet?"

"No, he's right here. Flirtin' with me."

"Would you put him on, please, ma'am?"

Five

The side-paneled van of the Florida Department of Law Enforcement's mobile unit was familiar to Barrett Raines. A team of FDLE investigators methodically gridded off the murder of the now-confirmed female who would be the Jane Doe of the investigation. Sheriff Sessions arrived at the scene in near total darkness to make his professional evaluation by flashlight which, of course, meant that the sheriff only delayed the team's arrival. Barrett could have had the investigators there that night, working under the halogens, saving precious time.

Even though the corpse's disintegration told investigators that the homicide was not recent, there still ought to have been every effort made to gather forensics on blood, tissue, and fluids as quickly as possible. The accuracy of many tests related to levels of adrenaline and serotonin that might be accurate within a day or two of death degraded precipitously thereafter. Some toxins that might be detected within five days or a week would fail to register beyond that time.

Forensic pathology was a time-sensitive art. *Every* man or woman in criminal investigation was drilled to gather fluids, tissue, and visual information as quickly as possible.

The sheriff's sensitivity for turf had delayed the gathering of crucial information a full twenty-four precious hours. What chafed Barrett, Cricket, and the other members of the team even more was that Lou seemed completely unconcerned about the effects of that delay.

You did what you could. The area was secured, first, and gridded off into squares. Every scrap collected in a given square received a coordinate in the grid, a description, and an identifying number. The finding officer signed a receipt for each bagged item of evidence. Chain of custody went straight from the discovering team member to Sheriff Sessions. The work was as painstaking as archeology, and the stakes were a lot higher.

A killer was loose. More than likely a sociopath. Certainly this was no ordinary crime of passion. Barrett and his team did not yet know (might never know, thanks to the sheriff) whether the woman was raped or had had sexual intercourse with her killer. That fact would greatly impact the profile made of Jane Doe's assailant.

The body, what was left of it, would be violated again, this time for forensic detail. Every hair on her body held a story. Every scrap of skin told a tale. A single fingernail or a sample of blood could point to her killer. Or cement a conviction. Barrett was certain that her killer was a he. And he would bet that this was not the perpetrator's first homicide. The dog was what bothered him the most. It *was* Rolly Slade's. That fact was verified by Rolly himself only that morning. Barrett was almost sure that whoever recruited the dog was a local resident. It was hard to imagine a serial killer drifting through the area who could capture or cajole the animal into captivity, then select a victim and construct the kind of horror show that was being uncovered grid by grid in this suffocating hammock. Whoever did this knew the dog, knew the land. Barrett would be surprised if he did not know the victim as well.

Barrett turned to Cricket.

"Where's Holloway?"

Midge Holloway was the chief forensics investigator from Jacksonville. Midge had gone much more than the extra mile, leaving that East Coast city to drive all the way to the West Coast for this homicide. The chief did not usually come to the scene. Their work was done in the Jacksonville morgue. Midge's responsibilities and authority were more fluid. When Barrett explained the elaborately staged scene, Midge had decided that she needed to have a clearer vision of the evidence than what could be gleaned from a grid map and plastic bags.

"I'll be there at first light," she had told Barrett.

"She's inside the shack," Cricket told Bear.

Midge was a short, slightly built woman. A premature onset of osteoporosis forced her to peer up at you from a nascent hunchback with eyes large and liquid as a lemur's.

Those eyes, Barrett thought. They don't miss much.

"Midge. You got any impressions?"

"Most interesting thing I've seen in a long time."

"Interesting" was not the word Barrett would have chosen. But he understood that Midge's vocabulary was shaped by the imperative need to remain objective. An emotional identification with the victim could be useful at some point in the process. But not here. Not now.

"We have a female. The pelvis, what I can find of it, shows no sign of childbirth. I'd be surprised if she was much older than twenty."

"Okay." Barrett was already scribbling in his spiral pad.

"I won't know for sure 'til I get to the lab, but I'm pretty sure she was not dehydrated at the time of death. Not badly, anyway."

"How you figure?"

"Body's been torn apart, which complicates things. And then there are the flies and maggots, not to mention the bacterial assault. But looking at what's left of her arms and hands, I don't see the kind of dessication you'd expect in someone who, for instance, died of thirst."

"How did she die?"

"At this point it could be anything from a shot of pentothal to the obvious."

"The dog."

"Right. That'll have to wait for the lab. If the dog killed the victim, she most likely bled to death or died of shock, but at this point that's conjecture."

"I understand." Barrett nodded. "Though that water bucket and pipe make me think that both the dog and the woman had some kind of access to drinking water."

"She wouldn't be sipping on her own," Midge stated wryly.

"No, my guess is she was kept. For how long and what purpose, I don't know."

The problem with looking for a motive early in any investigation was that it led to rabbit trails or, worse, a distortion of the actual facts on the ground. Something no more complicated than revenge might have led to this criminal act. Victims both male and female had been tortured to death in retaliation for any number of reasons. But there were some general patterns in cases like these that were hard to ignore.

"You figure the killer was male?" Bear asked.

"Oh, yeah. Male. Late twenties to mid forties. You know the profile. And there is one piece of religious paraphernailia that I find interesting."

Out of a blue plastic tub, Midge pulled a plastic bag with a cheap crucifix inside.

"Victim was stripped naked, except for this. Now who might allow a crucifix to remain on the naked body of a victim he meant to torment and kill?"

"You're thinking Catholic?"

"Possibility. Could also be a killer with a religious bent

or background. Lot of your Latin workers fit that bill."

"Lots of Baptists, too," Barrett countered.

Midge shrugged. "Nevertheless, this crucifix taken with the fact that the victim is Latin American suggests to me that we can't exclude Latin American males from the set of her possible killers."

"Would not fit the general profile," Barrett responded.

Barrett knew, and Midge knew very well, that this sort of crime tended overwhelmingly to be the work of male Caucasians, usually men without strong ties to family or friends, who were somewhere in age from their late twenties to forties. That profile, developed in the need to find serial killers, also conformed remarkably well to most elaborately staged homcides, especially those involving women.

"What would motivate a Latino male to go to this trouble?" Barrett asked.

Midge shrugged. "What made the guy from Texas whack victims along the railroad?"

"Those were targets of opportunity," Bear pointed out.

"Who's to say our victim wasn't?" Midge countered. "Or going the other way, you can look at scenarios for revenge, betrayal. Anything to do with drugs. Folks in the coke business torture people to death routinely. Just on the *suspicion* of a doublecross. You think every druggie in this district is Caucasian?"

"But this homicide took time," Bear mused. "It took planning. And resources."

"What resources?" she countered. "A shack. Some water. A dog."

"How about the handcuffs?"

"Ordered from a catalog. Or anyplace that caters to sexual fetishes."

"This is Lafayette County, Midge. Not Jacksonville."

She smiled. "Just looking at the possibilities."

"Well, let's see what we can do to eliminate a few. First

thing I'm going to want is an identification for the victim. A name links to people and places. Friends. Family."

Midge nodded. "I'll do what I can. But you know as well as I do, Bear, that if this young woman came here with migrant workers she's more than likely not going to have a fingerprint on file. She's probably not going to have a green card, either. No social security number. No dental or school records."

"You got somebody who can reconstruct her appearance?" Bear asked. "Somebody good enough to give us a composite?"

"Nobody in our shop," Midge shook her head. "And Tallahassee's crew are swamped. It'd be weeks. But maybe . . ."

"Come on, Midge."

"I might be able to find somebody."

Barrett knew better than to press. "Just see what you can do," he urged.

"I'll need the sheriff's approval."

Barrett chewed that one over a moment.

"Do it on my authority," he said finally. "We've *got* to know what Jane looks like if we're to have a hope in hell of making an ID."

"What about Lou?"

"Well. As General Powell used to say, it's a whole lot easier to ask for forgiveness than it is to ask for permission."

Midge nodded. "I'll call our guy first thing."

Barrett was not sure, even with a good reconstruction, how easy it would be to identify this young woman. There would be a great and natural reluctance for any illegally entered Latino to volunteer information for criminal investigators. A code of silence prevailed. And there was another factor, too. Women and girls in migrating communities were, in too many cases, valued only for their labor—for the beets they picked, the straw they raked.

Women were abused by men in great numbers across all socioeconomic categories. But Latino women working as migrants from Florida to California were particularly vulnerable.

Would a family member or friend in fear of deportation tell Barrett anything at all about this particular victim? How could he gain their trust? How could he protect them? After all, a man or woman capable of this kind of violence would not hesitate to kill again.

Absent specific information about the victim or her killer, Barrett was left with general trends, general information, generally occuring patterns of behavior. He didn't like that. Generalities got you in trouble. Generalities were only useful to indicate the broad topography of an investigation.

They could not be used as a compass.

"That's enough in here."

Barrett followed his forensic investigator into the fresh and welcome air.

"Hard to believe you'd leave an office in Jacksonville for this mess, Midge."

She shrugged. "I like dead people." She sealed a plastic bag. "Tell you one thing. Whoever's done this has done it before. Or something very much like it."

Barrett nodded. "Occurred to me as well. I think we ought to fax the Bureau with all the details we can muster, ask them to compare the staging of this scene with others nationwide. Our killer might have a track record someplace else."

But when suggested to Sheriff Sessions that federal authorities be asked to assist in his investigation, Lou went ballistic.

"The hell! What have I got *you* people down here for?"

Barrett stiffened. "We'll support you all we can, Sheriff. But the feds might have seen a case exactly like this that'd help us out. They may have a fingerprint on our Jane Doe. Hell, we might get lucky and get some DNA on the perp that shows up in VCAP's library."

"You can run the DNA from right here," Lou growled. "*I* can run prints through AFIS. That's all the FBI I god-damn need. What *you* need, Bear, is to sift this shit and bag it so I can go interview my suspect."

"Whoa. Sheriff. Suspect? We don't even have an ID on the victim yet. We don't have a face that anybody can recognize. Give Midge some time, she might can get us something we can use."

"I already got somethin' I can use. I got tire tracks to a Humvee. And I know who owns it."

"Set of tracks doesn't give us much."

"Puts Gary Loyd on the scene." Lou bit it off.

"We don't know that. We don't even know the time of death for sure," Barrett disagreed. "And according to Jar-old, there've been three or four different vehicles coming back here for at least a couple of months. Most of 'em right up to the shack."

"Good. Find out who they are. I'll see them, too."

"Sheriff, I—"

"You what? What the fuck is your problem, Agent?"

The activity that had so methodically proceeded in all grids of the crime scene halted abruptly *in medias res.* Technicians, forensics, photographers—frozen in their tasks with the sheriff's bilious challenge.

Barrett took a deep breath.

"I just don't want to lose a potential suspect, Sheriff. We go in now, we're just fishing."

"I can fish."

"What for?"

"Well, Agent Raines, for starters I'm gonna ask Gary Loyd if he's ever come out here for some Mexican strange."

Barrett saw one of the FDLE team snap off her latex

gloves; Irene Sanchez marched without a word toward the side-paneled truck. A long pause, then, before Cricket Bonet strolled over.

"Sheriff. Maybe you-all want to keep this conversation private?"

"Not likely."

Cricket made himself at ease beside the county's top dog.

"All right. Then what makes you think Gary Loyd's a likely susect?"

"Why else would he be out here?"

"Shoot a deer. Whack off. Only one of which can be construed as a crime in the state of Florida."

"You'a wiseass, aren't you, Bonet?"

"Wise enough to know that if you go looking for Gary Loyd you're better off with a warrant."

"Judge Blackmond ain't gonna give me no warrant," Lou scoffed. "Not off a week-old set of tire tracks."

"Then let us dig," Barrett rejoined. "If we get hard evidence that puts Gary in that shack, or anywhere near it, you can search his truck, his house, anything you need."

" 'Course, that would take some little time. Wouldn't it? To get me all those—those facts?"

Barrett faltered. "Some time. Sure."

The skin across the craters of the sheriff's face stretched tight as canvas.

"You're not bought off here, are you, Bear?"

"Beg your pardon?"

"Well, Linton Loyd's got to be a big part of your future, hasn't he? Maybe that's why you're wantin' to treat his boy with kid gloves."

"You—!"

Barrett was moving toward the sheriff with damage on his mind when Cricket stepped in to intervene.

"Gentlemen." Bonet turned to the county sheriff.

"So you're determined to interview this Gary Loyd?"

"Soon as I can."

"Without a warrant?"

"The hell I need a warrant for? I'm just asking the man some questions."

Cricket nodded. "All right. Mind if we tag along?"

A smile split Lou Session's cratered face.

"Hell, no. Be my pleasure."

Six

Rolly Slade barely glanced at his son as Jerry slipped a magazine and a pair of floppy disks into his knapsack.

"Be a little late coming home," Jerry announced on his way out the door.

Rolly was on the phone, hard in the market for another rottweiler. Jerry heard the talk—how the Slade family would get rich suing the county, state, and justice department for the wrongful death of the dog killed by Barrett Raines and that goddamn, grouper-headed warden. Rolly's peroration extended to a vaguely libertarian rail against all manner of authority. His son padded out of earshot down the short packed-dirt alley that led past their small machine shop to reach a chinaberry tree, under whose nasty shade the school bus would rumble to a stop.

Nothing like the doors on a school bus. Slap-slap. Jerry Slade nodded greetings and limp high-fives to the other sophomores in his class. There were no teenage spics on board, Jerry noted with disappointment, but a quartet of little señoritas, their hair tied in bright bows, their eyes deep and brown, always sat up front where Mr. Theo could keep an eye on them. And there was his special girl.

"Get youself a seat, Jerry." Mr. Theo was riding his ass before he got halfway down the aisle.

Jerry flopped into a vacant, straight-backed chair. He opened the knapsack—

"What you got, Jerry?" A gaggle of teenage boys stumbled over each other to see a full-length glossy of Brittany Spears.

"She's hot." A pair of feral eyes beamed across the aisle.

"Take it." Jerry handed the poster across the aisle. It had not cost him anything. He had downloaded the pic from his computer.

His peers preoccupied, Jerry plunged a hand into a canvas knapsack. He came out with a camera, a Sony Mavica. It was a digital camera. He had stolen it from a tourist in Pensacola. Stuck with the older VGA technology, the Sony did not produce the awesome detail you could get from pixel-based competitors, but, hey, it was free. It had a ten-power zoom. And the Mavica had one other feature which for Jerry's purposes was very important: You could store the Sony's pictures on standard floppy disks. That meant you didn't need adaptors or SmartMedia cards or anything exotic to transfer your pictures from camera to computer. Just pop your three-inch disk out of the Mavica and slip it into a machine.

You got a Mac? A PC?

No problem. He could go either way.

It was a total improvement over the Polaroid. No film to worry about. No photo lab, like the Polaroid. But also no delay. Well, not much. The-FD51 model he acquired took five seconds or so to save its images to disk. Jerry would have preferred his instrument to process instantaneously, gratification being best when it was instant, but for now five seconds would do.

The teenager checked the camera's lithium-ion battery. Good to go. He then slipped the Sony into a pouch on the outside of his backback and looked for his newest subject.

She sat only three seats ahead. Isabel, he had heard the fifth-grader give her name. Like "Ees A Bell." Jerry shook his head. If they couldn't speak the language, why the hell let 'em in school?

He peeked his canvas blind above the lip of the seat-back before him. The camera snugged into its velcro pouch peeked out through a hole which Jerry had cut for the purpose. The arrangement allowed him to take pictures unobserved. There was plenty of ambient light here. No need for a flash, which of course Jerry would not have wanted. He was pleased with himself. His arrangements. He could press the camera's actuator without even having to reach inside its marsupial pouch.

She was showing him her profile. He snapped a picture. Funny you still said "snap," as if that archaic description of sound still applied. Jerry framed the girl, clicked. Another archaism. No buzz or snap or click with these cameras. No way. They were virtually soundless. So Jerry was not pleased when Harvey Koon, the class cretin, leered knowing and wise from across the aisle.

"Hey, Slade. You gonna be the next Spielberg?"

"Got a Sarah Gellar gallery for ya, Harvey." Jerry lined up his next composition. "If you'll shut the fuck up."

Isabel turned animatedly to one of her chums. A bow had come loose from her black hair. In the chatter of Spanish that followed she turned in her seat so that another brown-eyed girl could refasten that gay ligament.

How sweet.

Jerry eyed the scene through the wide display of his camera. You didn't even need to sight through an aperture, which was an advantage. She stretched her little arms in delight.

He selected the uncompressed mode for sharper resolution. Snap. Another picture destined for his hard drive. And then he could do anything he wanted.

The school bus rumbled over a cattle gap, which spoiled Jerry's clandestine session. Goddamn Theo. Couldn't drive worth a shit.

He could see her back firm and brown above her sundress. He needed to get closer. The next cattle gap, Jerry jostled foward.

"Por favor?" He ignored the protest of a child across the aisle.

Isabel turned. The bright smile melted. She had seen this strange, bleach-haired boy with his black pouch. She knew there was a camera inside. It took her a while to realize that she was being taken into its silver-lined lens. This made Isabel afraid. Pictures are not for strangers, she had been told. And her grandmother agreed—the camera could take your soul.

Was this boy stealing her soul?

"Mistah Theo!" Almost the first words she learned in English rose shrill, even above the bus's multitongued racket. "Mistah Theo, Cherry's taking picture!"

" 'Cherry'!" Harvey's laugh bellowed from the back and Jerry's gut clenched into a knot.

"Little bitch." He moved forward another seat only to find Mr. Theo's tired, gaunt face spying from the platter-sized rearview mirror.

"Put that thang away, Jerry."

"What thang'd that be, Mr. Theo?"

"Awright, youngun, I've had about enough o' you. We get to school, I'm a'turnin' you over to the professor."

The school bus burst into laughter, this time at the driver's expense. The professor! He meant the principal, of course. The local principal, Alton Folsom, who, scared for his job, intimidated by parents and slavish to the local board, never meted out discipline in any hard measure to anyone.

94

"The professor!" Jerry clutched his heart. "Damnation, Mr. Theo, not the professor!"

Another peal of derision in the bus. But Isabel's brown eyes were wet. She fumbled, alone now, to fix the bow in her hair.

It was the first day she had pulled school bus duty in a long time and Laura Anne couldn't get enough of it. She loved standing in the schoolyard, smelling the GMC's exhaust. Their bright yellow, Bluebird chassis, their blinking white and yellow lights brought back all of the tangled memories that attend a teacher's life interrupted.

Even so, as a substitute teacher, Laura Anne could not feel quite bona fide. She was only subbing, after all, the Neverland occupation that comes with a "regular" teacher's absence. And of the six classes Laura Anne would teach in her seven-period day, only two were devoted to music. The rest, math, health, and three classes of English, were unfamiliar assignments whose folders Laura Anne scanned, even as the students filed through the quadrangle and beneath the covered breezeways that led them to their newly constructed rooms.

Laura Anne had forgotten how much she missed this, the first moments of a school day. It frightened her to think that the labor she had poured into the restaurant was an investment that forever barred her from teaching. And it bothered her that the resentment she thought she had buried for Alton Folsom still smoldered. Alton was essentially a coward. The principal was looking to hide from communal censure when on Laura Anne's return from Tallahassee he used a budgetary fiction to deny Laura Anne her old job on Deacon Beach's Consolidated Faculty. Alton's decision forced Laura Anne to scramble for income. It was what had driven her to restore the restaurant. It was the only reason she was not still teaching music.

Two years had brought some improvements to the school. Federal money added a new elementary wing to join the junior and senior high school complex. It was still a very small school. Grades K through twelve numbered fewer than five hundred students, smaller in its total population than many high schools.

A Yellowbird Bus pulled up. Mr. Theo's bus; Laura recognized her neighbor. He didn't look happy. But Laura Anne could not help but smile as, one by one, boys and girls from childhood to puberty slouched or leapt or climbed down the steps to the sidewalk.

The smells were the same. Straw on the ground. Heat on the concrete. A confusion of perfumes and colognes. Little kids with candy. Big kids with big-label shoes and Hilfiger jackets. The classrooms smelled of sweat and chalk. The odors wafted by passing children triggered memories that would seem totally unrelated: of the cafeteria. The bandroom. The promise of fresh-cut grass on a Friday-night football field.

"Miz Raines, you on duty this mornin'?"

This from Mr. Theo.

"Theopolis. Good to see you." Laura smiled to the deacon of her born-again church.

"You too, ma'am. Got a chore for you. Sorry."

"That's perfectly all right." Laura Anne's professional demeanor pulled over her face like a mask.

"Got a young man here needs to see the professor."

Laura Anne recognized the teen with a knapsack over his back who slouched off the bus.

"Can you tell me what this is about, Mr. Theo?"

"Taking pictures of this little girl."

Laura Anne inclined her head to see the beautiful Latin child framed by the yellow doors of the bus.

"Buenos días." Laura Anne's greeting to the child triggered an instant torrent of Spanish.

"(Slow down, little one. We will talk inside. But slowly. With good manners.)"

"*Sí, señora.*" Isabel nodded and Laura Anne could see the recent trail of tears.

"So," Laura Anne said as she escorted the teenager and child to the office. "What's this about, Jerry?"

The boy scowled. He didn't like the fact that she knew his name.

"Taking pictures is all."

Laura Anne glanced at the technology in her hand.

"It's rude to take someone's picture without her permission, Jerry. I'm sure you know that."

"It's my camera," he said sullenly.

"And it's her prerogative to refuse the cameraman, isn't it?"

He did not reply. Laura Anne took both children into Alton Folsom's office. A wide, gray desk was swamped with the requirements of a state bureacracy dedicated to everything except results. A flock of Post-its fluttered as if to hide the principal's computer screen.

"What have you got now?" The sallow-faced administrator frowned as if it were Laura Anne who had been referred for discipline.

She summarized the situation quickly.

Folsom extended his hand for the Sony and turned to the brown-skinned child.

"Did you give this boy permission to take your picture?"

"Yes," Jerry answered to her silence.

"Mr. Folsom," Laura Anne intervened. "I don't believe she understood you."

Laura Anne turned to the little girl.

"(Will you tell the truth?)"

"*Sí.*" The girl nodded.

"She said yes." Jerry's posture suddenly improved. "You heard her, she said yes!"

"She said she would tell the truth." Laura Anne forced eye contact with the boy before returning to Isabel.

"(What is your name, little one?)"

"Isabel."

"(Isabel. Did you tell this boy he could take your picture with this camera? Or with any camera?)"

Her hair shook in its tangle of bows. *"No."*

"She gave no permission," Laura Anne informed the school's principal.

"Thank you for your translation, Miz Raines."

Was there a hint of sarcasm there?

"I'll take it from here."

Laura Anne turned to leave the office and almost missed the next, tiny torrent.

"(He takes in the girl's room, too. When I pee.)"

Laura Anne stopped short. Turned around.

"What was that, Isabel?"

"Miz Raines, I have enough . . ."

"Excuse me, Mr. Folsom. Isabel, what was that you just said? Slowly."

"(I go in to pee. From the playground. He was there.)" She pointed to Jerry Slade. "(He took pictures.)"

"Mr. Folsom." Laura Anne tried to keep the tremor from her voice. "I think you'd better call the sheriff."

"The sheriff? What in the world?"

Laura Anne repeated the girl's accusation. Jerry Slade's mouth went tight.

"It didn't happen," he said.

"I frankly don't see *how* it could happen," the principal blustered. "What would the boy even be doing on the elementary side of the school?"

"I believe we have been told," Laura Anne answered coldly.

"There's my camera, Mr. Folsom. All you got to do is download it. You could do it right here. In your office. Every picture I ever made's in there."

And when he said that, Laura Anne knew that this teenager was lying.

"It would be a good idea to keep the camera," she allowed. "But Mr. Folsom—I'd be willing to bet that Mr. Slade knows full well that any picture he takes can be downloaded into *any* compatible computer and the file then erased. Do you have a computer, Jerry? At home?"

"None of your business," the boy sneered.

"All right, that's enough." The principal rose briskly. "I'm going to give you back your camera, Jerry—"

"Sir?" Laura Anne could not keep the outrage from her voice.

"—but you better not let me hear anything about you taking pictures without people's permission, you hear?"

"Yes, Mr. Folsom," Jerry replied meekly and turned to meet Laura Anne eye to eye.

There was hatred there. Instant and adamantine.

"I'll get one of our assistants to take this little girl to her class." Folsom returned to his seat. "You better hurry along, Miz Raines. You'll miss your homeroom."

Linton Loyd once said that he'd be happy living in a Quonset hut, but that the missus wouldn't have it. That statement apologized for the mansion he soon built on a bluff overlooking the Suwannee River. About a half mile down from the Hal W. Adams Bridge on the Lafayette County side was a home unlike any other in the county, a seamless contour of concrete and glass self-consciously re-creating the art deco architecture of the '20s and '30s.

You could imagine Hercule Poirot enjoying croissants and coffee on the marble-tiled lanai that looked from a high bluff over the river made famous by Stephen Foster. A coffee-brown swell of water carved sharply into the banks on the fast side, revealing sandbanks on the other with the river's reduced flow—a deep, wild river bounded by water oak and pine and palmetto. It was cooler on the river; a breeze seemed to follow the Suwannee's slow march to the Gulf.

A patio above the lanai was built to catch whatever breeze was stirred from the river below. Its wide balcony was shaded with magnificent arms of oak trees that stretched almost across the patio's broad expanse. Spanish moss fanned to and fro above that balcony in beards heavy with humid air. From its vantage you could see what Linton's wife described ostentatiously as a carriage house where their son had his own quarters, a two-bedroom apartment built atop an open carport and removed from any view of the river.

The balcony tiles were identical to those of the sunroom below, and it was on this open-air landing, with the river's magnificent panorama before them, that Lou Sessions, Barrett Raines, and Cricket Bonet waited uncomfortably for the owner of the house.

Linton emerged from French doors onto the balcony, his son trailing like a cur behind. A stray breeze caught the strands that never covered Gary's balding head and wisped them about his skull.

Like straw, Barrett thought.

"Gentlemen. Lou. What can I do you for?" The elder Linton started off with an insult.

"Need to ask Gary some questions," the sheriff answered stiffly. "Concerning his whereabouts sometime in the last three to seven days."

"That'd cover some territory." Gary spoke too loud. Bear wondered if it was the late heat that made him appear so pale.

"Wouldn't care to narrow it down some, would you, Lou?" Linton inquired, settling his compact frame into a deerhide chair out of place with the decor, pointedly allowing Lou and the other lawmen to remain standing.

"We found a homicide . . ." Lou began.

"Strawman's Hammock." Linton pulled a wad of chewing tobacco from its leather pouch. "I know."

Lou flushed red.

"Come on, Lou." Linton chawed, taking pleasure in the sheriff's consternation. "Anybody can monitor the police band. I must've had four hunters call me in the time it took your deputies to tell everybody they knew what was goin' on."

"Then you heard about the tracks. Tire tracks."

"Tires? Tracks? I don't believe so."

Gary laughed. More of a bark, really.

"Why don't you come on down to the station, Gary?" Lou turned to the son. "We can do the interview this afternoon."

"You can kiss my ass," Gary snapped back, and Barrett instinctively moved to flank Sheriff Sessions.

"Let's keep this civil, all right?" Cricket Bonet's was the calm, professional voice.

"You don't have any authority here," Gary shot back. "And you, Bear—the hell are you doing here?"

Which put Barrett in a bad situation.

"You might have heard something or seen something important to the case, that's all, Gary. If you did, I need to hear it."

"Well, you heard all you're gonna hear." Suddenly Linton was out of his chair, his jaw working the tobacco like a second baseman. "I've *had* you in my home at *my* discretion. You come again, it better be with a warrant."

"I don't need a warrant to interview suspects," Lou shot back, and Barrett knew there was trouble coming.

"Suspect?" Linton shoved his lined, handsome countenance into the sheriff's pockmarked face. "You tellin' me my boy is a *suspect*? For murder? Off a pair of *tire tracks*?"

"So you do know about the tire tracks!" Lou crowed in triumph.

It was Linton's turn to flush beet red.

"All right, gentlemen . . ." Barrett began, but it was too late.

"Track this!" Linton snarled and spit a blind of well-chawed tobacco juice directly into the sheriff's face.

What happened then was hard to untangle. Lou flinched aside to blunt the effect of Linton's filthy missile, leaving Barrett to take the nicotined charge square on his chest. Instinctively, Bear reached for the smaller man's wrist in a come-along. By that time Sheriff Sessions had Linton by the neck.

Things escalated when Gary leaped to his father's aid.

"Son of a bitch!"

The younger Loyd charged Lou from the blindside, just beyond Cricket's desperate reach, to tackle the sheriff high in the ribs.

What had started out as a peaceful interview was now an assault on an officer.

It was time, then, for training to take over from instinct. Barrett moved with Cricket as a single man.

Cricket jerked the son free. A kick to the instep brought the youngster howling to the hard marble flooring. Barrett caught the father's fist in midflight and slapped it into a steel bracelet.

"The hell—?" Linton turned furiously to face his new assailant, and when he did Sheriff Lou Sessions crossed with a solid right hook straight up the side of the older mans's head.

"Daddy!" Gary screamed curses from the floor.

"Jesus, Lou!"

Barrett caught Linton Loyd as he fell. Cricket kept Gary Loyd pinned to the floor, and was on the radio.

"This is Agent Bonet for PD One." He spoke rapid fire into the receiver. We are at the Loyd river house. We need backup. That is backup and an EMS at a residence—Linton Loyd. On the river."

*   *   *

Thurman Shaw bailed out the father and his son. Barrett was there to see that sorry procession as it emerged from the county's pitiful excuse for a jail to pass by boarded-up doors and the jerry-rigged evidence bin. Thurman paused at the duty desk. Lou Sessions was there with a deputy.

"We plan to bring suit, Sheriff Sessions," Thurman announced, accepting the sergeant's clipboard.

"For assaultin' an officer? Be my guest."

"And I demand the immediate release of all property."

"If you talkin' about the Humvee, you can ferget it. I dusted for prints off that thing already. Got hair off the carpet—black and straight."

"You had no warrant!"

"That vehicle is linked to a crime scene."

"The murder?" Thurman was incredulous.

"The assault," Lou grated. "On me. Could'a been a gun in that 'vee for all we knew. Could'a been a threat to me or one of the FDLE."

"That's a stretch."

"I got the Humvee. And everything in it."

Thurman smiled. "We'll see."

"You better see quick, counselor. We just about got that thing turned inside out."

Thurman signed a receipt for his clients and handed over pairs of wallets, watches, and gold-plated fountain pens matched father to son.

"You sorry sack of shit," Linton Loyd mumbled to the sheriff through a jaw swollen the size of a gourd.

"That's enough, Linton." Thurman ran a veined hand through his shock of rooster's hair. "We got him by the short hairs this time."

Lou snorted. "Sure you do."

Thurman Shaw turned then to Barrett.

"Agent Raines? See you outside?"

Barrett glanced to the sheriff for his reaction. Lou took the gesture to mean that he was asking permission.

"Go ahead."

Barrett followed Thurman and his clients through the chipped oak doors that exited onto the sidewalk outside the jail. Elizabeth Loyd waited in her lavender Lexus beside the Viking fence securing the jail's sally port, a porcelain smile painted on her face as though she were picking up her husband for a football game. Or shrimp and steak at Ramona's.

"Better watch that son of a bitch in there." Linton pushed past his attorney to speak directly to Barrett. "He'll fuck you in a minute."

"Oh, Linton," the wife smiled vacantly. "I do wish you wouldn't use that language."

"Get in the car, Linton," Thurman advised. "You too, Gary."

Only when the Loyds were inside the Lexus and the doors closed did Thurman return to Barrett.

"I don't want to have to put you between Lou and Linton, Bear."

"No."

"Off the record?" The rooster ran a mottled hand through his comb.

"All right," Barrett agreed.

"It looks to me like you're between a rock and a hard place on this thing, Bear."

"Again," Barrett agreed with a grim smile.

"So tell me. Off the record. Was this assault provoked?"

Barrett hesitated. "Provoked? With words, maybe. Attitude. But an assault on an officer, Thurman . . ." Barrett shook his head. "The hell was Linton thinking?"

Thurman actually smiled. "Probably 'bout how he'd rather have you for sheriff."

"I can't lie for him, Thurman," Barrett countered urgently. "Don't even give him the ghost of an idea that I'd be willing to do that."

Shaw wagged his head. "No, no. Last thing in the world any of us wants you to do is lie. No, sir. All we want, Bear, is to make sure you tell the truth."

"Of course I'll tell the truth!" Barrett shot back angrily. "Why wouldn't I?"

Thurman Shaw held Barrett's eyes a long, long moment.

"Awright," he said finally. "Fair enough."

With that ambiguous reply Barrett prepared to end his day. But then he saw the familiar mast of Channel Seven's live van. That meant an interview with the station's most despised and anemic mongrel, the dishonorable Stacy Kline.

"Looks like Stacy's got wind of the story." Thurman smiled ruefully. "You better get inside, Barrett."

Raines shook his thick head.

"Won't do any good. Bastard, Stacy. He'd follow a maggot to a gut wagon."

Seven

Night had fallen as dark as the inside of a cow by the time Barrett Raines settled his cruiser between Aunt Thelma's trailer and the rear of his own modest, modular-framed home. There had been some add-ons to the Barrett mansion over the years: a second bathroom, deck, carport. Barrett's hand trailed absently over the hood of his restored Malibu as he headed for the back door, shedding his tie and cotton-thin blazer.

A light switched on.

"Bear?"

Laura Anne stepped into a weaving cone of illumination. She had changed into a sundress from her workday attire. It showed off her legs, the curve of her belly and hip.

"Home at last." He emerged into the bulb's swaying light.

"What happened to you?" She pointed to the ruin of his shirt.

"Chewing tobacco." Barrett mounted the back steps to take her hand. "Where're the boys?"

"In bed. It's nine o'clock."

"Sorry."

"That's all right." She smiled. "At least you're home."

Barrett brushed her lips with his own, accepted a squeeze on his tightened shoulders. Then he went straight in to see his twin sons.

Ben and Tyndall. Fraternal twins. About as opposite as two boys could be. Tyndall was the larger, bulkier child, sleeping now with a football, his mouth relaxed into the small O that only sleeping children master. Ben's frame, long and svelte like his mother's, stretched beneath the tent of his sheet. He had a flashlight going.

"Benjamin."

Off went the light.

"Daddy?"

"What you reading, goose?"

The child emerged. "Harry Potter."

"You like it?"

"Mmmhmm!" Ben pulled out his light and book. And then, hesitating, "But I like Tolkien better. The hobbits and the ring? There's . . . more to it."

Barrett sqeezed his precocious son to his chest.

"That's very good, Ben. Still—there's room to enjoy both. Everything in its place."

"You always say that, Daddy."

Ben dropped his lamp and book to wrap thin arms about his daddy's neck. And then, abruptly, without pre-amble: "Do you need lots of sleep, Daddy?"

"Yes, I do. And so do you."

"Ooooookay." The boy burrowed into his sheet like a squirrel.

"Night-night, Daddy."

" 'Night, Benjamin. 'Night Tyndall."

A gentle snore was the only response.

Laura Anne and Barrett made slow love before the ten o'clock news. The pre-news hour was getting to be prime time for them both. Couldn't find time much earlier.

Couldn't get up the energy much later. *Twelve years married*, Barrett thought, *and we still find time.*

She was as firm in the belly as when Barrett had first seen her. Heavier in the breasts with childbirth. A long back, strong, strong shoulders and legs. And that mile of supple skin.

This was another reason to work near home.

Afterward they watched the flicker of the bedroom's television from between their toes.

"Boys have their party Saturday after next."

"Good."

"They want a puppy."

"I ain't gonna have no whinin' puppy in the house."

"We can put him out back."

"I'm not going to potty-train him, either."

"You trained the boys, Bear. How much harder can it be?"

Barrett grunted. "You get hold of Cory and Corrina?"

"All set. And I'm thinking of inviting another fifth-grader."

"Somebody special?"

"She's Latino. Isabel Hernandez. Her parents are migrant workers. I've met the mother. I think I can get her to come."

"That's nice."

"Rolly Slade's boy is taking pictures of her."

Barrett turned. "The mother?"

"No. Little girl." Laura Anne related the day's incident. "I suggested to Alton that he ought to contact the sheriff."

"Good suggestion."

"He didn't."

Barrett frowned. "Honey, I don't know that there's much I can do. I really don't have any independent authority here."

"I know that."

Barrett grunted. "I wonder if the boy has a computer."

"What difference does that make?" Laura Anne asked.

"I'll mention it to Lou," Barrett answered obliquely, and then the evening news came on.

Stacy Kline, a poster boy for bulimia, displayed a microphone that towered like a spear of broccoli from a fist as devoid of flesh as a talon.

". . . and late this afternoon there was consternation in the county jail as Linton and Gary Loyd were arrested for an assault against Sheriff Lou Sessions. . . ."

"Were you—?" Laura Anne began.

"Yes." Bear nodded.

". . . Sheriff Sessions is here with me now. Sheriff, can you give us your side of the incident?"

A cold smile remained like a ravine below Lou's cratered complexion.

"Aw, Stacy, it wouldn't really be proper for me to give details before the hearing."

"Then this will go to court? Gary and Linton Loyd will face justice?"

"As would anybody, let me emphasize that, *anybody* who assaults an officer of the law. Nobody's above the law in Lafayette County."

"FDLE agents present at the time were less helpful to this interviewer." Stacy's offscreen edit led into what passed for his interview. Segue from Lou's brittle face to Stacy's ambush of Barrett Raines.

"I almost got away," Barrett declared mournfully from his bedside vantage as the TV offered bouncing footage to show Stacy chasing him down from behind.

"Agent Raines? Agent Raines, Stacy Kline, Channel Seven News."

"Well, good evening, Stacy."

Turning to the newsman's summons, Barrett displayed a shirt that looked to be splattered in blood.

"I understand you were present at the assault on Sheriff Lou Sessions?" Stacy's thin wrist shook as if palsied.

"It hasn't been ruled an assault yet, Stacy. Only alleged."

"But there was an arrest."

"Yes."

"And you were present?"

"I was. With Agent Bonet, Tallahassee office."

"And so we can expect to see you testify in court."

"If I'm subpoenaed as a witness, naturally. Yes."

"That puts you in an awkward position, doesn't it, Agent?"

"Awkward? How?"

Stacy dropped his bomb.

"Well, isn't it true that Linton Loyd is backing you to run for sheriff against Lou Sessions?"

"What?" This from Laura Anne.

She turned from the caricature of her husband on the small screen to face the man in her bed.

"Just listen," Barrett replied.

"Mr. Kline, I don't know where you got your information, but it is incorrect. I haven't even sat down to think about whether I ought to run for sheriff, let alone who I'd be asking to back me. That is a fact which you can verify with Mr. Loyd himself."

"So there is nothing to this rumor?"

"Well, Stacy, I'm relieved to hear you call it a rumor. Because that's exactly what it is."

Laura Anne snagged the remote to silence the tube.

"What's this about running for sheriff?"

"What's this about teaching school? We both seem to be gettin' the itch for change."

"You know very well school's not the same as sheriff."

"Doesn't pay as much for damn sure. And neither one pays like the restaurant."

"I can sell the restaurant."

"Don't let's go countin' our chickens before they hatch, honey."

"Don't 'honey' me, Barrett Raines! How long have you been thinkin' of running for sheriff? *When* did you get the idea? Where?"

"Week or so ago," Bear answered tiredly. "At camp."

Laura Anne sat up straight. "So that's why Linton had you out."

"Well, it sure as hell wasn't to hunt deer."

"Then you lied, Bear! On TV. You lied to that despicable Stacy Kline."

"Hell I did. I haven't accepted Linton's backing or anybody else's. I haven't even decided if I'm gonna run."

"Gonna run? Or *should*?"

"Don't you start, Laura Anne . . ."

"Start what? We just about get our lives back to normal and you're thinkin' politics! Black man running for sheriff in Lafayette County? You got to be a bubble and a half off plumb to think that's gonna happen."

"Thanks for your support."

"Don't talk to me about support!" she flashed angrily. "That restaurant was my support! Sixteen- and eighteen-hour days is my support!"

"I know, I know." He reached for her. "I'm sorry. Really I am. It's just—I were sheriff it would give me even more time than we have now, Laura Anne. I'd be closer to work. A whole lot more flexible hours—"

"And every four years you're out of a job," she finished.

He sighed heavily. "Yeah. There's that."

Laura Anne turned away from him a moment. It took a while to see that she was crying.

"Baby! Baby, I haven't *done* anything! Not a damn thing! It's just talk. What-ifs, that's all."

"Well, what if I want to leave the restaurant?" She turned back to him. "You get messed up in politics, there's not a stable salary for the family, Bear. Even if I sell the business, that's not what we oughta be livin' on. That's for college, for old age. And wouldn't it be nice for the boys to start life with something? Just some small, certain inheritance beyond a—a pushout trailer and a hot rod?"

She was crying again.

"You're right. You're right." Barrett eased over to her side of the bed. "Look. Laura Anne. I can work in the FDLE 'til the cows come home."

She nodded. "It's just—I feel like it's my turn, is all. For you to help me."

It was. Barrett knew it.

"Tell you what. Until you have decided whether you want the restaurant or the classroom, I'm not changing anything. How's that?"

She nodded. "Would make it a lot easier for me."

Barrett spread his wide hands gently on her leg.

"I wasn't trying to do anything behind your back."

"No." She laughed. "But Linton Loyd was. Who do you think gave Stacy that story? Or had it given?"

Barrett nodded. "I know. I know."

"Run for sheriff!" Laura Anne shook her head. "Linton poured it on good, did he?'

"He tried."

"Said he'd back you."

"Yes."

"Which means he'll buy you votes."

Barrett squirmed. "I wouldn't want that."

"Makes you think you'll have any say in the matter? Tell you something, Bear, you get in bed with a man like Linton Loyd, you're gonna wake up with fleas big as nickels."

Barrett reached for the freshly washed sheets.

"Puppies get fleas." Barrett nuzzled his wife.

"They've got medicine for puppies," she said.

"Night-night."

Sparks were flying next morning in the Lafayette County courthouse. Barrett rose early to arrive with Cricket and

Warden Jarold Pearson for the hearing scheduled in Mayo. The attorney representing the state of Florida had his fountain pen tapping code on the arm of a hardwood chair like the last telegrapher on the Titanic. Judge Alfred Carey Blackmond, sitting for the third circuit, glanced up from the writ on his desk.

"Roland. Please?"

Roland Reed's platinum-tipped pen paused in *medias res*, lending an unnatural silence to chambers only recently made available to visiting judges. The county judge's office, just downstairs, was too busy and too cramped to accommodate the circuit judge's needs, so an old jury room one flight up had been recently renovated for third-circuit business. It was a serviceable interior, complete with phone lines and modems and computers. But it did not have the character of the chambers Judge Blackmond had enjoyed while a county judge in Perry. Barrett Raines had visited those wainscoted and oak-paneled digs on more than one occasion, enjoying the high tin-pressed ceiling, luxuriating in the airy view of a town square verandahed with the limbs of sycamore trees.

Judge Blackmond had reluctantly left the comfortable confines of his Perry chambers to assume duties spanning seven large counties. And duty called this frigid morning. Another norther rattled the windows badly set in these new accomodations. The belligerents were ranged for dispute. State Attorney Roland Reed had a table to himself, flanked on one side by Sheriff Sessions. Thurman Shaw represented defendants Gary and Linton Loyd across the aisle.

Barrett Raines and Cricket Bonet attempted to find neutral ground toward the rear of the room. Jarold Pearson sandwiched in between, his olive-and-tan uniform spotlessly pressed and creased, his tan Stetson resting in his lap. He perched on the edge of his padded seat like a good bird dog waiting to point, the Boy Scout knife diligently applied to his cuticles.

They heard arguments for a good half hour. Roland and Thurman wrangled acrimoniously for the entire duration, a period of time and mode of demeanor not usually granted before the man known as the hanging judge. Barrett was trying to read Judge Blackmond's always calm and never perturbed face. He was a hard man to figure, a judge of liberal sentiment who had sent men to the death chamber, a champion of the little man who had ruled against unions as often as against corporate interests. A passionate defender of speech who believed firmly in law and order.

He'll have to be Solomon this morning, Barrett thought to himself, and as if reading Bear's mind, the judge looked up to offer the state's advocate a wan smile.

"Mr. Reed, it seems you are determined to prosecute the Loyd family for their alleged battery of the county's sheriff."

"And agents of the FDLE, your honor."

"Yes, yes. Must have been some donnybrook."

Roland aka "Fountain Pen" Reed had scrambled to be assigned this case, and Barrett was not surprised. Any dispute promising headlines got Roland's attention, no matter the merits. The prosecutor dressed for Channel Seven's ever-present camera, tailored suits and vests completely impractical for the climate.

Thurman "The Rooster" Shaw was unkempt by comparison, his own baggy suit and frayed shirt making him appear even scrawnier than was usual.

The only person who looked completely at home in the visiting judge's chambers was Lou Sessions. The sheriff lounged unconcerned in his khakis alongside the state's attorney. Barrett and Cricket had their shirts cleaned and ties knotted in anticipation of being called as witnesses.

Felony charges had been filed against Linton Loyd and his son. You punch a civilian in the nose or spit Red Man on an umpire, you got charged with a misdemeanor. But similar actions when directed at any law-enforcement officer put you up with the big boys.

So there was that business. Not to mention disputes related to murder.

"Seems we have two issues here." Judge Blackmond had a way of looking you in the eye that made you think he was talking to you, and you alone. "The first issue relates to battery. The facts are not disputed in that case. Only, perhaps, the degree of provocation alleged in Sheriff Session's conduct and a history, which I am inclined to consider, of enmity between Sheriff Sessions and Mr. Linton Loyd. On this issue I have first to say, nothing, short of unlawful threat to life or limb, gives anyone the right to batter a sheriff, deputy, or FDLE investigator. Having so stated, I do acknowledge a degree of provocation from the sheriff that was extremely unprofessional. And then there's the history." The judge shook his head. "Worse than Agamemnon and Clytemnestra."

"Sir?" Roland was perplexed.

The judge waved him off.

"The second issue relates to the impoundment of a vehicle alleged to be connected with a homicide. I have no intention of minimizing the importance of this case. I recognize that Sheriff Sessions was investigating a particularly brutal and apparently calculated slaughter. I am willing to believe that the heinous nature of the crime, the length of the day, any number of factors may have led the sheriff, while acting in good faith, to nevertheless commit errors in judgment or comportment. The most serious consequence of those errors relates to the seizure of Gary Loyd's unique vehicle."

"It was linked to the crime scene, your honor," Roland reminded the judge unnecessarily.

"A half-mile hardly constitutes a 'link,' your honor." Thurman Shaw bristled like a hedgehog beside his clients. "Especially in the middle of hunting season. Especially when, by the sheriff's own account, there were other tracks of other vehicles reported by the game warden to have on more than one occasion come directly to the site of the homicide."

"Might I point out that the truck was taken in conjunction with the battery, your honor? And that it may have held a device or weapon posing imminent threat to the interviewing lawmen?"

" 'Interview' is an interesting choice of description," Judge Blackmond replied drily. "The weapons of choice, in this case, were an overzealous son and a wad of chewing tobacco. Were there a contemplated use of the arsenal in the Humvee, I am sure Mr. Loyd and his son would not have resorted to blindside tackles and Red Man."

"Your honor—!"

"Tend your notes, Roland. Now. Sheriff Sessions. It seems to me, Sheriff, that your judgment in this investigation is badly compromised by the obvious and ongoing contempt that you make no offer to conceal for the defendants.

"Add to that bias a more compelling problem: You simply have not demonstrated probable cause sufficient to accuse Gary Loyd of any crime whatever. Mr. Reed's insistence that you needed a warrant to inspect Mr. Loyd's property or his vehicle is incorrect. You did not. What you *did* need was clear, direct, and probable cause that would substantiate an arrest or even investigation of Gary Loyd for the murder of Jane Doe. You do not have such cause."

Gary Loyd, Barrett noticed, bowed his head with that pronouncement. Linton did not.

"Furthermore, Sheriff," the judge continued, "by impounding Mr. Loyd's Humvee without probable cause to search or seize, and by subjecting that vehicle to forensic examination, you have deprived yourself of the benefit of *any* evidence so derived. If the tree cannot be allowed, neither can the fruit of the tree.

"It is therefore my ruling that in the absence of independent corroboration or potential for discovery, any evidence derived from this truck or its examination must be suppressed and may not be used in this case."

"State will appeal," Roland Reed declared.

"You have that right. Before you do, however, we need a private conversation. Mr. Shaw, do you have any questions before me?"

"Like to know when my client can get his vehicle back, your honor. Along with everything that was in it."

"Immediately."

"Then we're good for now." Thurman nodded, taking the judge's hint and shepherding Gary Linton and his tighter-wrapped father toward the door.

Linton paused as he passed Barrett.

"I read your statement."

"Yes."

"Looked pretty much up the middle to me."

"I just told the truth, Linton."

The elder Loyd smiled tightly. "Man expects to be sheriff, Bear, he has to be willing to make some hard decisions."

"The hell is that exactly supposed to mean, Linton?"

"Means you were fair and impartial, Agent Raines." Thurman addressed his neighbor as though he were a stranger. "Linton, we're out of here."

Thurman bustled Linton Loyd and his son into the hallway. When the door sighed to a close, Sheriff Sessions exploded.

"You let a goddamn killer walk out of here!"

"Sheriff, you are before a judge."

"I don't give a damn *who* I'm in front of!"

"Clearly."

"There's hair on that truck! Stains of semen. He *had* that girl, judge! He took her out there, he raped her, he strung her up, and he put that dog on her. Sure as shit stinks!"

"Sheriff Sessions." The judge's voice suddenly turned to flint. "If you do not recuse yourself from the investigation of this case—immediately—I shall inform the state's attorney general that you are abusing your authority and must be replaced."

"The hell?" Lou Sessions' cratered face went white.

Roland Reed lurched from prosecution to defense.

"Your honor, that's outrageous! It's a breach of authority! It's—it's—the sheriff is the backbone of this county! You can't do this!"

"Of course I can, Roland. Now sit down. Unless you'd like me to hold you in contempt."

Roland sank to his chair. Judge Blackmond waited patiently for the sheriff to follow suit.

"Better. Now, gentlemen. I don't want to undermine the Sheriff's authority. The problem is, the sheriff has managed that on his own. And it is not my goal in life to displace any man or woman from duly elected office. I can refrain from going to the attorney general. But there will be some quid required pro that quo."

"Such as?" Lou growled.

"I recommend that you drop all charges of battery against the Loyds," the judge restated firmly. "I also order, *order*, that you turn over the day-to-day investigation of Jane Doe's homicide to the FDLE. The Live Oak field office will assume those responsibilities.

"I am not taking the case out of your jurisdiction, Sheriff, but I am limiting your ability to participate. With luck you can save face and preserve your authority in this matter. But you have to understand, Sheriff, that you are incapable of an objective evaluation of the evidence in this case. So it is strict injunction that you subordinate your efforts in the investigation of Jane Doe's homicide to the FDLE."

"Play by these rules and we'll be fine. But if you go within a mile and a half of either Linton or Gary Loyd, Sheriff, I shall visit the state's wrath on you like white on rice."

Judge Blackmond leaned back.

"You have a badge and a gun, sir. I hope to be reassured that you retain the judgment and common sense necessary to use them."

Later that day Thurman Shaw was informed through a clerk of the court that State's Attorney Reed had dropped all charges of assault against Linton and Gary Loyd. Thurman was also informed that the Florida Department of Law Enforcement would assume primary responsiblity for gathering evidence in the case, coordinating that effort day to day with the sheriff's office.

Like a true Solomon, Judge Blackmond left no one happy.

"Son of a bitch!" The sheriff corralled Barrett before he could leave the courthouse. "Your buddy took care of you up there, didn't he, Bear?"

"What are you talking about, Lou?"

"Blackmond's always been in your corner. Even when you was pounding tar in Deacon Beach. So now—he's settin' you up for sheriff."

"Pretty hard for him to do that, Lou, when I haven't even decided whether to run."

"You'll run, all right." The sheriff's holster squeaked with the grip of his hand. "You'll piss around and make noise but when it's all over and done Gary Loyd's gonna walk free, and Linton's gonna give you credit. Ain't that what you want?"

"No," Barrett answered steadily. "And goddammit, Lou, by now you should know me better than to think I would."

Eight

The hearing got Barrett home early. Time to throw the boys some football. Tyndall took naturally to the ball's odd shape and spiral. Ben competed gamely. Barrett hustled his boys off to schoolwork after their short recreation, spilled some coals onto the backyard grill, and rummaged with a pocket knife into the well-tended garden. Laura Anne came home to find hamburgers and fresh tomatoes waiting.

"How was school?" Barrett asked.

"I'm scratchin' that itch," she admitted.

"It's doin' you good." Barrett pulled her over for a sailor's kiss and the boys giggled at their mother's embarassment.

Barrett and Laura Anne made love that night. It started in the shower.

"Come here," she invited him in. Took him in her hand.

They coupled like adulterers against the fiberglass shell of the shower. Then Barrett picked her up in a store's worth of cotton towel and took her to bed. That was the night's reward. Rising early the next morning gave Barrett a chance to tell his boys they'd be getting a puppy for birthdays well anticipated. The squeals of excitement greeting that guarantee and the hugs around his neck sent Barrett Raines off to work.

"Have a good one." He tugged on the seat belt that snugged Laura Anne into their Dodge Caravan.

"I will!" She backed out to the blacktop with the boys waving in concert, two little hands like windshield wipers, back and forth.

Barrett wiped the arm of his blazer briefly across the hood of his Malibu before climbing into his cruiser. Work, this morning, meant a drive to Gainesville, and promised to be interesting, for this morning Bear would rendezvous with Cricket and Midge at the C. A. Pound Human Identification Lab, located in Gator country at the University of Florida.

Barrett took a left at the light in Mayo, put his vehicle on cruise control, and headed down Highway 27. Twenty minutes later he saw the Branford bridge. The Suwannee River swept majestically beneath the bridge, its high cliffs looking over bass boats and jet skis and a chocolate swath of water. The river was low, very low. A telephone pole mounted near a spring on the south side of the bridge was marked to indicate floodlines from the late '30s to 1998. The yellow or whitewashed stripes with their crudely lettered histories reminded Barrett how mercurial this wild river could be. As late as '98, the Suwannee had risen from its slow torpor sixty feet below the bridge to overflow the banks high above and flood thousands of acres around.

Too bad there wasn't some way to save that water, Bear thought.

He saw a man and woman in wetsuits loading their tanks onto a pontoon boat. Cave divers. They came from all over, California, New Jersey, crazy folks with scuba gear, to dive the springs on the banks of the Suwannee, squirming with a pair of tanks and a light through narrow chutes to explore the spectacular limestone caves that were secreted beneath the cold, cold water. Barrett shivered. He could never do that.

It was not yet nine o'clock. Bear rolled past Branford and through High Springs and never saw a chain restaurant or a golden arch. This was the Florida Barrett loved, a place still roughed out, its small towns offering a single red light, a pair of cafes, its forests and lowlands not yet gridded off into Holiday Inns or theme parks and not overrun with tourists. Fishermen came here in reasonable numbers to share with local sportsmen. Hunters. Those crazy divers. That was about it. That was about all anybody wanted. This region, like the Suwanee that flowed like an artery through its heart, needed to remain untamed. It needed to be wild. But not savage.

The crime he had witnessed in his home county bothered Barrett more than the usual homicide for a variety of reasons. There was a racial component that could not be ignored. Latin workers were already experiencing in the year 2001 the sort of prejudice that African Americans had endured since Reconstruction. Was this crime in any way a result of racial hatred? That bothered Barrett greatly. But what bothered him even more was the feeling that this elaborate homicide was somehow another indicator that the culture he knew and respected as a child was being subsumed into something much more amorphous and alien.

The crime provided one more indicator to Bear that his rural haunt was no longer immune from the influence of the culture at large, the same culture digested in Miami or Jacksonville or Daytona. Young people, particularly, took their cues for life off satellite dishes, not front porches. The old vices, bad as they were, had always been constrained in this region by a powerful consensus about what was right and what was wrong. And folks didn't hesitate to tell you when you stepped out of line. But that consensus was disappearing, and as it did Barrett wondered how long he could claim that his special part of northern Florida was different from the rest of the state.

"Your culture will be assimilated." Ben and Tyndall mocked the Star Trek fantasy. "Resistance is fu-tile."

Past High Springs, Bear turned to catch the interstate. Forty minutes later he was in Gainesville. The C. A. Pound Lab, though part of the University of Florida complex, was located northeast of the main campus, off Radio Road. Alice Lake steamed nearby, home to alligators and future mascots. The lab was constructed without a lot of money and no pretense at grandeur, a single-story Butler building, green and metal and prefabricated. Set on a slab in a virtual forest of bamboo. You had to come looking to find the place. Even if you knew where you were going, the facility was easily missed.

Barrett turned hard into the narrow drive that led to a scattering of parking slots. He got out of the car in a hurry, eager to get inside. The Pound Lab, as it was commonly called, boasted some of the most accomplished forensic experts in the state, though many of those associated with the university's faculty rarely referred to their research as forensic in nature. A fair number of these academic types were tenured in departments like anthropology, zoology, or botany. Their curiosity regarding hominids or insects or plants just "happened" to find a forensic application.

Dr. William Maples had made the lab famous throughout the southeast, combining theoretic pursuits in spectroscopy and biologic sciences with a passion for forensic application. His *Dead Men Do Tell Tales* was a book Barrett had thumbed to death. The doctor's death saddened many at the university, and in law enforcement, but his down-to-earth manner still reigned at the Pound Lab, and legions of academics inherited his passion for science and criminal investigation.

There were some odd ducks at the lab. It was interesting to Barrett that the same professor who might on a Wednesday morning lecture to a group of budding anthropologists comparing mitochondrial DNA in populations of ancient Neanderthals with those in modern chimpanzees, would that afternoon complete a similar analysis that could convict a killer in Jacksonville, or exonerate a man facing death in Raiford.

As Barrett approached the lab's utilitarian door he noticed a young woman in running shoes and jeans leaning into a common hedge that Barrett recognized from his nursery days to be photinia, family Rosaceae. Rosaceae— the scarlet fruit? The shrub appeared to be infested with aphids. Late in the year for aphids. Then Bear saw the parasites being gently removed from the hedge's shining green leaves and realized that the infestation was exogenous and purposeful.

He went inside. The jukes in the weather had fooled the A/C, which was still pumping cold air, even though it was barely fifty degrees outside. There was nothing so formal as a receptionist's desk, though an open office was occupied. A university employee reigned, her sweater draped across the back of her chair. Barrett waited patiently to announce his arrival. A message was relayed and Midge Holloway emerged shortly from a narrow hallway, waving him on over with even more kilowatts of energy than was her usual.

"It's fantastic, what he's done!" She shoved Barrett down a sheetrocked hall. "You won't believe it! Fantastic!"

The lab was divided into something like large bays. Faculty and graduate students were engaged in a bewildering variety of tasks. With a murmured apology, the gardener from outside edged past Barrett bearing a tin of aphids.

"Barrett. I'd like you to meet Dr. Nguyen Tran."

Barrett turned at Midge's voice to find an Asian face staring straight into his own. For a moment Bear had the uncomfortable feeling that he was being inspected. The anthropologist was taller than Bear expected. A fine mesh of French and Asian features. Delicate, but not feminine. Straight black hair receded from the forehead. Deep, hazel eyes.

"Nguyen, this is Special Agent Barrett Raines."

"Doctor." Barrett extended his hand. "I can't tell you how much we appreciate your help."

Barrett kept his eyes steadily in the center of the small, delicate skull before him. He tried to ignore the fact that Dr. Tran had no ears.

That impression did not give an accurate description, of course. The doctor could hear. There were orifices, certainly, allowing waves of air to beat onto the tympani within. But the visible ears had been savagely removed. From where the lobes should have been, and extending to the temples above, only a ragged vestige of tissue remained, like the rims of dead volcanoes.

Dr. Tran cleared his throat.

"A schoolboy's revenge, I am afraid. Enacted, unfortunately, by a gang of men. In prison."

"I have some scars of my own, Doctor."

"Nothing so visible, I trust."

Midge was embarassed. "This is my fault. It didn't occur to me to tell him."

"Of course not." The doctor laid a firm hand on her shoulder in obvious affection. And then to Barrett, "She sees through the eyes of love."

Barrett smiled. This man knew what to keep and what to chuck.

"Come see my work." The academy-trained crime fighter swiveled abruptly for a set of double doors. Barrett followed Tran and Midge to find an open, high-ceilinged studio littered with mannequins and plaster casts. A set of cubicles roughly divided an otherwise open interior. Barrett saw body parts floating in formaldehyde or lying exposed all over the damn place. The hands, Barrett knew, had been sent so that their owners could be identified. Frequently it was cheaper for a sheriff seeking a John Doe's identification to amputate a hand for delivery to the FDLE rather than bear the expense of shipping an entire corpse. Tallahassee normally received those gifts by Federal Express. A similar procedure, Barrett assumed, was followed here.

He saw a hand hirsute as a chimp's lying casually on a silver tray, a wedding ring still in place. A phallus occupied its own tray nearby.

"Sometimes we get a print," Tran quipped. "Sometimes not."

Barrett found himself chuckling.

Moving on they passed beneath a skeleton and anatomical chart that looked over dozens of prosthetics, hands and feet fashioned from combinations of Kevlar and titanium and even more exotic materials.

"We are experimenting with neural impulse from the brain." Tran led them weaving through the artificial landscape. "Very promising work."

Then they entered the anthropologists' studio. Ancient hominids and other animals gazed from stools or tables. Everything was coated in a white dust of plaster. Dr. Tran led Barrett and Midge past a dozen partial reconstructions before he stopped to drape a delicate hand over a mannequin's shoulder.

"Jane Doe."

Dr. Tran stood aside to allow Barrett's inspection.

Barrett could not believe what he was seeing. This was no static display. There was expression here. A sense of life. There was tension in the muscles of her face. Her mouth was opened slightly, head turned, as if she were responding to a summons or sound. An opened door?

"I have a wig." Dr. Tran rummaged through an ordinary cardboard box. "We are confident she was Latin

American. Probably from Mexico. See for yoorsef."

She had been beautiful. A high brow and wide-set eyes. High cheekbones. A nice mix of Spanish and Indian in that sad face. And straight black hair.

"It's . . . it's unbelievable," was all Bear could say.

Tran allowed a smile. "We've had an artist from the lab draw a composite from this cast," he said.

Midge beamed with pride. "Over here."

Barrett turned to find what might have been a portrait in pen and ink. A finely detailed, fully living being looked out at him now, reconstructed from flesh and bones mangled in a terrible death.

"Somebody has got to know a face like this," Midge declared.

"Several somebodies," Barrett affirmed grimly. "Now maybe we can get a shot at finding out who."

Hezikiah Jackson looked sternly at the supplicant at her door. "I tole you it'd take some time. Not gonna get well overnight."

She shivered in the wind like a tuning fork. A thin blue line drawn in the sky from horizon to horizon was all that kept a Canadian front from freezing Strawman's Hammock. Hezikiah could feel it coming on, a blue norther. There would be a bitter drop in temperature. A hard frost. Ice in the barrel. She glanced to her gourds and pumpkins. Better make 'em into pies. Hezikiah always knew what climate was coming. She felt it in her knees, her back. It made her irritable.

"You been usin' that salve I give you?" She wrapped a blanket tighter against her emaciated frame.

"I have another sickness." The barrel-chested Latino known as El Toro kept his hands folded over his cap.

"You a busy boy."

"Not that. Of the soul. A sickness of spirit."

"That girl, though, ain't it? Something to do with you' whore."

"She iss not my whore."

Hezikiah cackled. The Bull reached inside his shirt. A crucifix was strung by a silver strand of chain about his thick neck, a cheap thing inlaid with lapis lazuli, warped with heat and humidity.

"She needs a shrine." He kissed the cross. "So that her soul may rest in peace."

"Or mebbe yours?" Hezikiah asked shrewdly. A bony hand snaked out to snatch the *crux ordinaria*. She thrust it like a nail into her bony chest. Breathed deeply.

"Oh, yes! Lordy, lordy. She was a purty thang."

A groan acknowledged that vision, and fear. What manner of witch could see the dead?

Hezikiah opened her eyes.

"She was purty. She was full o' life. Why cain't she rest easy? Can you tell me why?"

He trembled as he shook his head. "No! I cannot say it!"

Hezikiah chewed over the first of the pecan shells that daily stained her teeth.

"You wanta repent? You wanta 'pease her spirit?"

"*Sí!*" He bobbed his head. "And make her a shrine."

A bitter wind whistled through the cypress shack. A pair of shingles chattered on the roof. Hezikiah hesitated a long moment, which was in its own way disturbing. Her instincts had never been wrong before. She had always known what to do. A pair of bleach bottles clanged in the wind like windchimes. Just a pair of bottles broken at the neck and strung with a twist of clothes hanger. Their bell was jarring, dissonant.

"We used to make syrup, days like this," the ancient woman declared absently. "Usta boil it in a open pot and pour it in whiskey bottles."

131

El Toro waited for her prophecy or vision to pass. Hezikiah noticed him, finally.

"Whutchu doin' on my steps?"

He nodded to the crucifix still in her bony hand.

"Oh, yes. Oh, yes." Her fist closed like a talon. "You need to repent. Is that it? Repent?"

"*Sí.*" His head bobbed like an apple in a barrel. "Repent. Confess! Give her peace."

The witch cocked her head to one side to regard him. Bloodshot eyes.

"Take down yer britches," she said finally. "I give you somethin' to repent about."

Sheriff Lou Sessions was abiding by the letter of Judge Blackmond's ruling, if not its spirit. Barrett Raines, Cricket Bonet, and Midge Holloway were required by the sheriff to brief him twice weekly on their progress. Sessions had the three agents seated like satraps in his bunkered office, shivering in the insufficient warmth generated by a radiant heater thick with dust. Barrett had just presented the sketch of Jane Doe to the county's top dog. The sheriff seemed singularly indifferent to that effort.

"And where'd you get this?"

"Dr. Nguyen Tran."

"Never heard of him."

"Pound Lab, Sheriff. University of—"

"I know where the Pound Lab is."

Cricket Bonet pointed a freckled hand at the composite. "Midge busted her ass to get us that sketch, Sheriff. Otherwise—it could have been weeks before our turn came."

"Am I supposed to be grateful?"

"Courteous would suffice," Midge replied cooly.

"My argument ain't with you, Midge."

"Well, it sure as hell isn't with me." Barrett stood from

132

his folding chair. "Lou, did it ever occur to you that I might actually want to see you get credit for busting this case?"

"You do, huh?"

"It is FDLE policy *always* to give the sheriff credit, Lou," Cricket pointed out. "That's how we stay so popular. Not to mention invisible to civilians."

Lou allowed a grudging smile in reply.

"Fair enough." He dropped the sketch into an outbasket. "I'll have 'em make copies."

"You're welcome." Midge's sarcasm gained no rejoinder. "And have you had a chance to go over the autopsy?"

"The dog's what killed her." Sessions shrugged. "Why else would he have been watered? Why else would she have been left for him?"

"She could have been killed any number of ways before the dog," Midge disagreed coldly. "But as it happens, the report confirms your first impression. The dog was responsible. He didn't go for her neck, at first. She was hung too high. So the animal fed first on her torso. The softer tissues. Shock and trauma followed. Essentially she bled to death."

"Sounds about right." Sessions nodded. "But 'til you get me a complete analysis of the DNA there's not much more here for me to use."

"No?" Barrett tried to keep all vexation from his voice. "The woman had repeated cases of veneral disease. A recent episode of gonorrhea. Her vagina was lacerated, consistent with a repeated rape or abuse with an instrument. There was a residue in her vagina which turns out to be a plaster of local herbs and soil, administered apparently as a kind of home remedy."

"That helps me?"

"Well, it is the year 2001, Sheriff. How many people still treat the clap with dog fennel, chinaberry root, and straw?"

"Not Gary Loyd. That's for damn sure."

"The woman also was HIV positive." Midge finished her summary gruffly. "I suppose were I a detective I might imagine someone wanting to wreak vengeance on a woman who gave him AIDS."

"If Gary Loyd's HIV positive, we'll have his ass," Lou agreed.

"Sheriff." Barrett leaned forward. "I want to nail Gary down on this thing, I really do. For one thing, even if he wasn't at this particular scene, he clearly knew about the location. He may well know some of the other people who on some kind of periodic basis appear to have visited the scene. But I think it's very dangerous to try and hang this case on any single smoking gun."

"That's a nice cover-your-ass." Lou's chair squeaked in his dungeon office.

"Not at all," Barrett responded quickly. "But take this business about venereal disease—that'd be enough motive for lots of men to kill, not just Gary."

"And then there's the crucifix," Midge chimed in.

Lou waved her off. "You already bent my ear on that one. If a Mexican did it, I'll be happy to run his ass in. But I don't know any Mexicans driving vehicles of any kind into Strawman's Hammock. Let alone a Humvee."

"Well, you've lost the Humvee and everything in it. So now you're down to betting that something off the victim's remains will tie her to Gary Loyd."

"Hair, fiber, semen. The girl did have semen, 'cording to your boy's report, Midge."

"Semen, yes. And from more than one man."

"So. She was gang-banged. Or pulling a chain. Doesn't mean Gary wasn't there to rape and kill her."

"All her possible partners had that opportunity," Cricket objected. "And supposing the sex was consensual?"

"Consensual?"

"All Midge can say is that there was intercourse with multiple partners. She can't say for sure whether the victim was raped. The signs consistent with rape are also consistent with vigorous sex. Or S&M."

"Oh, Jesus." Lou threw up his hands.

But Midge persisted. "It is a possiblity. Harder to make, I grant you, because of the condition of the body, but these photos . . ."

She fished a pair from the thick file on Lou's desk.

". . . come from the extremities still handcuffed to the wall of the shack. See these bruises here? On her wrists? Those are handcuffs. But there are older wounds inflicted with much softer ligatures beneath and on her arms that I suspect are related to some kind of bondage scenario. That's just my guess. But definitely the woman had been tied up before."

"So maybe this time things just got way out of hand?" Lou scoffed. "Is that what you want me to believe?"

"No, Lou." Barrett tried again. "Midge is just trying to say how this thing might have started—how the victim might have met her killer. Or pissed him off. Or given him AIDS—who knows! But it does tell us this woman didn't mind walking on the wild side, and it implies that a number of probably local men can identify her if we *just get the damn picture out!*"

The chair groaned under the sheriff's weight.

"There's one other detail in this-here report. Something I'm not sure that any of y'all FDLE sleuths happened to notice."

Barrett took a deep breath before replying, "If you can help us, Lou, I'm sure we'd both appreciate it."

"There's the straw."

"The straw?" Barrett frowned. "You mean the straw in her vagina?"

"Nope. In her hair. And those welts you mentioned, Midge? Those long, regular ones along her arms? I've seen that kind of sign before. Comes from working in straw."

"But there's straw all over the Hammock," Bear responded.

"There's straw, yes. But what kind?" Lou rocked in his easy chair. "See, that's yellowheart pine on the crime scene. Loblolly. Original growth. That's what was mixed up in whatever godawful mess they found inside the victim. But the straw they found in her hair? Came off slash pine trees. Hybrid pines. Am I right, Midge?"

Midge was astonished. "I don't know."

"No?" Lou rose from his desk. "But I do. Y'see, there's other folks in that Pound Lab besides gorilla hunters. And those folks, they gave me some real information. Something I can use."

"Be nice if you shared the information with us," Barrett remarked.

"Why we're havin' these little get-togethers," Sessions smiled. "You look and you'll see that the straw in that girl's crotch came from the Hammock. But the straw in her hair didn't. Now, I'm just a country-boy sheriff, but I'm thinking to myself, what besides screwin' puts pine needles in a woman's hair? And what kind of work scratches yer arms? And then I ask myself, where can you find Mexicans working?"

Sheriff Sessions retrieved the sketch with one hand, handed it to Barrett. " 'Bout five crews working at present. Gary Loyd's got a gang raking 'bout five miles out towards Oldtown. Back in the woods deep. 'Course *I* cain't go near the place."

"Spare a deputy?"

Lou smiled. "Nope."

"It would be better if we could work together on this thing, Sheriff."

"What I thought, too. But the judge, why—he sees it different."

"That's a pitiful fucking excuse." The roots of Cricket's hair now sprouted in a scarlet scalp.

"What'd you say to me, Agent?"

Lou was coming to his feet. This is what the bastard wants, Barrett realized. He *wants* to make us fuck up.

"Agent Bonet made an excellent point," Barrett intervened smoothly. "But it's no problem, Sheriff. I believe I know a man can get us where we need to go."

Nine

arold Pearson knew exactly where Gary's latest crew baled straw.

"Land used to be owned by a dairyman." The game warden picked up Barrett and Cricket at Shirley's Homestyle Cafe and loaded them into his Chevy off-roader. "St. Regis tried to buy it years ago. There was some kinda' bankruptcy. Gary got it on auction. Put it in pines. First stand to bale in the county."

"So it was Gary's idea to get in the straw business? Not Linton's?"

Jarold nodded, his eyes steady and alert in their narrowed cranium.

"Linton's run that boy all his life. Took credit for everything Gary ever did, or tried to do. But this straw business—that was the boy's notion. The only thing, really, he can call his own. Half his own, anyway."

Something like eighty percent of the land area in the county was now planted in slash pine trees. For years Barrett Raines had watched as farm and cattle land was replaced with long, regular rows of resined timber, cultivated mostly for conversion into pulp and paper products. At first the stands were seeded almost entirely by large milling companies—St. Regis, Buckeye—and these out-of-county employers were still the dominant economic force in the region, bigger by far than the prison.

But as grow crops like tobacco and peanuts and melons became less profitable, smaller farmers began to put their twenty and forty and then their hundred acres of fallow ground into pines. Within ten years or so, a cut of timber could be expected to yield a modest income. Nobody then was thinking about straw.

Straw served two basic consumers—plant nurseries needing mulch for their infinite variety of annuals and shrubs, and contractors needing material to control erosion along highways or large commercial sites. Nurseries preferred to get straw in bales. But unlike the eighty- or hundred-pound bale which used to be common in hayfields, pine straw was baled manually to produce a wired bundle barely twenty pounds in weight. A standard forty-eight-foot truck-hauled trailer hauled 912 bales of straw. Some owners extended their trailers to fifty-three feet. That bumped you up to 1008 bales of straw.

The landowner made anywhere from seventy to a hundred dollars for every hundred acres of pine he leased. The baling company made roughly a thousand dollars profit per trailer. The men and women who raked, stacked, baled, and loaded the straw got roughly a quarter a piece. Twenty-five cents for each bale of straw. You didn't have to be an accountant to figure out who made money on the deal.

The game warden's Tahoe rumbled out toward the city limit to pass the town's solitary and elevated water tower. GO HORNETS!!, read the scarlet scrawl.

Two miles later and seventy miles an hour, you could get dizzy watching rows of pine flash by. Flickering, almost. Like canned footage of a silent movie.

Other crops, tobacco, melons, required pipes and

pumps for irrigation. But there was no irrigation to worry about when you planted pine trees; pines survived where anything else would parch. You put 'em down, mowed the long, straight rows until they got a start. Then you waited eight or ten years to cut your timber. That was about it. Until Linton and Gary Loyd started the business, no one gave a second thought about that other product of the pine tree, the needles that fell to sweetly carpet the ground below.

Barrett loved the smell of pine straw on the ground. The morning's cold, damp weather heightened the aroma. The norther that had blown in the evening before threatened rain. Barrett recalled Matthew Arnold's description: the air truly was low as lead. Jarold Pearson pulled the Tahoe off the farm-to-market road, skirting a culvert to park beside a semitrailer. A pair of Latin men tossed bales of straw from a narrow, two-wheeled carry-out into the trailer where a stacker packed the straw in tiers of gold. The workers kept their eyes caged.

Barrett, Cricket, and Midge followed the game warden past the half-filled trailer and down a row of mature pines. A couple of hundred yards inside they found them, a crew of migrants racing to beat a coming rain, raking straw like gold from the ground into heaps and pressing it by hand into portable balers.

The labor was arduous and simple. You thrust the pine straw by hand into the baler's roughly square mouth, leaned on the jerry-rigged lever to compress the straw into its shaped container. Once secured, bales were tossed onto narrow take-out carts that transferred them to the semitrailer where other Latin workers carefully loaded the finished product for transport.

There were probably a half-dozen balers working this morning, fed straw by perhaps twice that many rakers, men and women who pulled the straw into heaps beneath the shaded canopy. The laborers were all wearing flannel shirts, Barrett noticed. Something they would not do in hot weather. In hot weather balers and rakers stripped to the waist. That's when you saw the sign of pine needles scratching their arms and torsos. Which provided further evidence for Barrett that Jane Doe was killed sometime during the warm spell that had punctuated their November season.

"*Cómo está?*" Barrett greeted the nearest Hispanic.

An upward lilt of the chin was the worker's only acknowledgment.

Then Jarold Pearson, to Bear's utter surprise, turned to the same worker.

"*Quién es el jeffe? Por favor?* (Who is your boss, please?)"

"El Toro," came the answer.

"When did you learn to speak Spanish?" Bear was amazed.

Jarold shrugged to hide a crimson face. "My wife was from Honduras."

"I didn't even know you were married!"

The warden nodded. "Six years. Met her on a church trip. We'd go down twice a year, you know. Build 'em schoolhouses, clinics, and such. She died four winters ago. Want me to ask where we can find the foreman?"

"Thanks, Jarold. If you don't mind."

The warden turned to a man baling straw. "(We are not INS, but we do need to speak to your foreman. Can you tell us where we may find him?)"

"Behind you." A different voice, the English heavily accented but perfectly understandable. Barrett turned with Cricket and the game warden to find a man of average height, but his chest was enormous. And the skull, heavily browed, turreted back and forth as the foreman eyed the gathered Anglos. Just like a bull.

"What you want?"

"I am Special Agent Barrett Raines. And as Warden

142

Pearson told your man here, we are not INS. We are not concerned with immigration."

"(He says they aren't looking for illegals.)" The Bull relayed that information loudly to his workers.

"What was that chatter?" Cricket asked.

"He's just reassuring his people," Barrett spoke up.

El Toro regarded Bear a moment.

"Hábla español?"

"Not as well as *mi esposa.*"

A ghost of a smile seemed to threaten the Bull's face. He reached into his pocket. The tip of a jackknife's blade snicked open on the hem of his blue jeans.

"Easy, chief." Cricket's hand went by instinct to his handgun.

The Bull ignored the warning, bending casually to cut a strand of offending wire from a bale of hay.

"Put away the knife for now, señor." Barrett addressed the foreman in English.

"Sí." The knife disappeared. "And why do so many men with guns come to the pine trees? Out of work?"

An ugly laughter erupted, but forced, as if the men had long learned how to respond to El Toro's humor.

"Got a girl killed, señor." Barrett closed the distance between himself and the barrel-chested Latino. "East of here. In an abandoned deer camp. We're hoping some of your people can identify her."

"My people?" The foreman raised his eyebrows in an imitation of insouciance.

Bear didn't bite. "Mexican girl, we think. Eighteen to early twenties."

Then Barrett showed him the sketch.

Suddenly every rake and baler was stilled. Like that moment when, before a heavy storm, birds quit their interminable chirp.

Barrett watched El Toro's face as he scanned the drawing. Nothing. Not a trace of interest or emotion shown. No curiosity, either, which was not quite believable.

"I do not know her," the Latin man declared.

"Have your men take a look, señor."

He shrugged. "(They a have a picture. Some girl.)"

Barrett spoke up sharply. "(She is not *some* girl, sir. She is a Latin woman killed, we believe, by someone local. Perhaps someone who works here, beneath the trees.)"

"You think so?" El Toro replied in complete indifference.

"(I am sure you have papers, señor. But did you know that if your men do not I can send *you* back across the border?)"

Bear's threat was not entirely credible, but it had the effect he wanted. El Toro's open disdain faded with a degree of confidence. His face became vacant, impassive.

"(I did not hire these men,)" was all he said.

"The hell's he sayin'?" Cricket could tell, even without translation, that Bear had quelled a Mexican rebellion.

"He's saying we can pass the picture around," Barrett improvised.

"Tell him we don't need his fucking permission for that," Cricket growled, to which the Bull offered a wide smile.

Not a single laborer recognized, or admitted to recognizing, the sketch of the murdered Latin woman. Some seemed barely to look.

"They're afraid to say anything," Cricket told Barrett privately. "They're afraid of that damned foreman. You see him look at that sketch? Doesn't know the girl? Bullshit. He's a liar."

"Yes, he is," Barrett agreed. "And I've got a feeling there's a lot more to hide than what he knows about Jane Doe."

"We could call in the INS. Threaten to deport 'em if somebody doesn't speak up."

"You can only play that card once," Barrett warned. "Let's just go easy. These workers know there's been a killing. They'll talk amongst themselves. Give it some time to percolate. In the meantime . . ."

"Meantime, what?" Cricket turned to see the new arrivals who blocked retreat through the row of pines.

A compact, confident man stood with his son, dressed well in pleated khakis and bomber jacket.

"Well, gentlemen." Linton Loyd removed a pair of aviator glasses. "The hell gives you the authority to come out here?"

Barrett displayed the sketch. "You know her?"

Linton stood calmly. "Call Thurman, son. Tell him we got some trespassers out here."

"That's a bluff, Mr. Loyd. We don't need a warrant to ask your workers, your son's workers, some simple questions. In fact, I don't need a warrant to question you, Linton. Or your son. You could call Thurman and waste us both a lot of time. Or, Linton, you might just cooperate.

"You want Gary off our to-do list? So do I. Let him answer some questions. What's wrong with that?"

"He's not answerin' shit."

"It's all right, Daddy." A gust of blue wind caught the straws clinging to Gary's receding scalp. "Ask anything you goddamn like, Bear."

"Okay. Do you know this girl?" Barrett displayed the sketch to Linton's son.

Anyone watching would know immediately that Gary Loyd did in fact know the woman captured on paper before him. The ripple on his face, the suddenly averted eyes.

He knew her, all right. Barrett glanced for confirmation to Cricket.

Even so, Gary's was not the reaction of a sociopath. It was not the reaction of a man without empathy. It was the reaction of a man with a conscience. Was it a man in remorse? How did that fit Midge's profile of a cold-blooded killer?

Barrett tried hard not to let generalities interfere with the specifics before him. There were many possibilities. Gary could be innocent of any wrongdoing. He could be innocent of the homicide, but know the woman's killer. Or perhaps the younger Loyd had simply taken Jane for sex.

"Never saw her," Gary lied.

Barrett turned his attention to Linton Loyd, but the father remained as stoic and impassive during his son's interrogation as his bullish foreman had earlier.

"Who owns the baling company?" Barrett asked suddenly, and something like the tail of a whip seemed to strike the father's face.

"Gary does," Linton spoke up tersely. "I'm just a silent partner."

"Thought you started this business, Linton."

"Daddy just owns part," Gary spoke up. "I'm buying him out."

"Any other details of finance you think will lead us to this girl's killer, Agent Raines?" Linton inquired.

"I just wondered," Barrett shrugged, "how in a place this small, with all these Latinos buying phone cards from the same place up by the Piggly-Wiggly, getting their groceries from the town's one, solitary store, crossing each other's path day to day in these piney woods—why is it, d'you think, Gary, that not one of your workers can identify this woman?"

"I wouldn't know," Gary responded guardedly.

Barrett smiled easily.

"Wouldn't be because you told them to keep quiet, would it, Gary? Or your foreman here? Mr. Bull."

"His name is Roberto Quiroga," Gary replied woodenly. "I don't know anything about a bull."

Linton's jaw was white. "Is this the way you'd go about bein' sheriff, Bear? Comin' out here like this?"

Barrett found that the slow anger that had simmered even at this man's deer camp was now come to a boil.

"The fuck ever gave you the idea you were above the law, Linton?"

"You can't talk to me like that."

"Hell I can't. You are attempting to influence an officer of the court, did you know that?"

"Bullshit."

"But I'm about to let you off the hook, Linton. If I do ever decide to run for office in this county—that's *if*—I will be asking for your vote, and that is *all* I'll be asking."

Linton spit a brown stream into the dirt between them.

"Easy to say now."

"Yes." Barrett felt the tension in his chest suddenly ease. "It is."

Linton Loyd turned on his well-booted heel.

"We've wasted enough time here, Gary."

Barrett watched as Linton and his son disappeared into a blind of needles and straw. Roberto "the Bull" Quiroga remained sullen and vacant from the box baler.

"They're hiding something," Cricket declared.

"Yes." Barrett nodded.

But what?

Within minutes Jarold was leading Barrett and Cricket out of the field. When they cleared the pines, Barrett took Jarold aside.

"What was your impression of Gary's foreman?"

"Bluffing. Hiding something."

Barrett paused to consider that description.

"Jarold. I'm going to need your help."

"Yes, sir." The warden didn't hesitate.

"Can you keep an eye on Señor Quiroga? Nothing intrusive. Just see where he goes. You run into Latinos downtown or out here, just keep a friendly conversation, see what comes up."

Jarold nodded. "I can do that."

"You think the foreman might be tied to the killing, Barrett?" Cricket asked.

"I don't know." Barrett shook his head. "I just got a feeling that we might have rattled his cage."

"I'll keep an eye on him," Jarold reaffirmed.

"Good."

By the time Barrett and his companions returned from the Linton's straw-lease, Laura Anne's day was half over. It had begun routinely enough with Laura Anne picking up her folder for the day's assignments and heading for homeroom. A mere week of substituting put her back in the saddle. The rhythm of classes and buzzers and students claimed Laura Anne's entire focus. For hours she did not even think of the restaurant. That illusion rarely lasted. The restaurant had a way of intruding into her teaching day.

Laura Anne had to give a pair of young managers the responsibility of keeping the restaurant afloat during her leave of absence. The cell phone was a godsend, linking the owner to her young protégés, allowing her to send and receive messages and voicemail. Not to say there weren't snags. Splinter Townsend tried to charge thirty cents more a pound for mullet in Laura Anne's absence than he would have offered to her face. When notified of that increase, Laura Anne called Splinter directly and told him if he couldn't keep a decent price she'd just start buying direct from Esther down at the Bay and wouldn't that just upset a nice business relationship?

Splinter suddenly found profit in his originally agreed-upon price. Laura Anne could not help but notice that during her second-period class, Splinter's sophomore son kept looking over Edwina Land's shoulder during their algebra quiz. Like father, like son.

Third period was free—a curious term, for there was

nothing free about it. When fully employed, Laura Anne used to cram lesson plans or practice sessions into her planning period. As a sub there were somewhat diminished responsibilities. She was headed for a cup of coffee in the lounge when a familiar voice stopped her.

"Hey, Laura Anne, is that you?"

Annie MacGrue was the elementary school's librarian, the only other African American on campus.

"Annie B. Yes, I'm here subbing."

Annie cocked her hip coyly. "Don't tell me you're gonna give up the big money for a county paycheck? Don't even tell me that!"

"Actually, I'm considering it," Laura Anne admitted.

"Our gain if you do," Annie beamed. "Say, I'm just over here robbin' some toner for our Xerox. Why don't you come on over and let me show you my library?"

"Annie, that'd be nice. Long as I'm back in time for fourth period."

A breezeway linked the high school and junior high facilities to the new elementary school's construction. In theory the campus was divided but, Laura Anne noted, there was nothing to keep a pedestrian from walking over. In fact, she noted, you could walk behind the gymnasium and stroll onto the elementary side virtually unobserved.

"Annie, can I put you on the alert?"

"Alert?"

"We've got a kid on our side who's taking pictures of little girls."

"Lord. Who?"

"Jerry Slade."

"Boy with the camera?"

Laura Anne broke stride. "You've seen him?"

"Sure. Playground. Bus duty. Says he's taking pictures for the annual."

"You ever see him on the elementary side?"

"Now and then he comes over." Annie nodded. "He'll pick up things I need delivered to the office, or like today, if I was too busy, Mr. Folsom might send him over with the toner."

"Mr. Folsom sends him over?"

"If I need somethin', sure. Always with a note."

Always with a note. Well. Laura Anne turned that one over.

How much should she tell Annie? Laura Anne, after all, was only a substitute. She had already been told to drop the matter by her boss. Still—

"Annie, Mr. Folsom thinks there's nothing to this. There may not be. But there's a little fifth-grader, Isabel Hernandez?"

Annie nodded. "I know her."

"I'm virtually positive that Jerry's been taking pictures of her on the bus without Isabel's permission. She also claims he was in the bathroom with her on one occasion. Taking pictures."

"Oh, Lord." Annie frowned. "Well, I'm glad you told me. Why didn't Alton send her teacher a note? Or all of us, for that matter? He wouldn't even have to specify a name. Something to get us looking."

"I think he's hoping there's not a problem," Laura Anne said lamely.

"Well, I'm going to talk to Isabel today," Annie promised. "Her teacher, too—Brenda Starling. You know Brenda? And we'll keep our eyes open from now on."

"Thanks, Annie."

"No ma'am. The thanks goes to you."

The subject changed, then, to the new library. Annie was thrilled with the construction, the computer bay, access to Internet resources. "We need more books, of course. And the periodicals are pitiful. But it's a start."

Laura Anne found herself warming to her friend's enthusiasm. The two women were chattering like bluejays by the time they reached the library. The restrooms were accessed from exterior doors just around the corner.

Isabel Hernandez had asked if someone could go with her to the bathroom. Señora Starling had smiled to say that Isabel was a good and trustworthy girl and that all she needed was this little pass and she could go.

Sometimes it was hard for Isabel to understand Mrs. Starling. The English went very fast and the señora did not speak Spanish. But Isabel accepted the little piece of paper pressed into her hand, marched resolutely out of her classroom, and took the breezeway past the library to the bathroom.

She used to like the bathroom. It was clean. Big. Cool inside.

A metal door opened to a stall and commode. She stepped inside. It was hard to close the door. You had to turn a little wheel and sometimes the bolt did not line up with the hole. But Isabel managed.

She felt safe then. Surrounded by walls of steel in this clean, cool place. She hefted her skirt and dropped her panties to squat over the commode.

"Hey, *conchita.*"

Isabel's head jerked up to see Jerry Slade and a silver lens.

Laura Anne was not present when Mrs. Starling referred the matter to the principal. By the time Brenda and Annie got to the restroom, there was no teenage boy present. Only a little girl whom the principal dismissed as hysterical, soiled over her little legs and canvas shoes, shivering in her closed stall.

"Jerry Slade could not have been over there," the principal insisted. "He was working at the office. To leave he'd have had to get a pass. I didn't give a pass to anyone during third period."

When Annie relayed that portion of the conversation, Laura Anne was flabbergasted. "So since the principal didn't issue a pass, Jerry couldn't couldn't have been on the elementary side? Is Alton an idiot?"

"Careful, Laura Anne," Annie responded in hushed tones. "He may be a fool, but he's the fool who hires us. Hires *me*, anyway."

"So what happened?" Laura Anne pressed in exasperation. "What are we doing to protect this little girl?"

Annie shrugged. "Alton told us always to send somebody with her to the bathroom. As *if*. And he said he'd speak to Jerry. Just to make sure, naturally, that on this occasion Mr. Slade was grinding brake pads or knives or whatever they do over there."

Laura Anne shook her head. "Why in the world would he choose to thick a fifth-grade girl would make up a story like this? Why would he choose to believe Jerry Slade about *anything*?"

"Because Jerry's dog kin, for one. He's family. And his sorry daddy's on the school board. *And*, as you well know, Laura Anne, because no one wants to side against homies on the side of Mexicans."

"It's not right, Annie."

"No, it's not right. But that's the way it is."

Laura Anne tried to remember the days before the county's school was integrated. What her mother had told her of separate schools, separate lunch counters. Separate bathrooms. Here was the pattern repeating.

"And now here I am, with this thing, sitting on my two hands," she said aloud.

"But Laura Anne—what can you do?"

Ten

The puppy was waiting when Laura Anne got home. Cricket Bonet was the hero of the hour, acquiring a short-haired Heinz 57 from an animal lover's litter in return for spaying and shots. She did not flinch at the coins Cricket rattled in a can. She played like a cat with the rawhide and tennis ball he brought. She rolled onto her back and let you scratch her belly, her pink tongue hanging to one side as if to say, I'll give you an hour and a half to cut that out.

She was, Barrett agreed, the perfect mascot for boys born a day apart. Ben, taking after his father's love of the classics and "old stories," named her Penelope, a combination of loyalty and love. Tyndall was not much interested in Ben's explanation of the allusion. Fraternal twins, Tyndall was born the 17th of November, Benjamin the 18th. The family alternated celebrations of that unusual circumstance. This year was Ben's, and the extra day's wait, you would have thought by listening, had driven the boys crazy.

"*He's perfect!*" Tyndall bounded into the carport like a shot from a cannon to leap into Barrett's arms.

Bear scooped him up in one arm.

"Daddy!"

And he snagged Ben in the other.

"Feel like I'm loading watermelons." Bear grinned widely as he climbed the stairs, a boy under each arm. Laura Anne and Thelma just shook their heads from their vantage in the kitchen.

"Look at those boys." Thelma wagged her silver head. "Thinkin' they daddy's some kina' teddy bear."

"That's fine by me, Auntie." Laura Anne found Aunt Thelma's ways a little too biblical, on occasion, to suit. She could have been a matriarch, Aunt Thelma, with her silver hair and cotton dress, belted at the middle, that fell to thick ankles. She was vain about her ankles, loved to show them off. "I got a nice turn, I do," she would say when primed with a little peach brandy. Running shoes had only recently replaced the black loafers that could no longer be found in the Emporium or Sears catalog.

She was strict regarding the boys' behavior. Demanding in matters of respect and reverence. She had never married. Her ways could be trying, but Laura Anne decided early that whatever inconveniences Thelma imposed were trivial in comparison to the treasures she brought to Ben and Tyndall.

Through Thelma the boys had a view, even if removed, of their heritage, their past. Aunt Thelma had become the repository of the family genealogy and history, a storyteller, matchmaker, and moral compass. She was an education, was Aunt Thelma, raised in a time and place about which Ben and Tyndall needed to know and appreciate.

She came from the line of old MacGrues, a distinguished and tragic family who began, some said, as virtual slaves on the old Buchanan place and wound up after the war (by which they always meant World War II) with a sawmill and property and God knows what-all. There were children, accomplishments. Respect. Some recalled, though Laura Anne never knew if this was true, that the elder MacGrue even piloted airplanes!

Flew in the war, Thelma insisted. Yes, ma'am, he did.

That dynasty did not last, of course. Hard for any family of color to hang onto businesses and property with Jim Crow and the Klan running the county. But children were born in those hard years to keep the line alive. Those offspring grew to marry and have children of their own. And then those children married. Or at least got pregnant. Laura Anne herself was related to the MacGrues, of course, in a chain of genealogy left for Thelma and a few other ancients to recite over holidays and funerals, like Icelandic scalds recalling in verse the arcana of some nearly lost and dimming saga. Thelma was a real and living link to a time rich in pain and triumph that Laura Anne wanted her boys to know "from the mouth."

Sometimes the aging spinster was a little rigid in her ways. She kept a switch on her kitchen counter, though Laura Anne forbade her to use it. The sight of that instrument was in itself a reminder to the boys of how things used to be for little boys growing up—and still was for too many others.

Barrett dropped the twins to inspect Thelma's cake.

"Got anything to lick?"

"Icing in the bowl for the boys." Thelma doled out her favors imperiously. "You can have the egg-beater."

"But you better hurry," Laura Anne cautioned. "We're going to have a house full of fifth-graders in just a few minutes."

By midday the Raineses' modest home was indeed spilling over with boys and girls shouting gleefully, ignoring the afternoon's chill as they climbed all over the rope swing out back, played tag and Red Rover, and ran, ran, ran—all around the house. An unfamiliar vehicle stopped on the county road out front, a rusted pickup arrested on the blacktop distant from the Raineses' brick-laid driveway. Its exhaust manifold leaked. It sounded like a Model-T. It was filled cab to bed with migrant workers.

Laura Anne saw a young girl slide off the tailgate. A woman of indeterminate age joined the girl, clutching her skirt modestly to climb over the bed's sideboard. The pickup sputtered away leaving a small, brown woman frail as a sparrow and a little girl dressed in white with shiny black shoes and bright ribbons in her silky hair.

"Isabel!" Laura Anne walked out to meet the newcomers.

The fifth-grader averted her gaze, but a smile just about split her face. Laura Anne saw a bundle wrapped in newspaper in the mother's arms.

"*Señora Hernandez? Cómo está?*" Laura Anne greeted the woman warmly and saw her eyes widen.

"*Hábla español?*"

"*Sí.*" Laura Anne took the offered gift.

"(This is the teacher, mama. Señora Raines.)" The shyness vanished. "(Raines—like in English the 'rain' comes. She is the one who helped me.)"

"(I tried.)" Laura Anne smiled. "(But I hope to do more.)"

"(No one believes her.)" The mother's eyes filled in a blink with tears. "(No one knows what she says.)"

"(I know,)" Laura Anne declared. "(I believe. Now, come in, won't you? My house is your house.)"

The humbly wrapped bundle brought by Isabel and her mother turned out to be the hit of the party. Barrett himself was the only celebrant present who had ever actually seen a piñata. The papier-mâchéed likeness of an owl was homemade, Isabel's mother modestly explained. It was filled with cookies and sweets made over the single propane stove available in the Hernandez's camp.

Barrett tossed a ball of cord over a crepe myrtle's smooth limb to raise and lower the piñata's bright-painted target. Laura Anne blindfolded each child in turn, and a broomstick became the bat that boys and girls swung blind in an effort to burst the hoard of candy from its owllike keep. Barrett made sure that every child had a chance to hit the target.

The honor for the blow that broke the piñata went, predictably, to Tyndall. One whack and a wealth of sweets scattered beneath the smooth-barked tree. Laura Anne and Barrett saw to it that no one hogged the bounty; every child got something sweet to eat. Thelma took over, then, with the help of visiting parents, to supervise a game of pin-the-tail-on-the-donkey. That gave Bear and his wife a space of time to visit privately with Isabel's mother.

They shared coffee in the yard, watching the children. Dolores sipped her coffee carefully, as if hoarding the precious cup.

"(I have plenty,)" Laura Anne volunteered.

"(I have enough, thank you.)"

"(But I want you to have more than enough,)" Laura Anne chided, and the smile she got from Isabel's mother let her know that the ice between them was finally beginning to thaw. A conversation ensued. Barrett's Spanish was much weaker than his wife's, so frequently Laura Anne served as translator for her husband and Isabel's mother.

Barrett began indirectly, with general questions, most of them not directed at Isabel's recent trauma.

"(Where do you live?)" he asked. "(How many are in your family?)"

There were around a half-dozen families living together, Dolores answered. Fifteen children. A camp near town.

"(What work have you found?)"

"(We are waiting.)" Dolores answered.

"(For what?)"

"(Word of the straw.)"

"(The straw?)"

"(The men bale. The women rake. Sometimes.)"

"(And who hires you?)"

Dolores averted her eyes with that question. "(I don't know. The men know.)"

"(Have you heard of Señor Loyd?)"

"(Oh, yes. He is a big man. He has much money.)"

"(Did you know that Señor Loyd hires men to work in straw?)"

She smiled coyly, as if amused at Bear's pronouncement.

"(Am I wrong in this?)" Barrett asked. "(Am I wrong when I say that Señor Loyd hires the men?)"

"(He pays them,)" Dolores responded patiently, as if explaining something to a child. "(But he does not get the work.)"

"(Who does?)"

"(El Toro,)" Dolores replied, and Barrett reached to squeeze honey into his coffee.

"The Bull?" Laura Anne asked her husband. "Have you ever heard of a man by that name?"

"It's a sobriquet, I'm sure, and yes, I've met the man. Ask the señora if all the work comes through the Bull."

Laura Anne asked.

"*Sí,*" she replied. "(Everyone who works must pay him.)"

Barrett leaned forward. "(Must pay him? How?)"

She seemed amused.

"(With money. The money you make from the bale; he takes the little bite.)"

The little bite, or *mordida*, translates from Spanish as "bribe."

"(Why can't you refuse?)" Laura Anne asked. "(Why can't you keep your money?)"

She seemed astonished at the question. "(You say 'no'

to the Bull—!)" She drew her hand across her throat. *"Muerte."*

"We've heard that something like this might be going on," Barrett confided to Laura Anne. "There are only a couple of balers in the county. A virtual monopoly. What's most likely happening is that Gary and Linton Loyd and the others are using this El Toro to twist arms and break legs. You either work for the wages *they* offer, or you don't work at all."

"That's outrageous!"

Barrett nodded. "Not to mention illegal. But hard to prove. Unless we can get this El Toro to turn on his straw-boss, which I don't think is likely."

"Or unless you can get these people," Laura Anne inclined her head to Isabel's mother, "to testify against him."

"Be hard," Barrett frowned. "We'd have to gain their trust. *And* convince them we can protect their families from El Toro. It would take something pretty major to accomplish that."

Laura Anne placed her cup on a milk crate that doubled as a server.

"Maybe I can help."

"You?" Barrett shook his head. "You stay out of this, Laura Anne."

"Why? Will it hurt your chances at sheriff?"

Dolores began to feel uncomfortable. "(I did not mean to begin a dispute.)"

"(There is no rancor,)" Laura Anne assured her. "(I can disagree freely with my husband.)"

Señora Hernandez greeted this last in an attitude of muted skepticism.

Laura Anne turned to Barrett. "You need this woman's trust and the trust of her family. They need you to protect a little girl who is being stalked, who may even be in danger of assault by a young man showing signs, I believe, of being very disturbed. You don't have to be a politician, Bear, to see how this can work."

"The problem isn't me, Laura Anne. It's Lou Sessions. He is the lock on the law in this county and he's not going to arrest Jerry Slade, or even seriously investigate the boy. Not on my say-so *or* yours. Not in an election year. Not without evidence so plain it can't be ignored and thick enough to insulate him from a goddamn barn-fire."

"That's the problem?"

"It ain't football, honey. I can't run an end-around."

Laura Anne rose from her chair.

"No," she said. "But I can."

Somewhere the puppy barked. Then the high laughter of children. The party wound down not long after. The same pickup that deposited Isabel and her mother came back to get them, remaining, as before, at a distance on the blacktop road.

Monday came with the flourishes of a busy family heading off to work—Barrett to his Live Oak office, Laura Anne and the boys to school. If Laura Anne had dwelled on the matter she might have realized she was tired. She was, after all, still working full-time over the weekend at the restaurant while finishing the last of her tenure as a substitute teacher for Deacon High. Thanksgiving was right around the corner, which brought other obligations—a recital, a church service. Not to mention the demands left over from a birthday party, a houseful of guests, and two high-voltage twins.

But the truth was, this morning Laura Anne was pumped. She was girded for battle. She had not told Barrett what she planned.

"Better you don't know," she said. "Just keep your cell phone handy."

Barrett objected. Laura Anne overruled. That was that.

She went through the first four periods of the day on automatic pilot. There were assignments to give. The usual in-class commotions to censure or break up. The constant, constant effort to keep students' attention. Laura Anne usually enjoyed those challenges. But today, all she wanted was to hear the lunch bell.

Actually, a muted buzzer had long superseded the traditional bell to announce the end of morning classes. Laura Anne left her fourth-period band hall on the buzz to see doors bursting open in synchrony all up and down the hall, a host of students spilling into that long corridor with the boisterousness and élan of firefighters racing to a conflagration. A pair of hall monitors were caught in that throbbing stream. There was the school's janitor and handyman, an old Appalachian, retreating to his closet for lunch, a brown bag stained with mayonnaise in his liver-spotted hand. Laura Anne took a position near a water fountain. Students strolled or stampeded by, most without a glance in her direction.

There was Jerry Slade. He was passing something to a knot of peers. A poster? Magazine? But Laura Anne was not interested in that.

She bent over the fountain as Jerry passed. She noted the teenager's backpack. Jerry broke from his acolytes as Laura Anne saw him do every day to reach a row of lockers in the hall. It was a combination lock. He spun the dial, snicked it loose. The door opened. A shouted challenge from Harvey Koon delayed the deposit briefly, but finally Jerry tossed his bag into the locker and rejoined the swell of students headed for the cafeteria.

Laura Anne waited until the hall was empty of students or faculty. She then walked with purpose to the hall closet where Alfred Land had eaten his lunch every school day for twenty-three years.

"Hello, Mr. Alfred."

He was wiping a smear of mayonnaise off his ham sandwich.

"Why, yes, Miz Raines. Nice to see you."

"You, too, Mr. Alfred. I need to borrow a tool."

The old man smiled. "Well, if I got it, you can have it."

The hall was deserted by the time Laura Anne returned to Jerry Slade's locker. She had assured Mr. Alfred that she didn't need his help. She popped open her cell phone and dialed 911.

"Yes, please. This is Laura Anne Raines. I believe I have just witnessed the deposit of a handgun in a locker here at the high school. . . . Yes, I'm right here. . . . Yes, I can wait."

Minutes later Principal Alton Folsom was trailing red-faced behind Sheriff Lou Sessions on his way down the school's long hall.

"Miz Raines, what on earth are you up to here?"

"I saw what appeared to be a handgun put into this locker," Laura Anne replied steadily.

"Whose locker is it?" Sessions was chewing tobacco.

"I have no idea."

"That a pair of bolt-cutters, Miz Raines?" The sheriff's mouth sealed a wad beneath his pockmarked face.

"Bolt-cutters. Yes, Sheriff. I borrowed them from Alfred."

"Thoughtful. You sure it was a weapon?"

"Reasonably sure, Sheriff. Metal and silver. Appeared to have a barrel."

"I don't want to start a precedent here—" the principal began.

Laura Anne cut him off. "You want to risk a shooting at school, Mr. Folsom?"

The words were directed at the principal, but Laura Anne faced Lou Sessions eye to eye.

"Do you really want to ignore a warning from a teacher

that a weapon may have been concealed in a place where parents want their children to be safe? Do you want to risk a killing? Do we need another Columbine to take that prospect seriously?"

"Well, I . . . I . . ."

"It's all right, Alton." Sessions reached for the bolt-cutters. "Cain't hurt to take a look."

The sheriff fit the bolt-cutter's jaws over the lock's hasp. Within seconds the keep was open.

"All I see's a knapsack."

"Yes," Laura Anne nodded. "That's where he put it."

" 'He?' " Lou asked and opened the sack.

For a while the sheriff just stood, frowning, as if trying to peer to the bottom of a dark well.

"Well, what's in there?" the principal blurted. The sheriff pulled out a photo.

The angle taken was disorienting, at first. The photo was stolen from a height, looking down at white panties pulled over brown ankles. Isabel Hernandez's startled face, framed with bows, looked up at her photographer.

"Whose bin is this?" Sessions growled.

Alton stammered some kind of equivocation.

"Is there a camera in the knapsack, Sheriff?" Laura Anne interrupted.

He groped inside and pulled out a silver shape of metal. A camera.

"That was what I took for a weapon," Laura Anne stated without apology. "It belongs, as I'm sure Mr. Folsom can confirm for you, to Jerry Slade."

After a short consult with the sheriff, Pricipal Folsom seemed suddenly determined to take action. Laura Anne was between classes when she saw Jerry Slade emerge from the principal's office in the sheriff's custody.

"You bitch." The teenager cast the epithet calmly, with no heat. "You nigger bitch."

"But she nailed your ass, didn't she, Jerry?" The sheriff

grabbed him by the belt. And then, facing Laura Anne, "Didn't she now?"

The day after Thanksgiving Jerry Slade went with his father before the elected county judge where mandatory counseling and probation were meted out.

"This will not," Thurman Shaw informed his client's father brusquely, "absolve you or your son from civil action."

"Civil? Civil what?"

"The family has the legal right to sue, Rolly. I just want you to be aware that your legal obligations do not end with a first offense and a slap on the wrist. And you need to understand the terms of the restraining order on your boy, here."

"Jerry's not gonna take any more pictures."

"He'd better not. And I am informing the school's so-called principal myself that Jerry is prohibited by courts order from any chore that would take him anywhere on the elementary side of the school. And do I need to tell you where to put that camera?"

"Who you working for anyway, Thurman?"

"You'll be back before the judge in one month. I'd advise you to come with a report from your chosen therapist to assure His Honor that counseling has been ongoing."

"Is there anything else a man can do?" Rolly was white with fury.

"Yes." Thurman loosened his tie. "Let your one remaining dog off that damned chain. And take some time with your son."

Stacy Kline covered the entire affair, playing as much as possible on the fact that Laura Anne was wife to an acting lawman and a potential candidate for sheriff, asking if Barrett had counseled Laura Anne regarding the legal propriety of her actions.

"No." Laura Anne offered a one-word response to that question and refused further comment. The community was split over her initiative, half the citizens voicing fury at her invasion of a teenager's privacy, the other half relieved that a school pornographer had been caught. Even if the victim were only Mexican.

No one seemed to challenge the idea that the smooth-metaled implement might have been mistaken for a weapon.

No one, that is, except Sheriff Lou Sessions.

"Your wife set that boy up." Sheriff Sessions detained Bear after a Wednesday briefing. "She couldn't get Alton to do anything, so she just figured herself out a way to get me down there."

"You had probable cause, Sheriff. It was a legal search."

"She jerked my goddamn chain to get it. And you try and tell me you didn't know a thing about it?"

"Lou. Not everybody thinks, or acts, or feels the way you do. If you don't figure that out, and quick, you're gonna lose a whole lot more than some damned election."

Barrett was heading out of the sheriff's dungeon when the lawman spoke up.

"She did the right thing."

"What?" Barrett was not sure he had heard correctly.

"Laura Anne." Lou nodded from his desk. "She did exactly the right thing. Same thing I'd've done."

"You think so?" Barrett was too surprised to offer more.

The sheriff nodded. "Yep. I'd've done it. Question, Bear: Would you?"

Barrett thought a long moment.

"I don't know whether Laura Anne lied or not to get you into that locker, Sheriff. But she's not taken an oath to protect and defend. She's not an officer of the court. You and I—we have different rules."

"And you never break 'em?" The seamed and hardened sheriff asked it quietly.

"Tell you what, Lou. We get some trust between us. Put some bad guys in jail. I might feel better about answering that question."

For the first time in a long time Barrett saw some genuine warmth on the face of the county's sheriff.

"Fair enough," Lou said. "What are you and that Canuck gonna be doing after you leave here?"

"Got some information on Gary's foreman we need to follow up."

"Got anything to do with our killing?"

"Honestly, Lou—I don't know if it ties in at all. But there's only one way to find out."

Jarold Pearson offered to drive Barrett and Cricket out to the deer camp that held Isabel's and a dozen other families. A steady rain drummed on the hood of Jarold's Tahoe. The cold front had stalled against a buffer of humid Gulf air to produce a deluge that washed out roads and culverts all over the county. The flatwoods were, for a welcome change, saturated. Barrett stretched out in the back of Jarold's Fish & Game vehicle, giving Bonet the shotgun seat. Much more room, in here, than in the Impala. And Barrett was grateful to have four wheels pulling.

Jarold informed them that the camp itself was on a lease that could normally be reached in about a half-hour from Mayo's town square, but today it would take longer. He was right. After twenty minutes on the county road, it took another twenty minutes of slipping and sliding through drenched ruts of mud before Jarold found the narrow cleft in a wall of pine that led to the camp.

A community of refugees materialized slowly out of the rain and pine, emerging in shapes at first indistinct before coming into sharper focus. Between swipes of windshield wipers, Barrett made out jerry-rigged shelters, tarpaulins mostly, draped over saplings to make rude canopies or tents. As they entered the camp he spotted two shacks that appeared original to the site, fairly large. Shingles and tarpaper. The doors would not close on their own. They banged open and shut in synchrony with the wipers' cycle, and through those unsecured doors you could see the yellow fade of newspaper that offered dangerous and flammable insulation.

Isabel was playing ankle deep in mud beside the one water pump. Barrett saw one small child squatting alongside. Took him a moment to realize she was urinating. The grownups padding back and forth between tarps or sheds seemed unconcerned for the girl's hygiene or their own. As the lawmen pulled to a stop, Barrett saw Dolores step from the nearest shack to bundle her daughter inside.

She stiffened momentarily as Jarold Pearson debarked. But then Barrett got out of the vehicle to bring recognition and relief.

Barrett let Jarold begin with formal greetings. Hospitality was offered in return—an astounding thing, Barrett thought, given the obvious poverty of the worker's situation.

He accepted instant coffee without sugar or cream, taken beneath a tarpaulin. Dolores introduced Barrett and the other lawmen to Isabel's father—*"Mi esposo."* Jorge Hernandez stood with his hat in hand during the entire conversation that followed. Probably a half-dozen men joined in. Two women, besides Dolores.

They all knew that the boy who took dirty pictures of Isabel had been brought before a judge and punished because of the Negro teacher. They knew, too, that the black woman who had championed Isabel was Barrett's wife, and that Señor Slade's son was forced to admit his crime and apologize, in writing, for his misdemeanor.

Isabel rushed inside, fetching the court-ordered apology for the lawmen's admiration.

Jerry Slade was also restrained by court order from riding the bus, Barrett learned. Isabel could now ride to school without fear of her stalker. But Laura Anne had new antagonists in Principal Alton Folsom and school board member Rolly Slade, the very folks whose blessing she needed to be hired full-time. The laborers seemed to fully appreciate that dimension of Laura Anne's sacrifice. Will she be fired? workers anxiously asked on her behalf. Will Señor Folsom take reprisal?

The fact that Laura Anne was willing to put her job at risk on behalf of Isabel was what ultimately gained her parents' trust and, by extension, the trust of the migrants in the Hernandez camp. And once these curious, nomadic people extended their trust, it was as absolute as a child's.

Barrett asked first if the community could give him more details about El Toro.

They all had the same complaint. You either took the Bull's wages and paid him a kickback or you never baled straw.

"(We would like to move on. Find work elsewhere,") a soiled Latin man told Barrett. "(But we don't even have money for gasoline!)"

Was the Bull a violent man? Barrett asked.

An old, weather-lined laborer chattered vociferously in response to that question.

"I couldn't follow him," Barrett turned to Jarold.

The game warden worked the toe of his boot into the sand as if extinguishing a cigarette in the damp earth.

"The grandfather here says that his son was killed by El Toro."

"Killed?" Cricket was suddenly alert.

A young Latino drew his hand across a throat tattooed with a wreath of serpents.

"Muerte. Sí."

"But never charged," Jarold finished his translation. "In fact, the señor blames the police. So I don't know how much credibility we ought to give to his story."

"Absolutely correct," Barrett replied, and then returned his attention to the gathered migrants.

"(How did the foreman get his nickname, the Bull?)"

"(Because of the women.)"

"(I see. So he is a ladies' man?)"

That did not translate well. Barrett tried again.

"(Women like the Bull?)"

"(Oh, no,)" came the reply. "(He abuses them. He turns them to prostitution. Rapes them. Even his own niece he pimps.)"

"(His niece. Does she live in a camp?)"

A collective shrug of the shoulders.

"(She started in the straw. But when she began to bleed . . .)"

"Menstruate," Jarold translated.

"(. . . El Toro takes her one night to town. When he comes back she is bruised in the face and arms. But he has a wad of green. Yankee dollars. He brags about the money.)"

"(But she did, too, poor thing.)" Isabel's mother bit her lip. "(She made money for him. But she liked the money herself. She said it was easier than straw.)"

"So you knew the girl?" Cricket's question was translated for the frail Latin woman.

"(Yes, I know her. Her name is Juanita. Juanita Quiroga.)"

Barrett reached inside his jacket and pulled out the manila folder that offered poor protection for the sketch inside.

"(Is this Juanita Quiroga?)"

Barrett displayed Jane Doe's reconstructed image for the workers. A half-dozen heads nodded in unison.

"(Yes,)" Isabel spoke up. "(That's her. Where is she? Where did you get that picture?)"

Eleven

ow at least we know who the victim was," Barrett declared.

All four wheels spun mud as Jarold's olive Tahoe pulled away from the Hernandezes and their extended migrant family.

"And we know who her uncle is," Cricket grated. "Lying son of a bitch. I vote we pay El Toro a visit."

Barrett agreed. "Even if he's not the killer, he's clearly hiding something."

"Protecting somebody?" Cricket raised an auburn brow.

"Protecting his job, certainly. Maybe his contracts."

"Or maybe his boss," Cricket finished that line of conjecture.

Barrett shrugged.

"Do y'all regard the uncle as a suspect, Bear?"

This from Jarold Pearson.

"Not yet. We certainly don't have enough to warrant an arrest. But this time when we interview Señor Bull, we'll have some leverage. We know he lied to us when he denied knowing his niece. And we can always go after the man for labor violations and assault. So what Cricket and I will do now is interview the man, see if we can carrot-

and-stick some useful information from him. That may lead to an arrest down the line or it may not."

Cricket belched.

"But first we gotta find the son of a bitch."

"He won't be baling straw." Jarold straddled ruts silver with water. "Straw has to be dry before it can be baled. There won't be any crews at work in this damp."

"First week in months it's rained and gives our perp a day to ramble," Cricket grumbled.

"Not that many places for him to go." Barrett's cell phone beeped.

"Agent Raines."

"Sheriff Sessions." Lou's voice came back like gravel. "Thought I'd see if you turned up anything useful."

Barrett summarized events.

"You have any idea where this character's staying?" Barrett asked.

"None," came the answer.

"Well, if you see him can you give us a shout?" Barrett requested.

"If I see him, I'll interview him myself," the sheriff came back and broke off the call.

"So much for intra-agency relations," Cricket commented drily, and then to his partner, "and dollars to doughnuts Lou knows where the bastard's staying."

"He lives in a trailer." Jarold Pearson surprised them both.

"A trailer?"

Jarold nodded.

"On the backside of Linton's deer lease. Not far from Strawman's Hammock."

"Does the sheriff know that?"

"I don't know, but we're a whole lot closer to the lease than Lou is. And I know the way in."

"Warden Pearson." Barrett settled back. "You have the helm."

Jarold launched his four-wheeler down the road like a bolt from a crossbow. The sandy loam ribbon on which they traveled was saturated with water. Creeks that hadn't run for months cut sand roads into gullies. The warden's wipers smeared mud across a windshield that offered only momentary glimpses of the road.

"Jarold, we won't find him any faster if we have a wreck."

"We're fine."

He braked into a curve. The Tahoe's ass end lost traction, broke free. Off the accelerator. Counter-steer. Accelerate gently.

"We're fine," Jarold said again and launched down the rain-soaked road.

Within minutes they were at the gate on the boundary of Linton Loyd's deer lease.

"Tire tracks." Jarold turned off his windshield wipers briefly. "Recent."

Only a chain on a nail to secure the gate. Barrett got out to open it, then hopped back in the Tahoe as Jarold pulled through. The way in was not a road so much as a swath of beaten undergrowth. Tangles of vine and low-lying cypress blinded the way ahead, slapping the windshield at intervals contrapuntal to the wipers' unvaried rhythm.

They splashed straight through the heart of Linton's deer camp. Bear recognized the gallows that remained. The pickle bucket was still there. Filled to the brim.

Once through the camp, they immediately plunged back into what seemed impenetrable undergrowth, following a snaking trail that opened up to flatwoods rowed in slash pine. The rows of that artificial arbor then guided their way, straight ahead and regular, until the warden turned his four-wheeler hard from their shelter into a primitive watered marsh where they floundered, all four wheels digging to reach solid ground and a grove of palmetto.

"We're there about." Jarold bottomed out in a small stream between a pair of wild hickories, then pulled up sideways to present the length of his car to a thirty-foot Prowler goosenecked to the bed of a big Ford diesel.

"Roberto's truck." Jarold nodded.

There was one other vehicle, too, a vehicle familiar, if unexpected. Gary Loyd's Humvee nosed up to the trailer beside his foreman's Ford.

"Looks like the boss man's spending some time with his help," Barrett remarked.

"You think they're talking about straw?" Cricket asked.

Barrett checked his radio.

"I don't know, but I think we ought to ask."

Cricket slipped a clip of nine-millimeter slugs into his Glock and cleared the chamber. Barrett unsnapped the leather strap that holstered his own weapon.

"You armed, Jarold?"

"Yes, sir."

That calm, professional voice. *Goddamn,* Barrett thought. *This man could have been a fighter pilot.*

"We'll do this by the numbers," Barrett went on for the warden's benefit. "We aren't here to arrest anybody, so we don't go in with weapons showing or anything like that. But we're not gonna be stupid, either. I'll approach from the front door. Cricket will cover the back."

"Be on your left," Cricket said and opened his door.

"Jarold."

"Yes, sir."

"Stay with your vehicle. Be ready to back us up."

The game warden unlimbered the twelve-gauge from its rack.

"I'm set."

"All right. Nice and easy."

Barrett followed Cricket out of the Tahoe's passenger door on the side away from Quiroga's trailer. Cricket strolled left to disappear behind the trailer. Barrett waited a moment, waiting to see some movement at the front door. Normally, if you drove up to a man's house in broad daylight, somebody came out. Unless they were preoccupied.

"Hit the horn, would you, Jarold?"

Jarold laid down on his horn. You'd have to be deaf not to hear.

"All right."

The horn stopped. Nothing, now, but the splatter of raindrops big as thimbles. Barrett's radio broke static.

"I'm set." Cricket's voice rasped over the ether.

A decision had to be made.

"I'm approaching the door," Bear declared, his hand pressed instinctively to his Kevlar vest.

He used Quiroga's truck to cover his approach to the side of the front door. Two quick, firm knocks.

"Señor Quiroga? Agent Raines, señor. FDLE."

Not a blind. Not the sway of weight inside the interior.

"Maybe they're out hunting," Cricket rasped over the radio, and in a small slice of that split-second, El Toro kicked open the front door.

"I kill him!"

The Bull had Gary Loyd collared at the throat. The foreman had his smaller frame well shielded with Linton's straw-haired son. An automatic weapon pressed like an iron against Gary's temple.

Bear's handgun snapped up.

"Put it down!"

Anybody with a badge and gun says at one time or another that it's the unexpected event or circumstance that gets somebody's ass killed. And that was partly true. But far worse, for Barrett, were those situations where you *expected* to find trouble, *knew* what to anticipate, and got nailed anyway. Barrett and his partner were now faced with that second, heart-sickening situation.

"Hostage out front," Barrett muttered into his radio.

Cricket had probably heard, anyway. But you didn't take chances in this situation.

"Put down the gun, Roberto," Barrett commanded, and then again in Spanish.

"Fuck you," the foreman replied, using his hostage as a shield as he edged deliberately for Gary's Humvee.

"Put it down now!" Cricket had his own weapon leveled from the corner of the trailer.

"No closer! One step more, I kill him!"

Cricket had no intention of coming closer. He had no intention of taking a position that might put Barrett in crossing fire. What Cricket would do, what he and Barrett were trained to do, was to bracket his target at ninety degrees to his partner.

"I kill his fucking ass!" the Bull warned again, and Gary's terrified scream died in a larnyx crushed with a brown, scarred arm. His eyes bulged from their sockets.

Negotiate, negotiate, negotiate. "We didn't come to arrest you, Roberto," Barrett stated as firmly and calmly as he could manage. "We just want to ask about your niece, that's all. That's all we came for."

"Fuck you," the Bull snarled, and began dragging Gary toward the Humvee.

Rule one in a hostage situation: Never—repeat, *never*—let the kidnapper take his hostage from the scene.

If you couldn't negotiate, you had to shoot. Or you could negotiate to get the shoot, to get that clear target.

Another scream gargled in Gary's throat.

"Roberto, use your head. You stay here, go inside the trailer if you like, we can talk. But we can't let you leave, señor. *Comprende?*"

El Toro was only steps from the Humvee now.

"I understand perfect, you dick. Didn't come to arrest me! What you think I am, a fucking moron? But I am leaving, *hombre.* I am taking this shit with me and if you try and stop me—I kill his fucking ass. Now—do you understand?"

Barrett trained his weapon.

"Cricket?"

"Got you covered."

Gary Loyd hung pale and bloated and helpless in the Bull's iron grip. They had reached the Humvee. The Bull kept his grip on Gary and eyes trained on Bear and Cricket as he reached with his gun hand to open the door.

"Heh?"

Jarold Pearson popped up from the Humvee's padded seat to shove his revolver into the Mexican's face. Two quick explosions rocked the reinforced cab. Barrett saw a spray of blood. And then his legs were pumping, as if on their own. He reached the Humvee. Two bodies on the ground outside. Barrett kicked the Bull's forty-five out of his twitching hand, his own weapon still trained on the fallen foreman. Jarold eased himself, pale but calm, from the Humvee's passenger seat. You could see on the warden's uniform the boundary between blood and fabric, a line of red and green delineated just above his well-knotted tie, where the door's ledge had blocked El Toro's splatter of flesh and blood.

"I'm fine," the warden reassured Barrett before he could ask.

El Toro, on the other hand, was now unrecognizable, his shattered face pressed into what looked like a bloody gourd that lolled limp as a rag doll onto a shoulder slowly accommodating to an unnatural relaxation. Cricket kept his own weapon leveled as he kneeled to press a pair of fingers unnecessarily to the carotid along the side of Quiroga's neck.

"He's *good* and dead."

"How about Gary. Gary? Gary, you all right?"

No reply. Gary Loyd lay on the damp earth, too, his knees pulled to his chest.

"He's not hit," Jarold said confidently.

But he was in shock. Cricket left El Toro to do what he could to reassure the scion of the Loyd family. He took off his own coat to blanket the terror-struck man.

"Just take it easy, Gary. It's over."

Meanwhile, Jarold was kneeled over the bull-like corpse. He pulled a pen from his olive jacket and slipped it beneath a link of silver chain visible inside the collar of the dead man's shirt.

"Something here, gentlemen." Jarold used his pen to expose a familiar talisman. "Crucifix."

There it was, a cheaply made cross of copper and rock looped around El Toro's neck.

Cricket walked over to inspect.

"I'm no jeweler, but isn't this damn near a twin to the one we found on his niece?"

Barrett nodded. "But that wouldn't be enough to make him a suspect."

"He tried to kill us," Cricket pointed out. "What the hell does that make him?"

Gary Loyd rolled into a nearly fetal retreat on the grass.

"What did he do? What did he do?" the younger Loyd cried, rocking side to side.

"Gary?" Barrett took his turn beside the recent hostage. "Gary, you're all right. . . . Gary?"

What did he do?" the younger man wailed, unconsoled. Holding his knees. Rocking sideways in the mud and rain.

Cricket rose. "Think we can take him in?"

Barrett frowned. "Better call an EMS."

"I'm on it." Cricket dug out his cell phone.

Barrett turned to Jarold Pearson.

"That was a hell of a move, Warden."

The warden shrugged. "If he hadn't got a hostage I probably wouldn't have tried it."

Cricket holstered his own handgun. " 'Probably,' the man says! 'Probably'? Well, I have learned something definite this morning, gentlemen. For certain and sure."

Cricket's tension eased in a snort of laughter.

"Never piss off a game warden."

It was not lost on Barrett Raines that the man he had once humiliated had saved a life where Bear himself was impotent. Barrett watched closely to see how Jarold Pearson would react to his recent trauma. He'd seen men who remained cool as ice under fire fall to pieces when you asked 'em for a cigarette. Once the need for action ceased, everything else shut down, too. But Barrett was relieved to see that this did not seem to be the case with the game warden. Jarold simply walked, if stiffly, to the metal steps of the trailer and seated himself before the door.

"You all right, Jarold?"

"I think so," Jarold removed his hat. His hands, Barrett noticed, though steady, became preoccupied with the bloodstained knot of his tie.

"It was a clean shoot. The man had a hostage for a shield. He showed every intent of using deadly force."

Jarold nodded. "I'll be fine. Need any help with the scene?"

Barrett shook his head.

"Why don't you just take a break 'til the cavalry gets here? I'll just make double-sure we don't have anybody else inside the trailer."

Barrett stepped up past the warden. The trailer's door opened with a nudge.

"FDLE!" Bear was irritated to see his own weapon trembling like a water-wand in his hand.

Slow down, he told himself. *Just make sure the place is secure.*

"FDLE. Is anyone here?"

He listened. His heart pounded blood through his ears. *Slow down. Slow down.* Bear could not make out a sound, not even the whistle of air through ductwork.

Barrett thumbed his handgun's safety again to make sure it was off. The place appeared unoccupied. No threat whatever. Barrett relaxed enough to note that the interior was surprisingly well kept. No filthy dishes in the stainless-steel sink. No ashtrays overflowing. Bear opened the fridge with a napkin and smelled the familiar aroma of marinating fajitas. There were no fajitas to be had in Lafayette County, that was for sure. The Bull would have had to prepare those himself.

The pushout was arranged in standard configuration, bedroom leading to bath leading to kitchen and then beyond to a space expandable on hydraulic joists and convertible from sitting room to extra beds. Barrett saw a couple of tapes on the sitting room's VCR. The titles were in Spanish and unfamiliar, but it was clear from the visuals that they were porn. He backtracked through the kitchen to check the bathroom. A damp towel was hung neatly; otherwise it was empty.

The bedroom door was closed. Barrett hesitated, then redrew his nine-millimeter.

"Anyone home?" He knocked.

No answer.

The door swung open to the toe of his Reebok. Barrett entered the room in a Weaver's stance. Nothing. The closet was open. Nothing there.

But Barrett felt a tightness suddenly close like a vice around his chest, and with that a shortness of breath. As if the room were suddenly emptied of air. And then the fear, the unreasoning combination of terror and vertigo. Barrett stumbled out of the bedroom, clawed to steady himself on the bathroom door.

Slow down, slow down.

Barrett looked through the windows to see outside. He

counted to ten in deep, slow exhalations. The chest lightened. The heart stalled its awful hammer. Bear weaved dizzily on the bathroom door. He knew what had happened.

Claustrophobia. It usually hit Barrett in tight spaces, in an elevator, in crowds. But that wasn't what had triggered the panic this morning, Bear was certain of that. It was not the modest space of the trailer's bedroom that had unleashed the fear and vertigo that fought the rational portion of Bear's brain on this occasion. The trigger, this time, had come from something completely unexpected and primeval. Barrett's heart began to pound again as he edged once more into the bedroom's interior. He took a tentative sample of air into his nostrils.

And stumbled back, heart pounding.

"Slow down!" he said aloud. "Slow down."

But he had been right; it was not the bedroom's cramped space that had triggered his claustrophohia.

The trigger this time was a smell.

A combination of smells, actually. There was a bowl on the nightstand beside the dead man's bed, just an ordinary cereal bowl, with a plaster of some sort heaped damply to the rim of its rude, metal cup to generate the odor from which Barrett retreated.

Barrett knew now where he had smelled this smell before.

Her dress was a cheap muslin, he remembered. Her blouse had been damp with perspiration and flannel. And around her neck was a kind of censer. When she bobbed her head an aroma came to him as powerful as sex, the same pungent odors as came now from the paste in Quiroga's bedroom. She always wore her garden of odors, this angel from Barrett's distant past.

Or witch.

A recollection had been jarred loose by the pungent and familiar odor in El Toro's bedroom.

He remembered the day his father was killed.

Barrett stepped back from the trailer's bedroom. His handgun went unremembered, limp in his hand, as he sank into a bolted chair. The day was before him, now, brought back with a conjure of dog fennel and herbs.

It had started outside in bright sunshine with the free play of wind and boyhood imagination. He was throwing darts. Not the store-bought darts familiar to barhoppers, of course. No, Barrett's was a boyhood invention. You took a corncob, then you sawed off the head of a nail. The sawed end of the nail got pushed or hammered into the base of the corncob; the other end made the point. You pressed a quill of chicken feathers into the crown of the corncob. Three or four would do.

Now you were ready. You could throw at targets. Or you could just throw the dart for distance or height, marveling at the swift spiral the feathers imparted, delighting in the corncob's distance and climb. He could remember the play, that morning, a rare and uncomplicated run of imagination. The corncob was a fighter plane, a spaceship. He was launched to Gainesville, to Valdosta, to Mars. Those flights were canceled rudely with his father's return.

Barrett recalled the smell of gasoline as his father drove up in his half-repaired sedan. He saw his mother emerge from the car, fresh stitches across her face, her jaw.

"Goddamn cost me thirty dollah," Barrett's father raged. "How'm I s'pose to find thirty dollah?"

His mother did not answer. Her face was bruised, her jaw swollen. Her eyes were silver.

"Git in the house." Randall Grant Raines was pulling off his belt, and his beaten wife obeyed mutely.

Barrett dropped the corncob and trailed his father and mother inside.

"Git back, you," his father snarled, but Barrett came on anyway.

From the shade of the sagging porch, through the door, he saw his mother running.

"Randall, don't!"

Barrett ran into the bedroom. He remembered reaching for his father.

"Leave Mama alone."

"Whelp," the father sneered, and as Barrett came between man and wife the father picked up his son by the neck and strode for the closet.

Then came the part that Bear was always able to remember. The tight, hot, closet. Dirty clothes. Fear and sweat.

The baseball bat.

Barrett remembered the weight of the wood in his hand. He remembered, as in his dreams, kicking the door. But this time the door opened full. Barrett came out running. His father was fully occupied with Barrett's mother when the nine-year-old boy sprinted across the warped floor, screaming, the bat held high over his little head.

The father didn't even bother to turn around.

Barrett had never played baseball. One of the many curious absences in his boyhood life. So he did not know how to swing his brother's bat, except as an axe.

He ran hard, aiming at the small of his father's back. He could feel the hatred and fear as he swung the bat down—

Some malicious instinct for survival told Barrett's father to turn. He took the first blow high on the ribs.

He fell howling and cursing to the floor.

And for a moment Barrett did not know what to do.

"You . . . little . . . fuckin' bastard . . ."

His father was heaving erect. Reaching for his belt.

"Wait . . .'til I get . . .'hold o' you!"

Down came the bat as if Barrett was splitting kindling. The father's skull turned directly into the path of the Louisville Slugger. Thirty-two ounces of hardwood smashed Randall Grant Barrett's brain to mush.

Barrett didn't stop with the first blow. Or the second. His mother had to pull her son, screaming, from off his father.

"Oh, my Jesus!" the mother wailed.

Then a woman was there, a stranger, but someone he had heard described in hushed conversation.

"Jolene, you got to git up." The command came quietly.

She was old. Looked like straight off a slave ship. Ramrod stiff and strong, with one of those bandannas tied up on her head, the knots standing up like ears on an Easter bunny.

She walked calmly into the room and knelt beside his father.

"Awright," she declared as if satisfied. And then turned to Barrett.

"Sad thang when a boy has t' do what men ought."

That was when Barrett smelled the smell. It was deep with odors familiar from childhood, but mixed in unnatural combination.

The pouch waved like a censer from her neck and the crone's voice became suddenly distant.

"Let him pass. Best thang."

The crone was walking then, it seemed to Barrett, in the direction of their kitchen.

"Jolene," she said. "I want you to gimme a knife."

He must have fainted, because the next clear memory unfolding from this box was the smell of urine on the pallet they always kept in hot weather on the porch. A crow was sitting on the bleach bottle on the fence beside their gate. Yellow eyes. Evil.

"Ain't time fuh you yet," the old crone spoke from the yard and the bird cawed away.

Barrett rose to see Sheriff Witt's police-packaged

Dodge parked beneath the pecan tree out front. The old and unfamiliar woman stood with his mother, foot shuffling as older Negroes were wont to do before a capricious authority.

"I just got my face stitched from last time . . ." Barrett's mother was saying.

"I got that part," the sheriff nodded impatiently. "And then he came at you with—what'd you say?"

"A knife." Barrett's puissant angel interposed to display a butcher knife red with blood.

His mother displayed her arm stiffly, as if on cue.

The sheriff frowned at the single, easy slice.

"Randall, he cut her," Hezikiah insisted. "I come up, I saw him cuttin'. Thought he was comin' fuh me. Then Jolene took up the club."

"You mean the baseball bat."

"Yassuh. And Randall, he turned back on her with the knife and got hisself a good one, right across the head. But it din' keep him down."

"Oh, it didn't?"

"Nawsuh. He still comin' with dat knife. Jolene, she had to hit him coupla mo' time good before he stay."

"So you're saying he would have killed her."

"He tried befo', ask Doc Hardesty."

The sheriff made a note. A pair of deputies lounged nearby. One of them bent to the earth.

"What's this?"

"Corncob dart." The words came unbidden from Barrett's mouth.

The sheriff seemed to notice Barrett for the first time. Barrett recalled the smell of leather in his belt as the lawman ambled over to the porch. His handgun was huge, much larger than the secondhand toy Barrett used to bust caps. He wore a pleasant smile as he leaned over the porch's ledge.

"You see any of this, son?"

"Some of it."

"He were in the closet," the mother spoke up. "Randall thowed him in."

"So you couldn't see much," the sheriff coached.

Barrett shook his head.

"I could hear."

The sheriff nodded. "Yes, boy. I bet you could."

The smile faded. The sheriff rose indolently, nodded to his deputies.

"Check with Doc. If he vouches for the beatin's I'd say we have a plain-old case of self-defense."

Barrett's mother remained uncomprehending.

"Self—?"

"You ain't guilty of a crime when you defend yourself, Miz Raines," the sheriff explained. "Plus the boy was at risk, too. I'm not gonna waste the county's money or my time worryin' over a nigger lost his head while tryin' to gut his wife."

Barrett realized that the old, ancient woman was staring straight at him.

"The daddy watn't worth much—"

She prounounced it deadpan, as if in a trance.

"—but that young'un gonna *be* somebody."

The sheriff did not reply.

"Come on boys," he said. "Let's wind this up."

There were no body bags in those years. They just drug him out. Hoisted him into the back of a truck. The truck was well down the road before Barrett first and truly realized that he had killed his father.

And that he was going to get away with it.

Barrett emerged from the trailer to find his partner anxious outside.

"You all right, Bear?" Cricket asked.

The air came now in deep cold drafts. His heart was calm. His chest was light. The sky seemed more open, even through the clouds, than it had been in years.

"Bear?"

"I'm okay, Cricket."

Bear suspected that The Dream was exorcized, now, along with the memory. Perhaps even some of the fear that came with it. But the memory of his hidden slaughter was now revealed in open daylight.

Who else knew?

Barrett, until this very morning, had repressed the fact of the killing. His mother was dead—had she ever told anyone? Probably not. Especially since she lied to cover for her son.

That left the old woman. The crone. Who was she? The smell was the clue.

"Cricket," Barrett spoke up.

"Right here."

"There's some kind of paste in the bedroom. Be sure and remind me to get it to Midge. I'm pretty sure she's going to find it matches that mess the lab found in the victim's vagina."

"You think the Bull and his niece were getting treatment from the same quack?"

Barrett shrugged. "Maybe."

He couldn't tell Cricket that he knew who had made the awful paste. He couldn't tell his partner about the ancient slave woman. He certainly couldn't afford to tell anyone that the *curandero* who divined potions of dog fennel and snake skins was also the woman who knew that Barrett Raines killed his own father.

That was not the kind of history, even if justified, that got you elected to sheriff in a white man's county.

"You all right, Barrett?" Jarold asked.

"Just secure the scene," Bear replied shortly. "I'll be fine."

Twelve

In the days that followed the Bull's death, Barrett Raines had time to ponder the significance of his recently recovered memory. A doubting Thomas by nature, Bear told himself that he was not obligated to trust his vision, that there was no way to judge the veracity of his violently recalled past. How could he have repressed such a memory? How reliable were memories suddenly recovered? Was it possible that his potion-triggered recollection was not reliable at all? For years Barrett had believed his mother had killed his father. That was the official story, and until his recent epiphany that was what Barrett believed.

His new memory, on the other hand, registered with the conviction of an eyewitness, made Barrett his father's killer. Bear was not worried about the ethical or even legal dimension of his patricide. Randall Grant Raines was in the process of battering his mother. The father's violence was repeated and escalating. A jury would not likely find the son guilty of anything more than self-defense.

But a jury never heard the case, and that bothered Barrett greatly. The truth, whatever it was, had been covered up to protect him from a white man's justice. Hezikiah had seen to that.

Yes, Barrett knew her name. Even as a boy he had heard stories about a crazy woman who caught lizards and snakes and took in people who had given up on tent revivals and Billy Graham. And the stories of her curses were as vivid as the ones of her healings. How she gave the Odom boy a club foot when he overcharged her at the grocery store. How she took away a woman's child for a debt of fifty cents. Burned houses and dead babies were laid at Hezikiah's feet.

She took credit for them all.

Barrett's urgent questions were personal, but he had an official gloss for approaching the old woman. Hezikiah, after all, was tied to a murder victim and her alleged killer. She might have something to add to the case. He had a rough idea where to look for her. Everyone in the African American community, at least, knew that Hezikiah Jackson lived in Strawman's Hammock. That was about as helpful as saying that General Custer could be found in the Dakotas.

Who could Bear ask to help him locate the old woman? Whom could he trust? Bear turned to Jarold Pearson. Barrett explained that the Bull and his niece were being treated for venereal disease by Hezikiah, and that Bear would like to see what the old woman knew of the uncle and his niece.

"You got any idea where to find her?" Bear asked.

"Sure," Jarold affirmed. "It's on the north side of the property from where we found the girl."

So once again Barrett was belted in beside the game warden, crashing through undergrowth and dodging bogs to follow a trail that wound into the bowels of Strawman's Hammock. December had come with a precipitous dip of mercury. The lowlands were spectacular this morning, the region's heavy dew gone to frost overnight, laying a virgin mantle in convoluted splendor on wild grape-vines and ragweed and dog fennel. Even the palmettos were fringed with frost. The air was crisp. Barrett breathed deeply, all the way down.

No wearies this morning.

They skirted the pond this time, following what looked like a foot trail that gradually widened to two sandy ruts.

"Been traveled some," Jarold remarked.

"Who comes out here?" Barrett asked.

Jarold shrugged. "All I hear is that black people think she's some kind of shaman and Mexicans think she's a witch."

"Little of both, I 'magine," Bear replied.

Jarold registered silent surprise at that response.

It took close to half an hour of winding around to reach her shack. If there had been a single turn off that scrap of road Barrett would have been instantly lost.

"Only one road in," Jarold nodded. "Trick is, of course, to find the one road."

"There it is."

Her home. Less than a sharecropper's shack, it nestled beneath a riot of trees, a corrupted box of tin and cypress centered in a yard of white sand. A single field fence surrounded it. Rough pine stumps were visible below the decrepit porch and floorbeams. A pair of mimosa trees untouched by frost draped the porch in blossoms out of season, a riot of pink in late November. Like a China-man's umbrella.

"You mind waiting for me?" Barrett asked.

"I'll be napping," Jarold replied, rolling down his window and easing back. "Don't startle me when you come back."

"Hezikiah Jackson." Barrett stopped on the top step leading onto her porch. "Hezikiah."

"No need t' shout."

He jumped, startled, to find a woman older than his dreams materialized, apparently, at his elbow.

"Hezikiah?"

"Who you 'spect?"

"Miz Jackson, I am—"

"You the Bear, I know you. Knew your mama. Knew your daddy."

"Daddy, yes. Actually, I'd like to talk about that, if you don't mind."

"Took you long enough. Come in."

She was wearing only the thinnest shawl over a shift so thin that in places her flesh was visible. A winter breeze shook the slats on her cypress shack like a death rattle.

She took him to what ought to have been a kitchen. A filthy gas stove was there. A sink. No electricity. A single kerosene heater glowing bright. Barrett noted a pair of arrowheads strung with what looked like fishline and hung from the ceiling, but it was the artifacts secured on the walls that kept his attention.

There were shelves floor to ceiling on the walls of Hezikiah's kitchen, and not a nail to hold them in place. Just irregular columns of whiskey bottles. Jar after jar lined those rude cabinets, none filled with things you might expect. Hezikiah, it seemed, did not spend her time pickling lima beans or acre peas.

Barrett could not take his eyes off what he strongly suspected to be a human tongue that floated murkily in a Bell jar. He pulled his chair to her flimsy table, rested his hands carefully. How could he start?

"You killed him," she said.

"What was that?"

"You heard me," she said.

And Barrett realized that he had.

"He was going to hurt mother."

She nodded.

"He was going to kill her."

"He didn't have a knife," Barrett offered in correction.

"Don' take a knife to kill a person, Bear. A word can kill. The right word. From the right mouth."

A sudden chill ran down Bear's back. He needed to reroute this interview.

"You ever have a girl come in here, Hezikiah? Latin girl." Barrett reached for the sketch folded in his pocket.

"I don't need a pitcher," she said scornfully. "I got nuthin' to hide."

"You treated her?"

The old woman smiled. "She was a purty thang. But et up with clap. He had it too."

"Her uncle?"

"Was that it? I knew it was somethin'. He was a hard man to read. A man, though. I can tell you that." She cackled. "We had some fun times. Right on this table."

"Sheriff's convinced The Bull had fun killing his niece. My partner's convinced. I'm not."

"He's killed befo'," she offered. "Mo' than once."

"It was a pretty elaborate homicide. He used a dog."

"Dog?" She seemed interested. "I had dog dreams two, maybe three weeks back. Big damn dog. Yellow eyes. He was gonna chase me, in my dream. Gonna rip my gut. But I turn' it around on 'im. I say, 'Git you ass offa me, you fuckin' dog. Fine somebody elsa eat.' "

The hair crawled at the base of Barrett's neck.

"You ever leave this place, Hezikiah?"

She chuckled. "What a conjurin' woman need to leave? Why she travel?"

"You came to my house," Barrett pointed out.

She smiled.

"You saw me. Don' mean I's in yo' hise. Don' mean I lef' my poach."

Barrett groaned. Was the truth of his new memory to rest on the word of a crazy woman? Or even of a killer?

"It wouldn't take you long to walk over to the lake," Barrett said.

"Naw," she admitted slyly. "I usta pick huckleberries on that lake. Usta drink right outen that pump.

"I need some hep with my pump," she declared in sudden distraction.

"Why? Can't you conjure it?" Barrett responded sharply.

She regarded him in scorn.

"Don' throw my pearl befo' no swine."

Barrett glanced around the house.

"I saw . . . the medicine you made for Roberto."

"Don' know no Robert-O."

"El Toro. The Bull."

"His medicine? Yeah, I got me some."

"May I see it?"

"Why, sho." She seemed suddenly shy. "You need treatin'?"

"No." Bear shook his head. "Just want to verify it's the same as we found in his trailer."

Right out the back door there was a sink, a hand pump. Bear recognized a rattlesnake's skin. A rolling pin. He shivered, trying not to imagine what sort of treatment would require that instrument.

"They's my potions." She raised a veined hand to indicate a rude motley of herbs and dessicated intestines drying on a shelf. A coke bottle and board served as mortar and pestle. Some remains of a pounded compound stained the shelf. A cast-iron pot sat to one side.

Barrett lifted the bowl's lid. The aroma came to him as surely as a signature. But the memory to which it attached was already jarred free. There was no revelation, this time. No sudden recovery of sight or breath.

Barrett placed the lid onto her pot of brew.

"That's all I need for now," he said.

"Jarold," he called from the porch and waited for the warden to nod before approaching the four-wheeler.

"Get anywhere with her?"

Barrett snapped his seat belt in place.

"Nothing new," he said. "Can you drop me by the courthouse? Gary Loyd's s'posed to give Lou a statement. I'd like to be there to hear it."

Sheriff Sessions was downright hospitable to Barrett on his arrival at the jail. "We're about to wrap this whole thing up," Lou declared. "Grab some coffee. We'll see Gary in my office."

Barrett entered a crowded office to find Gary Loyd and his father cozied up with Thurman Shaw next to the sheriff's desk. All smiles and coffee cups.

" 'Lo, Bear," Linton greeted him loudly. "Glad to see you got the right man."

"It was the sheriff's investigation," Barrett replied automatically, "and it's his call whether we got the right man."

"I understand," Linton winked. "I understand."

Barrett had the distinct impression that he was about to witness a rush, if not a race, to justice. He took a folding chair and squeezed honey from a plastic jar into a steaming mug of scalding hot coffee.

"Well, now." Lou settled behind his never-cleared desk. "Let's get this out of the way."

Lou conducted virtually the entire interview. Barrett was almost completely sidelined. The Q & A that followed did not, to his mind, go much toward nailing down Roberto Quiroga as his niece's killer. Gary Loyd did not resemble the frightened, fetal creature who only the previous day had a gun held to his head. The younger Loyd was cracking jokes now, almost bragging about his experience. Barrett noted Gary's braggadocio. He also noted that the onetime victim's account of events was self-serving.

"The only reason I was out there," Gary explained, his lawyer following closely, "was that Roberto said he wanted to see me about raising wages. But I get out there to the trailer, he starts right off telling me the police are interviewing migrant workers, asking questions. Telling me I should get the police off his back."

"Did he tell you he was getting kickbacks from the migrants?" Lou suprised Barrett with that question.

"You don't have to answer that, Gary," Thurman Shaw imposed quietly.

"It's all right," Gary replied. And then to Lou, "Yes, he did tell me. Said he got a piece of the action from everybody on my crew. Got bribes from crews all over the county!"

"So you didn't know anything about it."

"No, nothing." Gary was adamant. "I never told him to do anything but get workers and keep 'em happy. I didn't care how he did it."

"Maybe you should have," Barrett offered coolly, to which point the younger Loyd remained mute.

"Go on, Gary." The sheriff smiled.

"Well, like I say, I was in the middle of finding out about this side-business of bribes and twisting arms and God knows what-all. Quiroga's tellin' me I've got to protect him, that he did all this for my company and he wants me to get the police off his back. 'How'm I s'posed to do that?' I ask. 'Pay 'em off,' he says. I was telling him that I couldn't do that, that this wasn't Mexico, when about that time Jarold pulls up in his Jolly Green. I think I even remarked 'Looks like we've got company,' or something like that. Next thing I know I've got a gun at my head and the Bull's telling me that if I even twitch he's going to blow my brains out."

Gary turned to Barrett. "I was hoping to hell when he didn't answer Jarold's horn that y'all would just go. But then you came out from behind the Tahoe and Quiroga said, 'Okay, señor, you're my ticket out of here.' That's when—well. You know the rest."

Gary's statement did not confirm Quiroga as his

niece's murderer. But other evidence mounted that strongly implicated Juanita's uncle. Midge Holloway's report confirmed that El Toro's DNA matched one of the semen samples found in his niece. Samples of hair from the shack and on the victim matched her uncle's. Perhaps most important, Midge was able to confirm that the Bull was infected with gonorrhea.

"He undoubtedly would blame the girl for that," the sheriff declared.

"If he knew," Barrett qualified.

"He paid for her bloodwork," Thurman pointed out. "The same series that found her positive for gonorrhea found her HIV postive as well."

"First the clap. Then AIDS." The sheriff spat. "I'd say El Toro had plenty of reasons to be pissed off with his relations."

"He didn't have AIDS," Cricket amended. "He wasn't even HIV positive."

Thurman allowed that point.

"But even though Quiroga had not contracted the virus, he would fear it. The clap was bad enough, judging from the way he chose to have *that* problem treated. But to be put at risk for AIDS! The Bull would have seen that as a deadly betrayal."

"Taken together I'd say you've got some pretty strong motive for murder," Linton summed up confidently.

Barrett remained silent. He knew how complicated motives could be.

Lou Sessions weighed in with some legwork of his own, having produced witnesses in Perry who confirmed that Quiroga on at least three occasions took his niece to the Highway 27 Motel for what were described as orgies. With that information, Midge's report, and Gary's statement, Barrett wasn't surprised to hear Sheriff Sessions announce that he was satisfied to conclude that El Toro was the pimp and killer of Juanita Quiroga, and that Gary

Loyd was no longer a suspect in the case.

The sheriff seemed positively brimming with goodwill. He herded the Loyds and the FDLE investigators onto the street outside the jail to a waiting pool of reporters and cameras and lights. Stacy Kline led the pack, his arm a stick with a microphone bobbing on the end. Linton Loyd steadied Stacy's bony hand to announce that justice had been found, and to publicly bury his hatchet with local law enforcement. Almost as an afterthought, Linton praised Barrett and the "truly outstanding members" of the Florida Department of Law Enforcement, and expressed the relief of the Loyd family that their son was exonerated from any trace of wrongdoing.

Everyone in the county seemed relieved that a sadistic killer was in a pauper's grave. No one said openly that he was equally relieved to find an outsider responsible for the crime. And it was especially comforting for many county locals to have the killer identified as Mexican. No one, after all, wanted to be burdened with the thought that some little whore had been tortured and slaughtered by a white man, let alone a neighbor.

About the only people not ready to forget the whole mess were the gentleman and lady of the FDLE.

Barrett met Cricket at Ramona's that night. Midge Holloway was there, had driven up from Gainesville with Dr. Tran to sample Laura Anne's menu and music. Laura Anne was warmly included in the investigators' circle. The party was seated close to her baby grand piano. A sophomore from Florida State was performing an arrangement from *Miss Saigon*. Hush puppies and flounder were mixing well with bourbon and iced tea as a discussion ranged across her table.

"There are too damn many loose ends to even think about stopping this investigation." Midge Holloway was outraged at the sheriff's announcement.

"Nothing we can do about it," Cricket declared. "It's

still his case. We investigate. He concludes. And in fairness, we don't have a suspect other than El Toro."

"He had the psyche of a killer." Dr. Tran loosened up considerably over bourbon. "His sexual relationship with the girl was taboo. His disease—a very powerful motivation for retribution. He tried to purge himself, we know that. Midge found signs of a recent whipping."

"Something like a scourge of switches," Midge confirmed. "A real doozy. Over his back and buttocks."

"Like a flagellation?" Laura Anne proposed.

"Good for you, Ms. Raines." Dr. Tran nodded and Cricket joined in.

"See? It all fits. He's Catholic, right? So he's repenting the fact that he had a dog maul his niece to death. Kind of like confession."

"If that's so . . ." Midge sipped her tea. ". . . I'd like to meet his confessor."

Barrett shifted uncomfortably.

"You all right, Bear?" Laura Anne asked.

"I just wish I could be sure we got the right guy."

Cricket drained his Jack Black.

"Pointless to worry. Roland Reed's already folding the tent. His position is if we get any more hot leads, follow 'em. Otherwise, we're just pissing up a rope."

Bear worried his own drink.

"Dead girl. Dead foreman. Dead file."

"Nothing wrong with a slam dunk, Bear. El Toro wasn't holding a gun to Gary's head because he was worried about a green card."

"True enough," Barrett allowed. "But I can't help worrying there's one dangerous predator still among us. Someone who is not Mexican, not anonymous. Someone who is smart. Vicious. He could be next door."

Laura Anne settled beside her husband.

"Well, then, if you can't keep an open file, do the next best thing—keep an open mind."

*   *   *

By the lights of a homicide investigator it had been a stimulating and pleasant evening. Great food, wonderful music and friends. A case to ponder. But Barrett said not a word on the short drive home. Hezikiah's face hung before him like a wraith. So did his father's. Laura Anne placed her hand into her husband's.

"Something bothering you, Bear?"

"Yes," he said finally. He did not want to lie to his wife.

"Does it relate to the murder?"

"God, I hope not."

"Bear?"

He squeezed her hand. "Gonna have to cut me some slack on this one, baby."

"Okay." She withdrew her hand. "Sure."

Barrett was cursing himself for spoiling a perfect evening and pulling into the carport behind his Jim Walter home when two mismatched boys burst through the screen door.

"Ben? Tyndall?"

Laura Anne was out before Bear could kill the headlights.

"Why aren't you two in bed?"

"It's Penelope!" Tyndall's face was streaked with tears.

Thelma came shuffling out the door.

"The dog," she said simply. "We put her out. She's gone."

At first Bear was filled with relief.

"Boys, settle down." Barrett scooped up the twins in his arms. "Penelope's just rambling, is all. Soon as she's hungry, she'll come back."

Thelma shook her head.

"I had her on the leash, Bear. On the dog run. It's been cut."

200

*   *   *

Jerry Slade had a bright blue nylon leash draped like a whip over his lap. The puppy whimpered in a milk crate and Jerry felt a tickle in his scrotum. Revenge was always sweet. With one stroke he would hurt the bitch *and* her little pickaninnies. Jerry reached for his silver camera, imagining the possibilities. He typed in the address on his computer for his favored site of recreation.

www.bondsandbrutemaster.freeplay.com

That half-breed bitch might have got his equipment banned from school, but she couldn't keep him off the Web. There were always opportunities. Matinee this evening was a garden-variety torch & see. Cat burning in a cage. A freebie. The mongrel puppy whined again inside the cage beside his desk. Jerry regarded the animal a moment. He'd love to do this in moving pictures, in video, though most of the stuff off the Net was herky-jerky, like the silent cinema.

The mongrel whined once more and Jerry's foot lashed out as if on its own accord to kick the cage. A yelp. The stupid dog retreated to a corner and peed. Jerry smiled. He had intended to do this one as he had others in the past, with stills from his Mavica. But maybe tonight was his chance to move on to the next level. He could always rent a videocam.

Jerry scrolled to the freebie of the evening, clicking on the print icon for a still of the cat's agony. Jerry always saved his freebies on floppy; you could get twenty or thirty dollars for a disk, even with only a half-dozen scenarios.

Speaking of scenarios. The cat and kidnapped pup were forgotten as Jerry ran the mouse to his favorite link and jerked open the warped drawer of his desk. There were receipts inside, credit-card receipts. He selected a MasterCard. The idiots at his father's shop never bothered to think about how easy it was to lift their credit-card numbers from the manually pressed receipts his father produced on their antiquated equipment.

Jerry spread the wealth around. Most people wouldn't notice ten or fifteen dollars gone here or there. And what wife would believe the man who said, "Honey, I'd never spend money on *that!*" Jerry chuckled. Still, he had to be careful—there was so much to be had. For a while he was spending forty, fifty bucks at a pop. Sales at school would never keep up with that kind of passion.

This hard financial reality was what first prompted Jerry Slade to consider creating product for sale himself. Buying was not enough. He wanted to supply original material and make money from it.

Jerry knew he could do better, of course. His own site would one day blow away any of the stuff he was seeing here. They were always robbing his ideas—the teenager would occasionally find himself screaming at the computer's wavering screen.

Like this one! How could it be? Right here on his favorite site there was the tease: "Beauty & The Beast."

The stolen receipt rustled in his hand. He was already over the month's limit. Still. This was choice. He reached for the mouse—

"Jerryyyy."

The bawl floated in from the shed.

"What is it?"

"Goddamn time to feed my dog is what it is!" Rolly yelled to his son.

The newest rottweiler bayed on cue and the puppy cowered. Jerry gnawed the edge of his thumb. The big dog and the little dog? Some potential, for sure. Not bad for a premiere performance. Better than a burn.

He bet Harvey would go thirty bucks for this one.

Jerry saved the S&M teaser, added it to the same file

holding the Raineses' puppy in digital limbo. Then he went back to get the burning cat on hard disk. Then he consolidated four stills from another file into 'PUPPY-1.' He included Isabel in the stills, her face smudged, identity concealed.

Talk about a tease. It was the work of a master.

"Jerry!"

"I'm coming," Jerry yelled at the door.

"The hell are you doin', boy?"

"Homework."

Barrett was sleeping like a log and Laura Anne counted it a blessing. No wearies in a week. She let Barrett sleep in, looking forward herself to a wonderful morning. The band was taking on *The Music Man* to support the senior play, and Laura Anne had been informed that she would conduct. She got to school early, ran through three periods and her planning period before skipping lunch to check in at the library. The computers there offered Net access; Laura Anne needed to acquire some sheet music for the coming production.

The sole computer available for faculty was in the librarian's office. From the office you could look over the periodicals and a reference desk to see the row of computers set for student use against the far wall. When Laura Anne entered the libray, she noticed Harvey Sullivan absorbed at the far end of that row. Harvey was not a student to miss lunch for academic pursuits. Games were not allowed on the students' computers. And only the librarian could get you on the Net. Laura Anne was about to go about her own work when she remembered the furtive exchanges in the hall—Jerry Slade to his circle of sycophants. Harvey was always there. She assumed that Jerry was showing off the photos he took in school. But Laura Anne also remembered that Jerry's camera could download pictures to floppy disks.

Was *that* what she had seen going from Jerry's knapsack to Harvey's hand?

Laura Anne paused at the library's interior door. Considered a moment. Then she made her decision. The rack of periodicals provided a blind for her approach. There was Harvey, completely absorbed before the glowing screen. Laura Anne stepped from the cover of the newest rack of *People* magazine and *Time* to see what had the teen's rapt attention.

A glance was enough.

"Harvey."

He scrambled to kill the screen, to retrieve the disk.

"Take it easy, Harvey, I don't want to see you in trouble."

She extended her hand.

"The disk."

He hesitated a beat.

"The disk, or you can talk to Sheriff Sessions."

"The sheriff?"

"I'm not going to fool with the principal, Harvey. It's a waste of time."

"It's not my disk," the freshman protested.

"Oh, really."

"Watn't me stole your dog, either."

"Pardon me?"

"The puppy. On the disk. Jerry said he was yours."

Sheriff Sessions met Barrett Raines at Rolly Slade's shop. The rottweiler snarled at their approach.

"Whatchu want?" Jerry's father was sharpening a mulching blade for a five-horse Snapper.

Sessions displayed a warrant.

"It's a search, Rolly."

"Search my ass!"

"Nope." Sessions shook his head. "It's your boy."

Barrett followed Sessions into the house, Rolly cursing

in tow. The boy's bedroom wasn't hard to spot, its door littered with admonitions to KEEP OUT and that TRESPASS-ERS WILL BE SHOT.

Barrett saw his sons' puppy right away. It was unharmed but in obvious distress, whimpering in a pile of shit in a milk crate.

"The hell?" Rolly growled. "He tole me it was *his* dog."

Barrett nodded to Lou.

"There's his camera. Floppy disks."

Sessions frowned.

"We're gonna need to confiscate his computer, Rolly."

"What?"

"Your boy's sellin' porno, Rolly."

Barrett's concern turned immediately to the animal. He extricated the puppy gently, wrapped it in a T-shirt on the floor, and took it home, where he observed the animal closely.

The twins came home overjoyed.

Tyndall ran to his recovered puppy. *"Penelope!"*

He reached down, hands extended to take the cowering puppy.

"Tyndall, careful—"

There was no warning.

The puppy leaped from the floor to bite Barrett's oldest and innocent son.

The rest of the day was miserable. Tyndall had to have a tetanus shot. There was some discussion as to whether the dog should be destroyed. Barrett was relieved when the vet offered an alternative.

"Let me keep her a while. See if I can turn her around."

So Barrett and Laura Anne left the dog with the veterinarian. All the way home they debated how to bring the news to their children.

"We'll just have to tell them the truth," Barrett said finally. "At least we didn't have to kill her."

Laura Anne was in tears. "I hate what Jerry did to that puppy, Bear, I do, but a dog can be replaced. But *he stole our boys' innocence.* He needs to be put away."

They weren't home an hour when Sheriff Sessions called.

"Bear, we been over that computer. Jerry Slade's?"

"Yes."

"Something here you got to see."

"First thing in the morning," Bear offered.

"No." The voice that came back was uncertain. Shaken. "I need you down here right now."

There were hundreds of still images saved on the hard drive of Jerry Slade's computer and copied to the disks on his desk. Most were simple pornography. A fair number involved children.

"Two of these you need to see." The Sheriff pulled up a chair for Barrett's benefit.

The first was of Isabel Hernandez. The girl was not hard to identify, even with her cyber-smudged face. The details of her dress and shoes, taken with details of the stall and Kohler commodes standard in the school, made identification easy.

"Plus the bows in her hair." The Sheriff winced.

"We knew he had Isabel," Barrett remarked. "That shouldn't be a surprise."

"No. But this is."

Sessions nodded to a deputy who clicked on another file. A thumbnail came up. Another double-click.

It seemed the same as the other bondage scenarios. A woman, face averted, was handcuffed in a stony dungeon to massive beams of wood. Gargoyles leered salaciously from perches on the wall as if entertained by the agony below.

"Wait a minute." Barrett leaned forward.

The source of the woman's apparent terror was withheld in this frame, an indistinct smudge at the bottom of the screen. It could have been a man's head, or a woman's.

"It's a dog," Barrett rasped, and then leaned in closer to inspect the grainy screen. "No. Maybe another woman. I can't tell. But I can see a crucifix. On her neck—you see, Sheriff?"

"I think so, yeah. Jesus, Lord."

Barrett nodded. "Yeah. That's Juanita Quiroga."

It was obvious to Barrett that Sheriff Sessions was dumbstruck with doubt. "I was sure we had the killer," he said over and over. "But now look at this!" Sheriff Sessions was completely ignorant of the technology used to produce the images on Jerry's computer, but he knew enough to admit that the pixeled images in his possession could not have been created by an ignorant migrant worker. The computer-generated scenarios downloaded to Jerry Slade's computer were not the work of the Bull. But Sessions had no idea how to follow this cyberspace trail to its source.

" 'BruteMaster.' " He turned to Barrett. "What kind of goddamn name is that?"

"It's a place to start," Barrett replied. "When you put something on the Web, you leave crumbs. Cookie crumbs, they're called. They have to lead somewhere. It may take some time, but we've got people who do this for a living. Let us help."

Sessions's leather holster squeaked. "Take anything you want. Bring anything. But goddamn, bring it quick."

Barrett pored over the scene generated by Jerry Slade's computer. It was impossible to say whether the images here were staged and consensual, or represented Juanita's actual torture. Similarly, it was impossible to say whether the original location had been a motel, a bed-room, or the scene of the girl's murder. What was obvious was that the original location was effectively camouflaged. The medieval wooden beams from which Jaunita hung on-screen, for instance, were obviously pasted in. The castle walls and stonework—all stock imagery.

The victim's body was not altered, so far as Barrett could discern; only the face was pixeled to obscurity, as if to say a whore was no person at all. And what was that unfocused image intruding from the bottom of the frame? Was it a dog? A shadow? The FDLE's cyber sleuths would have to crack that one.

But there was one remaining, ordinary detail that Barrett almost missed. It sat on the floor to one side of the frame, a vessel of some kind. A pail, maybe? Bowl?

"See that?" Barrett pointed. "The hell would you put a bowl in a bondage scenario?"

"Water?" Sesssions offered.

Barrett leaned in close to the screen. There was something familiar to him about this bowl or pail or whatever it was. A substantial volume, flat, cylindrical sides. Composed of metal, certainly, not porcelain or clay.

"It's not for water." He squinched. "It's a cooking pot, an old, cast-iron . . ."

And then Barrett felt his heart pounding in his ears.

"Sheriff." He rebounded from the screen. "I need your help."

"*You* need?"

"I . . . interviewed a woman," Barrett continued. "Didn't get much. I was going to drop it. But she lives in Strawman's Hammock, she knew both the victim and her uncle, and I'm not sure now that she told me everything she knows."

"Hell." Sessions reached for his hat. "It's better than nothing. And who is this mystery woman?"

"Some people call her a witch," Barrett answered. "I've about decided they're right."

Thírteen

ezikiah Jackson turned a deerhide rocker to face the failing shade of her mimosa trees. Summers she loved to sit on the porch, admiring the evening fire-flies that glowed beneath those twin parasols. But it was much too late in the year for those gentle creatures. The old woman pulled a shawl closer about her bony shoul-ders and reached to take the frosted glass of water pulled fresh from the pump in her sandy yard. Her potion pot sat handy, its blackened belly filled from the afternoon's labor with dog fennel and hemlock.

She was working on a potion now. A pod of pickled beets stained her lap like urine. A butcher knife was cra-dled in the thin fabric that sagged between the sticks of her legs.

Creak, creak. Creak, creak.

The rocker found its rhythm on the porch's widely spaced planks. *Creak, creak.* But then something artificial intruded on the evening breeze. An engine of some kind. Car. Truck. Hezikiah did not alter the cadence of her labor.

The porch steps squeaked with his weight.

"E'nin."

She took hold of the knife.

"I figgered you might be back."

Barrett was barely able in the failing light to direct the sheriff onto the faded path that twisted to reach Hezikiah Jackson's sharecropper shack. At one point he was sure he'd lost that meager road. But then he saw above a setting sun the preternatural blossom of her mimosas.

"There you go," the sheriff declared, pulling his Crown Vic into the clearing of her sterile yard.

"*Hezikiah?*" Sessions bellowed.

No answer. Only the rocking chair, propelled by a stiff breeze. *Creak, creak. Creak, creak.*

"There's the pot," Barrett said. "Same one, gotta be."

"*Hezikiah?*"

No answer. Sessions unlimbered his .357. "If it ain't one thing, it's another."

Barrett followed the sheriff inside. The floor tilted at an angle, like a crazy house. The lawmen worked their way as drunken sailors down its shotgun hall. The rooms on either side were empty. Finally they came to the rear of the shack and the kitchen.

"Shit Miss Agnes," Sessions's Tony Limas slipped.

Barrett caught him by the arm. "Careful."

The floor was slick with fluid and strewn with a variety of parts—frogs' innards, snakeskins, chicken heads. The shelves that formerly held the *curandero's* potions were knocked off their bottled columns. Shards of glass and pottery added hazards to the awful-smelling mess strewn onto the floor.

But there was no witch to be seen. Only the remains of her spells, her alchemy. The back porch waited now, the only place left to check. A single flimsy door barred the way. "Cover me," Sessions directed, and kicked that flimsy impediment from its rusted hinges.

There she was, nailed like a deer through the heels

and hung from the beam of her porch. A garrot of gingham twisted about Hezikiah's straw-thin neck. She twisted obscenely in the half-shadows, naked, tongue lolling and purple from a toothless mouth.

She was disemboweled from her crotch to her throat.

"Jesus." Sessions turned away.

A butcher knife fresh with blood stood straight in the rough pine beside him.

The two lawmen worked out from the homicide in practiced patterns, being careful in the failing light to preserve the scene. They had worked out to the car when the sheriff nodded Barrett over.

"Got some tire tracks."

Barrett walked over to a place about a piss away from the sheriff's cruiser. A pair of widely spaced treads were well preserved in the hard-packed sand beside the leather-bellowed pump. Barrett knew instantly where he'd seen them before.

"I'll be goddamned after all," he said.

The Loyd family's riverside mansion glowed like a jack o' lantern. Lights set into the surrounding water oaks bathed smoothly curved walls. Incandescents inside beamed through the mansion's wide windows like a lighthouse to limn the approaching driveway.

The wife's Lexus stood in its familiar place on sand-packed brick alongside Linton's SUV. And in between the mother's vehicle and his father's crowded Gary Loyd's Humvee.

Linton met them at the door.

"Where's Gary?" the sheriff asked.

"I don't know," came the wooden reply.

"This time I got a warrant, Linton," Lou warned. "Independent discovery. I called the judge myself."

"Damn well better have," the elder responded curtly.

They checked the Humvee first. Linton claimed not to have a key for the toolbox wedged behind the front seat, but Barrett found a spare in the vehicle's map box. He opened the steel-tempered container. There was a smoothly machined lump of metal inside. A camera, Barrett realized. Similar to the Slade boy's.

"Linton."

"What?"

"Does Gary have a computer?"

They spotted Gary's computer on a desk in a bedroom bare of any plaque, picture, or memento. Sheriff Sessions waved Barrett off.

"No. Get your people in here. Let's do this thing right."

Barrett became the virtual case officer on the scene, coordinating with two mobile units to keep a strict chain of custody for all evidence bagged from Gary's carriage house residence and from Hezikiah's shack. Barrett also personally swept the shack in Strawman's Hammock for the second time, just to make sure nothing was missed.

It was immediately apparent that things did not look good for Gary Loyd. For starters, dozens of files featuring Juanita Quiroga in various scenarios of pornography, bestiality, or bondage were discovered on Gary's computer, including, for clinchers, the medieval scenario found on Jerry Slade's machine.

Investigators also reported that the PhotoLab software on Gary's PC was exactly the sort of program used for sophisticated cut-and-paste procedures, though they were unable to retrieve files from his machine that contained images of the actual crime scene or Juanita's real-life agony. The computer's hard drive was clean of that evidence. But not the camera's.

The camera Barrett recovered from Gary's Humvee was digital, a Nikon Coolpix-900. And it was from that camera that investigators finally recovered the original and untouched photographs of Juanita Quiroga's ordeal.

A sense of morbid curiosity competed with the professional obligation to view those photos, but Barrett resisted them both. He was more than willing to let the pros in Violent Crimes pore over that material. The only thing he wanted to determine was whether Hezikiah's potion pot showed up at all in the digitized pictures from the actual crime scene in Strawman's Hammock.

"Did you see the pot?" Barrett double-checked with Midge Holloway.

"Only in the medeival scenario," Midge answered. "No place else. And definitely not at the actual scene."

"I guess I should be relieved," Barrett grumbled. "I made the initial search, for crying out loud. I *know* I couldn't miss a damned cast-iron pot."

"You didn't, Bear. It wasn't there. Gary imported that pot into his fantasies, just as he imported the castle and the gargoyles and the rest. Hezikiah was a participant. Maybe she provided stimulants. Maybe kinky sex. Hell, maybe Gary used her house at one time or another, I don't know. But at some point, he simply decided to include something of hers as part of the scene."

That made sense, of course. It made perfect sense.

"I guess you're right," Barrett relented. "It just bothers me that he'd leave a clue like that in a setting otherwise disguised."

"Part of him probably wants to get caught. Or at least get public recognition. It fits the profile."

Cricket agreed. "It was Gary Loyd all along."

Sheriff Sessions reveled in the bright-haired Canadian's endorsement. Cricket and Bear had just completed their biweekly brief with the sheriff, a much more amicable affair than usual. It had become apparent that the sheriff's humor was entirely determined by how the news of the day affected his relationship with the Loyds and his bid for reelection. In this regard, Sessions was a perfect politician, cozying up to the Loyds and ignoring Bear when El Toro was pegged as his niece's killer, distancing himself from the Loyds and embracing Bear when Gary Loyd again looked good for murder.

"For sure Gary killed Juanita." Cricket gulped his coffee. "And then he got afraid that Hezikiah would talk. Or maybe she tried to blackmail him, who knows? So he killed her, too."

"Damn woman." Sessions shook his head. "She musta had somethin' on everybody."

A point too close to home for Barrett to blithely acknowledge. About that time a deputy stuck his head out of his underground office.

"Call from Jacksonville. Miz Holloway."

Sessions put Midge on the phone's duct-taped speaker.

"Just some additional goodies," Midge began. "First off, you can eliminate Jerry Slade as a suspect. The camera used to photograph Juanita was definitely not Jerry Slade's, or any Sony Mavica. And get this—we traced credit-card payments for the freeplay site to a hidden account in Gary's straw-baling company."

"What kind of change we talkin'?" Sessions drawled.

"Almost a quarter of a million dollars," Midge reported. "That's in the *one* account we've been able to trace."

"Looks like we got our BruteMaster by the balls," Sessions declared loudly, and Barrett had to admit that the evidence was mounting.

Most damning was the fact that forensics on the ground stood right in line with evidence pulled from computers and cameras. The FDLE team that cast the tracks leading up to Hezikiah's porch matched the pattern of those treads to the tires on Gary's Humvee. Also recovered near the witch's uneven stoop were partial prints from a size ten R.E.I. hiking boot that matched a pair found in the garbage behind the Loyd mansion.

Barrett's team found loose, straw-colored hair in Hezikiah's kitchen. They found traces of semen, badly degraded, in her bedding. Samples from a hairbrush and razor in Gary's bathroom were sent to Jacksonville for DNA comparison to samples taken from the murdered women of Strawman's Hammock. The Humvee was transported to Jacksonville for extensive forensics.

"And this time," Sheriff Sessions promised, "ain't nothing gonna be thrown out."

Barrett received congratulations for an effort that was well coordinated and professional. Within the week, Gary Quentin Loyd was charged with two counts of first-degree homicide. Fountain-Pen Reed champed at his platinum-plated bit as he waited for the DNA analyses that would unarguably tie the alleged BruteMaster to Juanita and Hezikiah. He needed one other thing to proceed, of course. He needed an arrest. He needed Gary Loyd.

Only Gary was nowhere to be found.

An APB was put out for the younger Loyd on the night of Hezikiah's murder, but with a week passed there had been no sight of Master Loyd. Sheriff Sessions was convinced that Linton was hiding his son from prosecution. For the narrow purpose of pursuing that possibility, Judge Blackmond granted a single interview, formally for purpose of discovery, to be conducted by Sheriff Sessions with Gary's father. An attached caveat required the FDLE to assign an agent to accompany the sheriff to the Loyd compound. Lou asked Barrett if he'd like to take that ride.

"Dollars to doughnuts Linton's either hiding that boy hisself, or helping him hide," Lou said as they rumbled over the cattle gap leading to Linton's riverside home.

"Just do us all a favor," Barrett cautioned. "Do not provoke. And do *not* get personal."

* * *

215

A hail from the driveway got no response from inside the big house.

"Let's ease around back," Lou suggested.

They spotted Linton Loyd viewing the Suwannee River from the height of his balcony. The elder Loyd did not seem surprised to see the lawmen.

"Come on up."

Barrett followed the sheriff into Linton's marvelous home, up the long curved arm of stairs, onto the marble tiles of the overlook.

"Do for you gentlemen?"

"Where's your boy, Linton?" The sheriff was not about to beat around the bush.

"Don't have any idea." Linton ran a neat hand through perfectly coiffed hair.

"Have a notion where he might hole up?"

"Don't know that he *is* holed up."

"Linton." Barrett tried to keep his voice calm. "If Gary did kill these people, he's either a sociopath or insane. If he's insane, and you can help us prove it, he can avoid the death penalty."

"You don't git the chair for foolin' around with a whore," Linton spat. "Now, I don't doubt that Gary might have chased his dick around a little. Don't mean he killed that little girl."

"How about Hezikiah? Don't tell me he was out *there* looking for strange. Nobody's that desperate."

Linton actually smiled.

"You might be surprised."

At some point in the debate the mother floated onto the balcony. More frail and porcelain, it seemed to Barrett, than ever.

"He took the boat," she announced without prompt or preamble.

Linton turned angrily. "Mother, be quiet!"

"Took it a week ago," she said. "Said he was gone to fish."

"Elizabeth, be *still*!"

She turned to her husband.

"You lord over him. You think you can lord over *me*?"

Real hatred there. Genuine contempt.

"Goddammit, Liz—"

"Damn *you*, Linton. Wasn't for me, you'd be *broke*! It's *my* money made the business in the first place. Bailed you out when you were bust. *My* money!"

"Elizabeth, for God's sake."

"God?" she barked. "God's got nothing to do with us." She turned to Barrett. "I want my baby."

"I understand."

"Don't hurt him, please. Whatever he is, Linton and I . . . we made him."

"I'll try, Mrs. Loyd. I'll do everything I can."

A renewed manhunt concentrated on the coastline of Taylor, Lafayette, and Dixie Counties. A week went by and still there was no sign of Gary Loyd. State troopers, county deputies, and dogs joined the marine patrol in an effort to find Gary Linton Loyd, to no avail. The coast guard and marine patrol officially ended their search. The highway patrol and local authorities pulled in their horns soon after. But Jarold Pearson kept at it, offering to take Barrett along one morning for a final inspection of the coastline.

They launched Jarold's jet-propelled bird dog from the ramp at Roy's restaurant, followed cypress poles through aisles of saltwater cut through plains of grass to reach the Gulf. Once in open water, Jarold wheeled to port and headed south. Barrett was grateful to have Jarold involved in the manhunt. There were innumerable creeks, eddies, or tributaries along the Gulf that might hide a felon, and fishing holes at which a man might camp too numerous to count. No one knew those twisting sloughs and waterways better than Jarold Pearson.

Barrett squeezed honey into a Thermos of coffee that was strapped beside a fire extinguisher on the helm of Jarold's midmounted skiff. It was bracing cold, but not frigid. Jarold had an ordinary fatigue jacket pulled over the olive and tans of the Florida Fish & Wildlife Conservation Commission. Bear pulled the hood of his Army-issued parka over his official wool cap. A stitching of white letters above the bill of the cap identified its wearer as FDLE. Bear tried to keep the chart in his numbed hands stable against a slipstream of winter air. Jarold navigated, as usual, by the seat of his pants.

There was no sophisticated equipment to keep the bird dog bound within the coordinates specified by the marine patrol, only the warden's intuition of wind and water and his mental catalog of buoys and landmarks. Jarold's one concession to modernity was a ship-to-shore radio. Barrett had his cell phone for backup, but kept it secreted in the deep pockets of his parka.

By noon they had worked past Dead Man's Bay. Gary's scarlet runabout was a distinctive craft. As Jarold and Bear searched the coast they gave a description of the boat to every fisherman or runabout found on the water. By noon they had canvassed more than twenty craft on the water, none of whose skippers had seen Gary's boat. Barrett would have bet that the younger Loyd had never been on the Gulf at all except for Roy's insistence that he had seen Gary's fire-engine red Whaler launch from the ramp near his restaurant.

"He's out here somewhere," Barrett said.

Jarold checked his gauges. "Tide's running out and we need fuel."

"Okay," Bear conceded. "Let's head back."

You could see the spines of oyster beds and the javelin tips of cypress knees exposed with the running tide.

"Think I'll play it safe," the warden declared, and headed out for deeper water.

The green comb of treeline that marked the fall of land receded. The grass that rolled in waves from the shoreline to the sea disappeared. Jarold nudged the throttle of his jet-propelled outboard and the bird dog leaped to fifty miles an hour, pounding through the choppy water, each thrust forward a blow to the hull. Barrett could feel the spray of brine beating his face like BBs. He flexed his knees to absorb the heavy blows being hammered to the bird dog's rugged hull. A brilliant blue sky spread an unflawed canopy overhead and even Barrett, always uneasy away from terra firma, was exhilarated to smell the salt and feel the wind tearing his face.

Within minutes there was nothing in sight except an endless horizon and a rolling plateau of choppy saltwater. Most men, Barrett knew, would not head to open sea without sophisticated navigation. But he realized that Jarold's abjuration of the GPS was only part of a larger distrust for all things modern. Part of a character that for months on end lived and survived in solitary self-reliance. Without plumbing. Without air-conditioning.

Jarold Pearson wanted to find the way home on his own, following the smell and feel of the water to a time, more than a place, that would say, 'Here, turn here.' To follow that voice off the deep water, back into sight of land, to seek some familiar landmark, some configuration of tree and green absolutely without distinction to Barrett or any other outsider, from that recognized place to yet another, a bald cypress, say, or an oyster mound identical to the other thousands that crowded this stretch of coast.

Finally, from those scattered constellations to fix the point that would lead to another point that would call him further yet to a trail of careless poles stabbed motley into the sand below the water to reach, finally, Roy's concrete ramp.

But he didn't make it. The warden was still in deep water when the voice came, that imperative born from equal parts of instinct and experience, 'Here. Hard to starboard. This is the place.' Jarold trusted that voice. He was set to turn. But then Barrett saw something off the starboard bow, something dark and swollen lifting on a swell of briny water.

At first Bear thought it was a bale of marijuana. Drug running was so profitable and the instruments that Jarold hated so precise that it had become common off the Florida coast to drop four or five hundred pounds of grass for later retrieval. Occasionally a bale would be lost, of course. Or a cache might be dumped if a smuggler was threatened by imminent boarding from a legitimate authority. Barrett had seen several bales washed up onto shore, but he'd never seen one at sea.

"See that?" he shouted above the midmounted engine, but Jarold was already banking toward the floating mass.

Barrett was wondering how they'd get the thing on board when an ermine flash in the clear sky above got his notice.

A pair of terns wheeled to catch the sun on white wings. Barrett loved watching terns. More slender in body and bill than other gulls, the tern was also fitted with narrower wings and sometimes even a forked tail, which made him a spitfire in flight. Barrett watched the birds dive to strafe the bale below. A second pass swooped low over the floating mass. The birds cawed raucously. The seafowl paired overhead, beating to a virtual hover against the gulfward breeze, furious above waves that began to chop white.

At first Barrett thought the gulls were dissatisfied with their unstable roost. But then the terns plummeted in tandem toward the target that bobbed swollen below, and this time they stayed. They were closer, now, to the birds and their roosting place, much closer, and Barrett knew when he saw the fowl plunge their beaks that these tern were not feeding on marijuana.

There was meat here, not fresh by the looks of it, but meat nevertheless and the terns were after it, their sharp bills tearing past a wreath of weed into what Barrett now could see was a bloated and putrefied human being.

An explosion of bodily gases broke free as the birds punctured the corpse's drumtight skin. A sickening odor washed downwind, undiluted by sea breeze.

"Shit."

Jarold banked hard to get upwind of the floater. Barrett clutched his stomach. The body appeared to be floating freely. No restraints apparent, or weights, though Barrett had retrieved more than one body that was supposed to never leave the seabed. That was the thing about dumping a body in the water—you could wrap a man in chains but if you didn't disembowel him, the bacteria in the victim's gut produced gases that converted the entrails into twenty three feet of ballast.

Jarold throttled back to pull alongside. A pair of beaks daggered greedily into the sockets of vacant eyes. Jarold gunned the bird dog toward the floating bale of flesh and bone. The terns briefly gave up their feast, putrid flesh hanging from a pair of probosci. But the fowl returned, this time to be unmoved by the warden's impotent charge.

Barrett reached for the cell phone in his parka. Even had they been able, Barrett would be loath to salvage these putrescent remains. Better to phone the sheriff's office, have Lou contact the coast guard.

"I'd call the marine patrol," Jarold suggested as if reading Bear's mind.

"Good idea." Barrett redialed.

The FMP could bring out a boat along with a net and a body bag. But in order for the patrol to rendezvous with the bird dog, Barrett would have to supply a precise location.

"One occasion when I wouldn't mind having a Magellan GPS."

But Jarold was ahead of him.

"See the chart?"

Bear handed it over. Jarold inspected the chart and glanced shoreward, then far off to port. He placed a thumb gently onto the nautical map.

"Tell 'em we're at latitude approximate twenty-nine degrees, longitude eighty-three degrees. Got that?"

"Got it."

"We're a little over two nauticals east of Marker 16."

"Sorry." Bear's hands were shaking. "Can you repeat that?"

"Here." Jarold extended his hand for the phone. "Let me."

Barrett surrendered his phone. The body rolled with a swell of brine. The terns attacked what might be a buttock. Barrett steadied himself on the gunwale. An identification would have to be made, he knew. But that would not happen without forensic assistance. There were no familiar marks to guide the way on that dumpling skin, no points of reference to mark a face black and swollen and beaked to shreds. In fact there was nothing distinctively human at all of this thing rotting on the open sea. But Barrett knew, nevertheless, why the outspoken heir to the Loyd fortune had been, for nearly a week, silent.

Fourteen

Medical examiners concluded that Gary Linton Loyd had died from a single, self-inflicted wound to the temple.

"Looks good for a suicide." Midge's final report was given in the sheriff's office. "The weapon used was an automatic, nine-millimeter. We found the slug. And we were able to find traces of powder embedded in his shooting hand. He was drunk, too. Levels were way high."

"Bothers me he wound up in the water." Barrett frowned. "Usually, situation like that, you'd expect to find the body in the boat."

"We figure either he sat back on the gunwale to ensure that he'd go in the water, or that, being drunk and standing, he went over the side with the impact of the slug," Midge replied.

Cricket raised his hand. "Do we have his boat?"

Sessions affirmed. "Tide washed it into the shoreline. Fisherman found it this morning, half-sunk with rain in a marsh of sawgrass."

"Anything onboard?"

"Empty bottle of Jack Black. Casing from a nine-millimeter shell."

* * *

The preacher at Gary's funeral laid the son's desperate act at the feet of a conscience wracked with guilt.

"He could not trust his sins to Jesus," the preacher declared mournfully. "And so he tried to atone for them himself."

The wake of Gary's funeral found Bear and his FDLE comrades in a state of exhaustion. Sheriff Sessions called them all together to his office to thank the investigators for their work and to wrap up what was nominally his own investigation.

Barrett ground his hands into his temples. "I never like to call the game on account of a suicide."

"Well," the sheriff drawled, "when your choices are an electric chair or a needle, I guess a bullet can look pretty good."

"Good for him, maybe. Bad for us."

"Not followin' ya, Bear."

"You can't ask a dead man questions, Lou."

"The hell cares? If he was gonna confess he wouldn't've took his boat out to the Gulf and shot hisself."

"I'd be a lot happier if Midge could match some of Gary's DNA to semen in Juanita, or at least to the crime scenes."

"His hair's already matched to hair got from Hezikiah's shack," Midge reminded Barrett. "And Juanita's hair was found in Gary's Humvee."

"We should wait for the rest of the DNA before we hang it up." Barrett was stubborn. "The semen, at least."

"Semen won't prove anything," Cricket replied reasonably. "Look, Bear, we're not saying that Gary raped Juanita over the time he had her in that shack. *We're* not saying he had sex with the girl at all. We're just saying he killed her."

"Of course he killed her." Sessions growled irritation.

"He took kinky pictures and sold 'em and somethin' got out of hand. Hezikiah knew what he was doin' with that girl, you can bet. Her uncle, too; wouldn't surprise me if the Bull had his boss man pegged. Maybe wantin' some money to keep quiet. I'd bet my hat that the morning Gary went out to Quiroga's trailer it wasn't to talk about baling straw. He went out there to kill him. Hadn't've been for you and Jarold, he would have."

"The Bull, yes." Barrett nodded. "That's another witness didn't give us much, did he?"

"You're out of line, Agent Raines." The sheriff growled.

"We have to go with what we've got, Sheriff, you're right. I just hate loose ends, that's all."

"In real life there are always loose ends, Barrett," Midge said kindly.

Bear nodded. "I apologize. I do. To you all."

Sessions nodded curtly. "Thank you, sir."

The briefing ended on that note. Barrett was heading for the street when he felt a meaty hand on his shoulder.

"Bear."

It was Lou Sessions.

"Yes, Sheriff?"

"Didn't want things to wind up sour, is all. You a damn good lawman, Bear. I could've been easier to git along with in the past. Think it's time we started fresh."

Barrett extended his hand. "I can do that."

"I don't suppose you thought any about the coming election." Lou kept the offered hand.

"Not much," Barrett lied.

"Well." Sessions let him go. "I guess I can always manage an honest race. Not like either of us is gonna git much support from Linton Loyd, is it?"

"I never counted on it," Barrett declared.

Sessions shook his head. "Aha. Well. Fresh start, then."

"You bet." Barrett nodded and headed for his sedan.

Barrett drove straight from Sheriff Sessions's feudal office to the open blacktop leading to Deacon Beach. A whirlwind of doubts swirled unanswered before the Bear, but there was nothing he could do about it. It was Sessions's investigation, ultimately, and Lou was satisfied to name Gary Loyd as the county's most recent and horrific murderer.

"If I were sheriff, this case would not be closed," Barrett announced to the interior of his car. "*If* I were sheriff."

What he needed now was some time with the boys and a slow meal with Laura Anne. But before allowing himself those hard-earned pleasures, Barrett detoured off Ocean for downtown, slipped through the green light, and parked along a weed-split sidewalk before the brick facade of the *Deacon Beach Herald*.

Pauline Traiwick was the paper's owner, reporter, and until the invasion of the digital age, the typesetter as well. Barrett spotted her neat, small frame when he opened the lead-paned door—a sixty-something in khakis who used to ride barrels and rope calves in Florida's rodeo circuit.

"Barrett. I've got an estimate for those cards you were asking about. Want to see the type?"

"Sure."

Pauline picked up what looked like a business card from her cluttered desk.

VOTE FOR **BARRETT RAINES**

Sheriff, Lafayette County

EXPERIENCE, DEDICATION, TRUST

"...No man is above the law. But no one is beneath it, either...."

"Pretty nice." Barrett nodded.

"Think you're going to run?"

"I'll know more in a couple of days."

"Will I have to get the news off Stacy Kline?"

"Pauline, you know better than that. Fact I came here with an exclusive."

"Gary Loyd?"

"Yeah. He looks good for three killings. Counting his own."

She reached for a pad of paper. "Just the facts, if you please."

Barrett made a habit of keeping Pauline informed. She was the last of a dying breed, the kind of journalist who did not construe an op-ed of two opposed opinions as a substitute for reporting the truth.

"Sessions thinks we got our man. Evidence points to it. We're closing the case."

Bear went on to summarize the factors leading to that decision.

"You think the sheriff's made a good decision, Bear?"

"I have to be off the record on that one, Pauline."

"All right."

"Based on what evidence we have, taken with Gary's apparent suicide, yes, I think the investigation's gone about as far as it can. But I gotta tell you, Pauline, it's hard for me to believe Gary was capable of something like this."

She nodded. "Hard for lots of people."

" 'Course, in fairness, that's one of the dangers comes of being *too* close to the folks you investigate. I've wanted to believe people were innocent before—when they weren't."

"I know, Barrett. We all do." She reached out a hand. "But I'd rather have a man err on that side than the other. Still, it must be hard, seeing so much violent behavior, to keep wanting to see the best in people."

"Couldn't do it on my own," Bear declared.

"But you need to be sure before you run for this office, Bear. Lots of folks around here still hate anything isn't white. They'll be looking at your wife, your children . . ."

Barrett sighed. "It was like that when I worked the Beach, Pauline."

"We're a town. Now you're taking on a county, a *big* county. Everything you ever did or didn't do will come up. Including this mess with the Loyds."

"Least they can't accuse me of playing favorites."

She smiled. "No, indeed. But if there is any secret you think you have, believe me—someone will unearth it."

Barrett looked out the small, square window of her newspaper. A boy, a black boy, was running a tire barefooted down the blacktop. Just a skinny boy with a rag of a coat, in December, barefooted.

"You remember when Daddy died?" Barrett asked quietly.

"I remember when your mother killed him," Pauline answered. "Why?"

"Like you to run through your paper, see what you wrote. Would have been 'sixty-nine, 'seventy. Somewhere in there."

"Somewhere, indeed." She kept her voice empty of surprise. "Am I looking for anything in particular?"

Barrett shrugged. "I just never had the facts is all. Nothing except from family, you know. I couldn't remember anything on my own."

"You were locked in a closet," Pauline said kindly. "According to reports."

"Was Hezikiah Jackson mentioned?"

Pauline regarded him a long moment. "I asked Sue about that, Sue Pridgeon? His father knew the sheriff at the time. There was *someone* there. She was described as a neighbor, which I did not print partly because I

228

couldn't get a name and partly because you-all were too isolated to have anything like neighbors. You must know there've always been rumors about Hezikiah. She's practicing voodoo. Aborting babies. Prophecy. That kind of foolishness. But nothing connected with your father."

"You mind checking anyway?"

"Why, Barrett? Do you recall something yourself? Has something—come back?"

Barrett sorted the freshly printed cards in his hands.

"Let's just say I don't want something hitting me from behind. Will that do?"

"For now, certainly." Pauline nodded. "I'll look over a couple of years, see what we have. If Hezikiah's mentioned anywhere I'll pull it for you. How's that?"

"Owe you one."

"No, no." She shook her head. "No favors, here. I look up things for people all the time."

He headed next for Ramona's. Laura Anne got them a table on the patio. The fresh breeze off the bay was more invigorating than a shower. Barrett breathed deeply. He was tired, but at least he wasn't weary.

"You better put a mark on your calendar for Wednesday." Laura Anne leaned over his ribeye. "Six P.M. And I want you looking nice."

"Because?"

"Because that's when the investors from Atlanta are coming down to meet us. That's why. That and a little over four hundred *thousand* dollars."

Barrett's fork parked in midair.

"Didn't realize it was this soon."

"Knew you wouldn't." Laura Anne dimpled. "Once you get involved in a case, the house could catch on fire and you wouldn't notice."

"But the case is over," Barrett assured her. "Lou made

it official this morning. He's got Gary. He's satisfied with the evidence. There's nothing more I can do."

"You don't look too happy about it."

"I'm a perfectionist. Makes me a pain in the ass."

"Oooo. Grumpy. Try some of that sweet tea."

Barrett gulped the iced tea from a quart-sized glass.

"Four hundred thousand?"

"Little over. With points."

" 'Points'? You're sounding like a movie star."

"Yo' mama." She tossed her head. "Thurman's got a contract ready to sign. And Barrett—I got a job."

"The high school? Teaching?"

"Yes!" she squealed. "Full-time. Music and math! I start this spring."

"Good for you, L.A.!"

Barrett leaned across the table to kiss her. She stopped him with a finger to his lips.

"One other thing."

"There's more?"

"I want you to run for sheriff."

Barrett sagged back into his seat.

"I just took a look at the cards."

"And?"

"That's cheap enough. But then I'd have to take leave to campaign. It'd cost. Not four hundred thousand . . ."

"No."

"Prob'ly more like fifteen, twenty thousand."

"Make a budget. Stick with it."

"I won't have Linton Loyd's money."

"No." Laura Anne winked. "You'll have mine."

"You sure, Laura Anne? Last time we talked you didn't want me running for anything."

"You don't try, you'll regret it, Bear. And I've about decided I don't want any 'what-ifs' hangin' 'round our heads."

"Well, young lady." Barrett could feel a smile stretching across his face. "With news like this? Seems to me like we need to go home and celebrate."

They drove home along the beach. Laura Anne called to make sure that Thelma kept the boys in her trailer for the evening.

"Coast is clear," she remarked.

"Yes, it is," he replied.

"Bear!"

They didn't make it to the bedroom. Laura Anne jerked a sheet from the wash and tossed it down on the living-room floor. Barrett's hand snagged in her bra. She laughed.

"Here."

She came out of her blouse and bra in one languid extension of arms and breasts and belly.

"Homecoming weekend," she said.

He kicked out of his slacks, his shorts. He did not need any encouragement. He had been aching hard since they banged through the back door.

"Oh, God, Barrett!"

They made love on the living-room floor. Made love again. Then they showered. He lifted her into bed, that mile of golden skin.

"Gonna sleep good tonight," she murmured.

"Yes," he agreed. "But not just yet."

When the phone rang at nine the next morning they were still in bed.

"Ignore it," Laura Anne said.

"Betcha," he mumbled. But then Midge Holloway's voice scratched chalk over the machine.

"Bear? You there? I have the final DNA analysis."

Barrett stumbled out of bed.

"I'm here."

"You sound like a drunk."

"Just woke up."

"Get your coffee. Call me back in a half hour."

"You're an angel, Midge."

"Recovering alcoholic actually. But close enough."

By the time Barrett had showered and spooned his honey into a fresh cup of coffee, Laura Anne was already at the domestic tasks of the day. She threw the sheet from the night before into the clothes hamper.

"We oughta save that thing for a trophy," Barrett said as he dialed Midge.

Laura Anne's laugh rippled through the house.

"Midge here."

"Barrett."

"You sound chipper."

"Don't ruin my day, Midge. It's started too nice."

"No, no. Nothing new here, really. But you were so damned interested in the DNA."

"At this moment I could give a shit." Barrett ran his hand down the back of Laura Anne's long leg.

"Too bad. You're gonna get it anyway. The bottom line is: Gary Loyd's DNA does not match anything we found in or around Juanita Quiroga. The hair found in Hezi-kiah's shack is matched by DNA to the samples we took from his house."

"That's it?" Barrett sipped his coffee.

" 'Bout what we expected, wasn't it?"

"Yeah. It just bothers me that we can't find a match for the semen," Barrett groused. "At the very least, there's the possibility Gary had an accomplice."

"Well, we're back to her uncle. The Bull's DNA *did* match semen found in the girl and on bedsheets in He-zikiah's shack."

"I know, I know." Barrett's reply was sharp.

"Well, Barrett, if you've got a suspect sitting around somewhere who we can match—"

"I don't."

"Then we are stuck, sweet pea."

"Bear—" Laura Anne interrrupted.

" 'Scuse me, Midge. What is it, hon?"

Laura Anne pulled a shirt from the laundry.

"I found this buried in your closet."

A stain of chewing tobacco spread like blood from a gunshot wound on Barrett's white shirt.

"We need to throw it away. Or burn it."

Barrett went pale.

"Barrett? Bear?"

"One second, Midge. One second."

Barrett cupped the phone.

"Do not wash that shirt!"

"It's ruined!"

"*Do* not. And *do not* burn it, either. Midge—"

He was back on the phone.

"Yes, Bear."

"Can't saliva carry a DNA signature?"

"Depends. For secreters it can. Probably eighty percent of the population."

"Keep your fingers crossed. I've got another sample."

"Make sure you've got a warrant to go with it."

"Nope." Barrett shook his head. "I don't need one."

The days crawled until Midge came back with the report that confirmed Barrett's hunch.

"Son of a bitch, Bear, we got a match. And there's more."

Barrett called Lou Sessions to explain the finding. A call from the sheriff to Judge Blackmond followed. The Judge agreed that Barrett's new evidence was admissible and directed that Barrett conduct the required interview and arrest. Sheriff Sessions handed Bear a warrant with no comment.

"Come on, partner." Barrett rendezvoused with Cricket at Shirley's cafe.

Close to an hour later they pulled up to the twin construction trailers that were the pride of Linton Loyd's deer camp. Linton was alone before his homemade gallows. There were no hangers-on this time to attend the compact man's outdoor dissertations. No sycophants or weekend warriors. Linton was seated on a canvas chair, polishing his rifle's walnut stock before the carcass of another deer. A pickle bucket brimmed with blood and guts. A pouch of the same chewing tobacco that weeks earlier had stained Barrett's shirt worked now in Linton's mouth as if he were a shortstop.

Barrett approached the armed hunter with Cricket flanking. Loyd did not alter the rhythm of his labor. Did not even acknowledge the presence of the uninvited guests who had invaded his camp.

"Need to put the rifle aside, Linton," Barrett directed.

"Why? You the new game warden?" Linton smiled through his wad.

Cricket freed the safety of his Glock.

"Right about now would be a good time."

"Shit." Linton laid his thirty-ought carefully aside. "You boys don't have nothin' on me."

"Got your Red Man," Barrett countered. "You spit it all over my shirt, Linton. Remember? That gave me the sample I needed to match your DNA to semen recovered from Juanita Quiroga."

Linton chewed reflectively.

Barrett reached down to collect the rifle.

"One way or the other you had sex with that girl. And then you got the drips. No big deal. A little clap. But when you went to get that little problem taken care of they took some blood, and next thing you know you've got your very private doctor calling to tell you you're positive for HIV."

"Medical records are sealed." Linton frownd.

"Your medicine cabinet isn't," Barrett countered. "We've already been out to the house, Linton. We found the prescriptions. Quite a cocktail. It must have been a kick in the nuts; first you're taking some simple antibiotics for the clap, then you find out she's made you HIV positive, and *then* you find it's gone to AIDS. It wasn't too long after that, was it, Linton, that you killed her?"

Loyd spit carefully into the spitoon offered by the pickle bucket. A stream of Red Man contaminated the deer's innocent leavings.

"Am I under arrest?"

"Linton Loyd, you are definitely under arrest . . ." Barrett pulled out the cuffs. ". . . for the murders of Juanita Quiroga, Hezikiah Jackson, and your son."

"I didn't kill Gary. I didn't kill anybody."

Bear stood him up. "Be careful what you say, you son of a bitch. It will be used in court."

Thurman Shaw moved to have the evidence of Linton Loyd's DNA thrown out, even though he knew the motion was doomed. Judge Blackmond informed Thurman Shaw and his client that the sample from the saliva in the Red Man that Linton Loyd voluntarily spit on Bear's shirt was thoroughly allowable as evidence, as was the evidence gained from the warranted search of Linton's art deco home. A computer in Linton's study was loaded with the same PhotoLab software as that found on his son's hard drive. The files on the father's Gateway had been deleted, but anyone who could use Norton Utilities could have pulled them up, and the folks at FDLE were considerably more sophisticated than that.

Experts confirmed that Linton had been producing pornographic material on his personal computer for more than three years. Juanita Quiroga modeled for dozens of those scenarios. She was bound with leather and chains in a variety of locations—motels, deer camps, once even in Linton's own bedroom.

Barrett and Cricket Bonet interrogated Linton Loyd in the presence of his feisty attorney. With Thurman Shaw editing his remarks, Linton admitted that he created the BruteMaster site, and admitted sexual relations with Juanita. But that was all.

"You're not doing yourself any good, Linton." Barrett straddled a chair.

"Aren't I?"

"Jury's not going to sympathize with a man killed his own son."

"Thought we were talking about the whore here."

"But Gary found out about the whore, didn't he, Linton? From his foreman, I'd guess. Or maybe he checked it out for himself, drove the Humvee out to that shack. Watched one of your bondage sessions, you and your buddies and Hezikiah having it all over each other. Letting that girl have it over you. The Brute Master.

"Maybe that's when Gary knew for sure that his own overbearing, macho daddy—pillar of the community, model citizen, Rotary Club president—was a pervert and a pornographer. And that's when he made you sign over the straw-baling business, wasn't it, Linton?"

"Don't know what you mean by 'sign it over.' It was his business."

"Come on, Linton, Gary had no more idea how to make money out of straw than Rapunzel. It was *you* started that business. It was *you* made it profitable. But then Gary took a peek at your nightlife and he had you by the balls, didn't he? 'Cause Gary knew that if your perversions became public, you'd be ruined. Your wife, your political connections, your customers—they'd cut you off in a minute.

"So he blackmailed you. Your own son. The only way you could shut your little boy's mouth was to pay him off. That's how Gary really got into the straw-baling business, isn't it, Linton? He made you *give* it to him."

"If that's true why the hell would I have to kill him?"

"Because at some point pictures weren't good enough for you, Linton. Each fantasy, no matter how elaborately staged, left you a little disappointed, didn't it? Maybe even angry. And then that little bitch gave you AIDS, didn't she, Linton? You made her die slow and hard and you were more than willing to let El Toro take the blame. But Gary knew better. 'What did he do? What did he do?' Gary wasn't talking about the Bull at all that day at the trailer, was he Linton? He was talking about you.

"And once he knew, you couldn't trust him to shut up, could you? Not for all the straw in the world. So you met him out on the boat. Little father-to-son talk. You got him drunk. You got him distracted. And then you killed him."

"That's conjecture, Barrett," Thurman Shaw attempted to intervene. "Be nice to see some kind of proof."

"All right." Barrett turned again to Linton. "Where do you get your balers welded and repaired, Linton?"

"What's that got to do with the price of eggs?"

"Rolly Slade does your work, doesn't he? Probably only a handful of folks go in there can get past Rolly's dog, but you could, couldn't you, Linton? That dog'd come to you just like a puppy."

"I like rottweilers." Linton cracked a grin. "And whores. No crime in that."

"No crime giving a dog a bone. But now you start chaining up little girls for him to gnaw, the court gets entirely unsympathetic."

"Last time I cuffed that girl on anything she was giving her uncle a blow job through a rubber. Son of a bitch was eat up with clap, she blowed him anyway. Hell, you got the pictures."

"Yes, we do."

"Not a law in the world against taking pictures."

"That the way Elizabeth sees it, Linton?" Cricket chimed in. "Your wife? The woman who made you, saved you, backed you . . . bailed you out! How's she feel about your small perversions? One more reason for you to kill your son; maybe Gary was set to tell Lizzy what Daddy did nights. Or maybe he just saw what you were doing with Rolly's dog."

"Kiss my ass."

Barrett threw a photo onto the table. Not a digital photo, but a fast-filmed glossy displaying Hezikiah Jackson, naked from the waist down and hanging from her back porch.

"Easy enough to get Gary on the water, wasn't it, Linton? Get him drunk and put a bullet through his head. Fit the gun into your son's hand, discharge another round so there'd be grains of powder consistent with suicide. But Gary wasn't the only one knew what you did to that girl. Hezikiah Jackson knew, too.

"Hezikiah was treating El Toro for his disease, we know that. We found strands of Juanita's hair in her kitchen. And I saw Hezikiah's potion pot planted in one of your scenarios. Did she participate, Linton? Or on the day you turned Rolly's dog on your little whore, while you were busy with your pictures, did you look up to see her standing at the window?"

For the first time Linton squirmed in his chair.

"I didn't kill her."

"No? You mean you killed a whore, killed your son, but an old beat-up nigger woman, she just wasn't enough sport? Give me a break, Linton, we *know* you were out there!"

"I believe this little talk's about over." Thurman Shaw muzzled his client. "You got a lot of smoke, Barrett. But it's all circumstantial."

"A jury will see those pictures, Thurman," Barrett promised. "If you want to take a chance on what they will conclude from *that*—! Then have at it."

"He cain't prove a thing. Can he?"

Barrett leaned into Linton's handsomely lined face.

"Three counts of first-degree murder, Linton. Then they give you a choice. Needle. Or chair."

"That's enough, Agent Raines," Thurman barked.

"Just keep listening to your attorney, Linton. Go ahead and roll the dice." Barrett buttoned his blazer as he rose from his metal chair. "Plead innocent. I'd love to see it."

"I bet you would," the surviving Loyd replied. "But Hell ain't half-full yet."

Stacy Kline had a field day with the newest twist in what was being called the voodoo murders. State's Advocate Roland Reed was faced with the problem of appearing as confident of his third suspect's guilt as he was of the first's. Barrett declined comment altogether. He had done his job.

Barrett drove over the speed limit to reach his shaded home. He only had an hour within which to change and meet Laura Anne with her out-of-town investors. Not much time to waste. There was no puppy bounding in greeting from the back door as Bear pulled beneath his carport, which reminded the investigator that he needed to be looking for a new dog for the boys.

"Afternoon, Thelma."

Barrett greeted Auntie in the kitchen.

"Laura Anne got you a tie and shirt all picked out."

"Thank you."

"Says wear the gray slacks. You jacket she got hung up here by the door."

"I believe I can dress myself, Thelma."

"You believe is right. Thass why Laura Anne took kere of it."

He met a ravishing woman at Ramona's. She was tall and athletic. A strapless gown bared a back that rippled like sand on a copper desert. Her hair was pinned with a turquoise clasp. Broad shoulders narrowed to a waist that Barrett could still hold in his hands.

She was still Barrett's homecoming queen.

"You all right?"

He could tell she was nervous.

"I don't know. I thought about dressing like a dyke. But then I don't really have a suit. And then the girls said I should play something on the piano—

"How do I look, Bear?"

"Make a train take a dirt road."

She laughed. He took her hand.

"They'll be eating out of your hand."

"I'm bringing Thurman Shaw along, anyway. Just so they stay out of my pocket."

The gathered investors and banker were eating from Laura Anne's hand. You'd think that a banker from Atlanta and venture capitalists from Boulder would be jaded to local experience, but they couldn't keep their eyes off Laura Anne.

"We see your business as the hub for a much larger project," a corpulent investor mumbled over hush puppies. "We've already got options for land along the beach. The county's bringing in another road—"

"They *are?*"

"They will." A banker smiled with that correction. "They will, believe me."

The chatter went on. Barrett was so proud of his wife he could burst. She had created this opportunity. It was from her sacrifice, from dire necessity, that this triumph had come.

Everything was going great until they started talking about the money.

"Four hundred fifteen thousand I believe is what we were looking at?" A banker pulled out his laptop.

"Yes," Laura Anne answered. "Plus some participation."

"Points, yes. Have to be careful with those. Give away the farm if you're not careful."

"Or a restaurant." Thurman smiled benignly.

The banker sipped his tea.

"Fair enough. All right. Four hundred fifteen, five points of net . . . over twenty-five years."

"Excuse me?" Laura Anne interrupted firmly. "Twenty-five years? There has been no discussion of twenty-five years."

"In my deal notes." The banker displayed his laptop as if it were God.

"Mr. Sorenson, the discussions have always been geared around a flat buyout." Thurman turned to the table's kingpin. "In *my* deal notes with you, sir, the offer is very specific. Four hundred fifteen to own with a participation of five points net. With independent right to audit, of course."

Mr. Sorenson hailed from Atlanta. He kept a pleasant smile from across the table.

"Well, Freddy, why don't we see what we can do fuh these people?"

Barrett could see the first signs of a coming volcano in his wife.

"I believe you have the situation characterized awkwardly, Mr. Sorenson."

The businessman turned to Barrett.

"Sir?"

"The terms are clear. Laura Anne is not confused. Nor is her lawyer. Is there some reason you can't meet the payment, sir?"

He flushed beet red. The banker, "Freddy," spoke up.

"It's very common to have these details when a deal comes to closing . . ."

Laura Anne cut him off.

"Do you really suppose, Fred, that I came to this meeting to renegotiate an offer that was represented to me as *firm* months ago?"

An embarassed silence fell across the table.

"Our investors want to be certain we are not over-extended, that's all."

"Then tell your investors what your situation is," Laura Anne replied smoothly. "I am willing to listen to a buyout of four hundred fifteen thousand dollars. If you can't afford that, I'm certain you can't afford the lots and condos and the 'encouragement' necessary to get the county to build a new road in here."

More silence with Laura Anne's response. Freddy turned to his Atlanta fat cat.

Mr. Sorenson waved a soft hand. "We'll have to run this by our people."

Laura Anne's smile was never more radiant as she rose from the table.

"Please take your time. There's more snapper. I'll be at my piano. Thurman?"

"Be glad to remain with our guests." Thurman Shaw's sarcasm was never clearer.

Barrett rose to escort his wife from the table. She was shaking with anger.

"I'm so proud of you," Barrett whispered into her ear.

"Those bastards!"

"Yeah. But we ain't gonna show it, Laura Anne. We ain't gonna show those dicks anything but class." He escorted her to the piano. "How are you?"

She fought the barest tremble in her mouth.

"I've played under pressure before. This ain't no big thang."

From the time she launched Clementi's Sonatina in F major, every eye in the place riveted on Laura Anne Raines. Her skin was gold. On fire. And from the moment her hands touched the keys there wasn't a fork in the place that didn't fall still by its plate. Barrett passed their table on his way to the bar. He leaned over, briefly, to the startled banker.

"Freddy?"

"Oh, yes. Yes, Mr. Raines."

"When you get back to Atlanta? Gonna have to tell your investors that the price just went up."

The barest pressure from Bear's rock-hard hand into the damp fabric of his three-piece suit, and then Barrett was on to the bar. To take a seat. To hear his wife bring a swell of music to standing applause.

To hold her later that night. When she cried.

"You can still teach, honey. You've got some good managers now can keep up the restaurant. I can help."

"Not if you're running for sheriff."

He held her close.

"Family comes before dreams, Laura Anne. You had to make that choice once. Now it's my turn."

Fífteen

Barrett begged Friday off from work. There were already homicides stacked to take the place of Juanita Quiroga's and Hezikiah Jackson's. There were still migrants working for rigged wages. But Bear needed a break, so he took a long weekend off to be with Laura Anne and the boys.

They talked. They went to church. They put on a good face and began the business of getting over their recent disappointment. Barrett was puppy-hunting one Saturday when he rolled by the *Deacon Beach Herald*.

He drove past the paper, intially. Reconsidered. No point in putting it off. He doubled back.

"Any thieves at home?" Barrett called as he entered Pauline's inner sanctum.

"Barrett!"

She was editing her paper online.

"Good timing. I got something for you."

"Well, first I better tell you that I'm going to have to put off my ambitions for office."

"Ohhhh. I'm sorry to hear that."

He shrugged. "Opportunity for funding fell through. Can't know for sure if it was even real."

"I can't tell you how many times Bernie and I haven't been bought out." She saved her file, and then, briskly: "Now. The stories you asked me to review—"

"Oh, yes," Barrett replied with diminished enthusiasm. What difference did his sorry history make? It surely wasn't going to be used against him now.

"Hezikiah Jackson . . ."

Pauline left her high-tech computer for an antedeluvian machine mounted on a waist-high counter.

" 'Sixty-nine to 'seventy-one . . ."

She paused to focus a frame of microfiche in the scanner.

"Actually, I found two stories. Well. One story and one rumor."

Barrett rounded the counter.

"I did find your father's homicide covered in the paper. It was odd, reading it. I must have been in my twenties at the time. Nothing much to it. See for yourself."

Barrett leaned into the microfiche's viewer. A small-town paper came to life in garish black and white:

JULY 10, 1969.

A colored man, Randall Grant Raines, was killed in his home this past Saturday. Sheriff Pridgeon would not confirm the cause of death, but did confirm that Mrs. Ellen Raines had taken her husband's life in what the sheriff described as "a clear case of self-defense." No arrest was made.

Mr. Raines is survived by his wife and two sons.

An ache came unexpectedly to Barrett's chest.

"I'm sorry," Pauline said.

"It's all right."

"No, I mean the part about describing your father as a colored man. I don't mention race anymore, Bear."

"It's all right, Pauline. But I don't see anything about Hezikiah."

"Wasn't anything to see."

"No mention of her?"

246

"Not around your dad's demise, no."

So there was no one left to know. His mother was dead. Hezikiah. Even Barrett's brother never knew the truth.

"Thanks for checking." Barrett had not realized he was holding his breath.

"Hold your gear. I did find *something*. Not sure how it could possibly relate, but—"

"Go ahead." Barrett halted at the edge of the counter.

"Hezikiah was cited in regard to another murder. Very similar to yours—"

"Mine?"

"Your father's. Sorry. This other case involved the Pearsons. You know Jarold?"

"Yes. Helped us on the Loyd case. Big help, actually."

"Hmm. Well. His mother was murdered, you might recall."

"Yes. Father went to Raiford and hanged himself."

"That's right."

"What's it got to do with Hezikiah?"

"She was there."

Barrett's heart picked up a beat.

" 'Scuse me?"

"Hezikiah was on the scene, according to the story I got."

"What do you mean 'you got'? It's your paper, isn't it?"

"No. The killing actually occurred in Dixie County. Cross City paper carried the story. I remember because I could not get a thing out of Sheriff Sue myself. Just as in your situation he wouldn't talk specifics, only that the mother was killed, her husband was drunk on the scene and was arrested.

"The Cross City paper went quite a bit further in their column. 'Course, they'd print anything. They'd print a phone number off a shithouse wall if—"

"Pauline."

"Sorry. Anyway the Cross City paper went on about Hezikiah being a witch, and all that hokum. Talked about her second sight. She walked right in on the homicide, apparently. Why on earth she was there at that place or time was a little spooky. Jarold Pearson's daddy said he didn't do it . . ."

Barrett's heart was now hammering on anvils.

". . . but he was a mean, abusive son of a bitch, like your father. Any excuse would have been enough to set him off; it was his wife's bad luck to have given him a good one."

"An excuse for homicide?"

"By the lights of the time, yes." Pauline nodded primly. "Seems Jarold's mother was having an affair."

"Another rumor?"

"No. They were pretty blatant about it."

"And who were 'they,' Pauline?"

"Jarold's mother, of course. And Linton Loyd."

"Linton?"

"Oh, yes. Just about every time Jarold's father stepped out, Linton was stepping in. It was disgraceful the way he took advantage of that woman. Then Jarold's father would come home and beat her, of course. You know the cycle."

"Yes," Barrett managed to affirm.

"So I s'pose the sheriff wouldn't have had any trouble believing Hezikiah when she told him the father killed Jarold's mother."

"No. Not in that circumstance."

"Bear." Pauline eyed him closely. "Why are you interested in these stories? Do they relate to these latest homicides?"

Barrett eased himself up onto the counter.

"Let's just say I'm double-checking a source. The important thing is—it was Hezikiah's word that got Jarold's father sent to jail?"

248

Pauline affirmed with a shrug. "She was an eyewitness, after all. And knowing the father's history of violence and abuse, the sheriff probably figured justice was served."

"Justice." Barrett swallowed. "Right."

Something itched deep in the back of Barrett's broad skull. A dry papyrus wrapped about his tongue.

"Pauline, were there any details at all related to cause of death for Jarold's mother?"

"What was reported."

"I'll have to take it."

"All right, then. The local paper reported she was trussed to her bed. Her hair cut off. And disemboweled."

"Disem—?"

" 'Gutted like a deer' was the actual description, yes."

The hairs on the back of Barrett's neck bristled.

"Barrett. What *is* this all about?"

He swallowed. "Just one more question."

"Fine, then." She folded her arms.

"How did Jarold's wife die?"

"Accident, what he told me. She fell. Crushed her skull."

" 'Crushed'?"

"Fractured, anyway."

"Don't suppose you could give me some details?"

"No." Pauline shook her head. "Not unless I was willing to learn Spanish and go to Tegucigalpa."

"Teguci—?"

"Honduras, yes. Where she fell. Where he said she fell." Pauline paused.

"They were building a church."

A church. A cross.

Barrett ripped a stitch out of his blazer as he slid off her counter.

"I gotta run."

"The hell is this about, Barrett?" she demanded.

"If it's rumor, I can't tell you. But if it's fact—"

Barrett loped toward her door.

"—you'll be the first to know."

Barrett Raines burst out of the *Deacon Beach Herald* stabbing the pad of his cell phone.

"Cricket. Bear here. We may have a situation."

"Let's hear it."

Barrett summarized his conversation with Pauline.

"Are you headed where I think you're headed, partner?"

"It fits."

"Barrett. Dammit. You better be right."

"Well, if I'm wrong I'll just be an asshole. But if I'm right he'll kill again. And no telling who."

Laura Anne was glad to have the day off. She had wondered if her respite from work would be marred with rainfall, the latest front pushing down from Canada having met the Gulf's warm, moist atmosphere to trigger a deluge. But today there seemed no threat of precipitation. In fact, it was a beautiful day in northwestern Florida, one of those days when the sun comes out bright and gentle above a vault of clear blue sky. Seventy degrees. The middle of December and there were still redbirds singing.

Laura Anne could see one now on the grapevine behind her garage. It gave her comfort. She had decided it was pointless to brood over the failed sale of her restaurant. Barrett was off work. So was she. It was a good time for the family to pack up in Bear's restored muscle machine and hide for a long weekend in Fort Walton. Maybe do some Christmas shopping on the sly. She had already snugged down the Malibu's convertible top in anticipation of the trip when Bear called to say he would be home soon. There was an edge to his voice that gave her some pause. Barrett had canceled vacations before when the Work called.

She hoped that was not the case this morning.

Laura Anne slipped a sweatshirt over her golden skin. It was big as a tent—covered her arms and fell past her waist. She tucked her feet into sneakers. No need for socks. She would finish the laundry, go to the Scout Lodge to pick up Ben and Tyndall. Then the Raines family would hit the road in their Malibu for a badly needed retreat.

The screen door opened.

"Bear?" She turned.

A familiar man stood in her back door.

Jarold Pearson took off his spotless Stetson hat.

"Mornin', Laura Anne. May I come in?"

Barrett called dispatch for Fish & Wildlife, hoping to get a fix on Jarold's location. Jarold's office, after all, covered several hundred square miles. But maybe Bear would get lucky. Maybe the warden had the day off. Maybe he'd be at home. Jarold might even be manning the dispatch himself.

No, the lady on the end of the line was terse. Lieutenant Pearson had not called in. Would not be in for several days. Would the agent like to leave a message?

Barrett was composing a neutral pretext for suggesting a meeting in Mayo as he called home. He couldn't remember if it was his job to pick up the boys from Scouts.

The phone rang, rang. The message machine kicked in. Barrett waited. Laura Anne was home, he knew she was, getting ready for their pre-Christmas holiday. But he wasn't surprised that she didn't immediately answer the phone. They both used the answering machine to screen calls.

"Laura Anne, it's me, pick up."

A beep on the line. Then silence.

"Dammit."

But maybe she was outside. Maybe *she* was getting the boys. Barrett was about to try again when an incoming call buzzed over his phone.

"Barrett Raines?"

The voice was strained and familiar.

"Speaking, who's this?"

"Rolly Slade."

"Rolly?"

"You gave me yer number, Bear."

That's right. He had.

"What's up, Rolly? What can I do for you?"

"First off, I want to thank you for clearing my boy of them killins."

"The evidence cleared your son, Rolly. Doesn't mean he's out of the woods on those other charges."

"I know that, I know."

"Anything else?" Barrett tried not hide his impatience.

"Well, there is one other thing. Prob'ly not important. But because of that *first* time—"

"Rolly, just tell me what it is."

"Well, Bear, you won't believe this, but—somebody's done gone and took my other dog."

"Your—your dog."

"My rottweiler," came the whining confirmation. "Somebody took him. Right after lunch."

Barrett cut the connection and slammed the accelerator to the floor. A litany of horrifying possibilities raced through his mind. He called home again.

"Answer me, hon. Goddammit, pick up!"

Laura Anne regained consciousness in Jarold Pearson's Willys Jeep.

"Rise and shine."

A rock road jarred her painfully.

"Ah!"

A headache. Her hands raised on instinct to nurse the lump behind her ear.

Something bright and shining jerked them short.

Handcuffs. Laura Anne gasped, still dizzy, to realize that she was handcuffed through the loop of gripbar welded on the dashboard of Jarold Pearson's Jeep. A wrap of duct tape trapped the calves of her naked legs.

"Good morning."

That skull! Pressed with an unnatural forceps. The eyes almost seeming to touch across its thin bridge of cartilage.

"What are you—? What am I doing here? Jarold?"

She tried to keep the pleading out of her voice. A sudden wave of nausea struck.

"Don't you do," he warned. "Puke in my Jeep, you're gonna clean it up."

A growl behind her brought ice to Laura Anne's skin. She turned her head painfully to the bed of the Willys. A massive chain ran through eyebolts and a collar to pin the biggest dog she'd ever seen to the Jeep's steel floor.

She looked outside. Nothing but an endless expanse of palmetto and pine.

"Where . . . where are you taking me?"

He laughed.

"That is the question, isn't it, Laura Anne? That will be the question on everybody's lips. For now."

He eyed her.

"But there'll be more later. I guaran-goddamn-tee."

Barrett Raines came home to find the screen door banging back and forth, flimsily, open to the breeze. A basket of laundry was spilled by the sink. There was fresh blood on the floor.

"Oh, Jesus! Oh, Jesus, God!"

For the space of seconds Barrett Raines was not a competent lawman, but a terrified and irrational husband.

He would later curse the five or six seconds it took him to regain the presence of mind necessary to dial 911.

"This is Agent Raines." His breathing was as labored as a long distance runner's. "My wife's been kidnapped. The suspect is armed, ruthless, and extremely dangerous. Yes, I do. He is the county game warden. That's right—it's Lieutenant Jarold Pearson."

The urgency attending the manhunt for Laura Anne Raines made the search for Gary Loyd seem an Easter-egg hunt by comparison. There were straws of hope at which to clutch. Bear was lucky enough to have discovered his wife's abduction within minutes of the kidnapping. There were plenty of witnesses who saw Jarold Pearson come to town in his Jeep; that time was fixed. Rolly even admitted that Jarold had visited the shop. "But I didn't see him take my dog!"

At least two persons, however, did see a large black dog leashed or restrained in some manner in the bed of Jarold's Jeep.

"He wants to get caught," Cricket told Barrett. "He's not hiding anything."

"He's hiding my wife!"

A pair of helicopters came in from the highway patrol to aid the ground search. The sheriff even garnered a separate pair of choppers from the national guard.

"Thanks, Lou," Barrett thanked him numbly.

"Don't lose hope, Bear. *She* won't."

The marine patrol had every boat they could get on the water. The coast guard weighed in.

"They got his boat," Cricket reported. "The bird dog. So he's probably still in the Jeep and on land. Most likely."

"Likely." Barrett felt sick. "Jesus."

Cricket had Thelma take the boys straight to her trailer.

"Just tell them their mother's lost for now. And that we will find her."

Cricket turned to his partner.

"You ought to go home, Bear. We can keep you in touch there."

"No." Barrett pushed off the sagging couch. "Get me a vehicle. I'm going on the ground."

"Bear, he could be anywhere."

"He could. But you said yourself, he's gone brazen. He's out in the open. Hasn't bothered to hide a thing. He *wants* to get caught, you said so yourself, Cricket. And Midge told us, too, remember? From the very outset she said this bastard wanted to get caught."

"So she did."

"So let's oblige the son of a bitch."

"Do you have any idea *where?*"

"The first place. The most obvious place. The place where he'd figure it would hurt Laura Anne, and me, the most."

The wind rushing past helped eased the pain in Laura Anne's head. Helped her stay alert. She glanced to the road ahead. To the side. There was no one. No hunter out for deer. No pulp-wooder. Only a game warden with murder on his mind. Still—somebody might hear. Some hunter off the beaten track. *"Killer!"* Laura Anne screamed. Jarold slapped her casually across the mouth. Stars floated in front of her eyes. She threw up, finally, all over herself and the Jeep.

"Time we're through you'll eat it off the floor," he promised.

"Why me?" she panted. "What have I ever done to you, Jarold?"

"Ask your fucking husband."

Then she knew. She remembered.

His mama took a fright. Rolled sideways.

Jarold inspected his narrow skull briefly in the Jeep's rearview. "Long as it was whites made fun, I could manage. Least I knew I wasn't on the bottom of the pile. But when the only damn nigger on the bus can shit you to your face—!"

Laura Anne turned to him desperately.

"God's sake, Jarold, you were boys when that happened! Boys!"

"Not a boy, now, though am I?"

Laura Anne tried to clear her head.

"What about Hezikiah? Or Juanita, or Gary? Did they *all* hurt you, Jarold? Surely they didn't. They couldn't!"

The game warden spit.

"Used the boy to git his daddy. Goddamn Linton. Been taking his shit for years. And then he comes out here, in *my* woods! With that Mexican whore."

He turned hard off the rock road to sand.

"They'd run out three, four trucks full of men at a time. Take 'em to Hezikiah's place. Get 'em drunk or crazy on whatever weed that witch was smoking, pay a hundred, two hundred dollars apiece to get tied up to a post, or have their pale asses whipped. Let the whore do it to 'em. Or tie her up and do it to her.

"They'd be screamin', hollerin'. You'd've thought it was a damn revival. Linton with his camera takin' pictures. Dollin' 'em up. Like some kinda Hollywood director. And then he sells the whole mess over the Internet. For perverts. For kids."

Jarold shook his plate-narrow head.

"A woman dirties everything she touches. Mama was like that. She had long nails? Always dirty. Always filthy with dirt underneath."

He spread a hand on the steering wheel to inspect his

own nails. Reached then for the reassurance of the Boy Scout knife at his belt.

"Daddy'd be gone working, Mama'd call Linton to the house, jump him at the door. They knew I was watchin'. They wanted me to. Those nails. Time they got through, he looked like he'd screwed a bobcat.

"So first chance I got, I took care of my mama. Yessiree bob. Was a long time 'til the next one. And then my wife. Then I figured it was about time to let the sins of the father visit the son, so I took Rolly's dog and Linton's whore to that shanty by the pond and we made us some *real* pictures."

His squashed head lowered briefly as he fished a camera from beneath the seat of his Jeep.

"Wish I could tell you this is the original picture-taker, but it's not. I saved everything from the hammock on my first camera, but I knew Bear'd be wantin' to find some original footage, so I gave up my camera. Put it inside Gary's Humvee. So this thing here is not my original picture-taker. It's bought special.

"Just for you."

"Oh, Jesus." Laura Anne threw up again.

Jarold dropped the Nikon to cup her breast.

"No!" She jerked away.

His lips curled as if he had sucked a lemon. The Jeep downshifted into a muddy rut.

"Hadn't been easy, layin' this off. Gary was a problem from the start. Boy knew *he* hadn't killed anybody. Hell, he hadn't even screwed the whore. But he kept asking questions: How long had I known about the shack by the pond? How many times had I got into Strawman's Hammock? That kinda thing. Then he started talkin' to Hezikiah.

"Hezikiah. Now, there's a piece of work. You can hardly kill anybody without that old woman showing up. She was there when I was finishing Mama. You know that? Damn woman walked right in on us. Took the knife out of my hand. Told me if I'd fuck her, she'd lie for me.

"It was like putting my dick in a pile of shit, but she made me do it."

He wrenched the wheels savagely.

"Sheriff comes out to the house, she put it all off on Daddy, just like she said, but I was always nervous she'd get the itch to change her story. And then she saw me, at the end with the whore at the shack? She tried to tell me she hadn't seen anything, but I knew better. I saw the change in the light. I know a witch's shadow.

"So I took care of Hezikiah, and then I called Gary and told him I had some information on the case might possibly help his daddy. It was easy to meet him on the water. Get him drunk. After I killed him I went fishing. Hadn't been fishing in a long time."

Jarold slowed to negotiate a ditch filled with water. Laura Anne saw a snake hissing beneath the Jeep's tires. A moccasin. His mouth opened wide and white and full of venom.

Jarold spat.

"I could've killed Linton anytime I wanted. Killed Barrett, too, for that matter. We got a season on bear, you know."

He seemed to enjoy that pun hugely. Then became as somber as a mortician.

"But this way is better, don't you think? This way everybody knows what the Straw Man and the Bear are *really* like."

"You don't have to kill me, Jarold. I know what Barrett did was wrong. He does too! He'll admit it! He'll admit it publicly!"

"Think that would hurt him, do you?"

"Yes," she said fervently. "Yes, it would."

Jarold's smile broke wider than the cramped width of his eyes.

"So imagine how much worse he's gonna feel when he sees what I do to you."

Laura Anne knew then that there would be no appeasement. No remorse.

"He'll kill you," she said simply. "Badge or no, Barrett will come after you and kill you. With his bare hands, if he has to."

Jarold's smile split even wider.

"Guess that means you and me better get busy."

They left the sand road in a bone-jarring detour through a jungle of tangled growth. Laura Anne's head snapped forward into the windshield. Stars again.

She revived to find the world very still. It took Laura Anne precious moments to realize that she was alone in the Jeep, that Jarold was gone and that the Willys was parked and silent. She could hear the tick, tick, tick of the radiator. It took her a moment more to realize that Jarold's vintage vehicle was nosed within yards of some kind of dwelling.

She could see in the painful glare of bright sunshine a cypress shack. But it was circled incongruously with bright-yellow tape. Like an oversized Brownie ribboned for a birthday party. Then Laura Anne realized that this was the crime scene that had for so long consumed her husband's attention.

She turned painfully to see a pond behind her. Dense undergrowth all around. Jarold still nowhere in sight. The dog! She looked. Gone, too. Then a growl rising from inside the shack that made her shiver.

"Stay still, you dick." The command came muffled with the slap of something hard on flesh. A howl of fury and anger.

If he got her into that cabin, Laura Anne knew, she was worse than dead. She tugged in sudden desperation on her handcuffs. The cuffs were looped through the dashboard's handgrip. Laura Anne slowed her heart, her mind. She only needed to free one hand. The handgrip was plenty large enough to pull a handcuff through—if it were not encumbered with a hand.

But that meant she had to get one hand out of these steel bracelets. Laura Anne relaxed her hands, her arms. Barrett's sweatshirt rode long over her hands; the handcuffs were actually braceleted over that fabric. There might be something there. Laura Anne lowered her head as far as she could on the arm of her sweatshirt, put her teeth into the sweatshirt's stiff cotton, and jerked up hard to expose her flesh.

The shack rocked with a fresh fury. She saw a shuttered window open, then close.

Laura Anne's arms and hands were slick with vomit. It was that sick mess that gave her hope. With the fabric pulled from beneath the handcuff there was now some slight play between the steel keepers and her exposed hand. She made her hand as small as she could and pulled, pulled against those steel hoops. Pulled with all her might.

It felt as though her hand were being cut from her wrists. But she felt some concession on one side through a fire of pain. Some give. She bit her tongue to keep from screaming and jerked hard.

The hand came free! It was cut and bleeding, but it was free! Laura Anne quickly pulled the still-closed bracelet on its short chain through the loop of the dashboard grip. She gathered the empty cuff into her still-cuffed hand. If it came to close quarters she would have a weapon. Of sorts.

There was a lull of quiet in the shack. Would she have time?

Laura Anne used the handcuff's chain to start a tear in the duct tape that bound her calves.

That was easy.

She slipped over to the steering wheel. It was a starter button! A regular vintage starter. But Jarold had an ignition rigged for the Willys. And he had the key.

If Laura Anne were a car thief she might try hot-wiring the ignition. But she wasn't a thief. What she was, was injured, sick, and terrified.

Laura Anne stumbled from the driver's side of Jarold's Jeep and stumbled dizzily for the shelter of the woods. Her legs were jelly at first. But then adrenaline kicked in its blessed benediction. And anger.

Briars and brambles cut her legs like barbed wire as she broke into a ragged run. She ran anyway. She was thirty yards into an utter blind of vegetation by the time Jarold Pearson had his dog settled. She had torn another thirty yards into the bush before he came from the shack for his prize and found it gone.

"You *biiiiitch!*"

She heard his angry scream.

"I'll gut you, whore! I'll cut your fucking guts!"

"Not without a fight . . ."

She panted it over and over, with legs and lungs on fire. And then she saw it, just a flake of flint exposed in the understory's damp earth. She dropped to a knee.

It was an arrowhead. One of many to be found in the region of the mound near Hezikiah's shack. Laura Anne snatched that artifact from the sand. A good four inches of shaped stone. Something she could use to cut, to punch, to puncture. Laura Anne gripped her found weapon tightly.

"Not without a fight, Jarold," she vowed and rose from the sandy floor.

He'd have to find her first. Even with a Jeep it would not be easy. She would not go where it was easy. Laura Anne knew that if she could just hold on she could outrun that grouper-headed son of a bitch. There weren't many men anywhere she couldn't outrun.

But then the hoarse challenge of an angry animal floated over the tangled underbelly of the hammock, and her heart quaked.

Could she outrun a dog?

They were hurtling down a sand road at seventy miles an hour.

"Faster, Cricket," Barrett grated.

The sheriff's cruiser was not ideal for touring the flatwoods, but no other vehicle was readily available to Barrett and his partner.

"Besides, if he's taken her to the shack, it'll do," Barrett said as he accepted the sheriff's offer of his police-packaged sedan.

Cricket gunned around a tight curve, keeping the back end from breaking away. Heel and toe, heel and toe. Straight again and back to seventy. Barrett unlimbered the twelve-gauge from its hold and was loading buckshot.

"How much of a headstart you think Jarold's got?"

"Can't be much over a half hour," Cricket answered.

Barrett steadied himself on the dash.

"Jesus, Cricket. What if he's killed her?"

"Barrett, he thinks he's got plenty of time. He couldn't have counted on you coming home early. He doesn't want to kill her. Not right away."

Barrett squelched the car's radio.

"You told everybody to stay off the police channel?"

"They know, Bear. They've got phones."

"Turnoff's just ahead."

"I got it."

"Faster, Cricket. Jesus! Get this bitch in gear."

Sixteen

Cricket slid the cruiser in a controlled skid to the space between pines leading to the wandering track that terminated on the site of Juanita's horrible death. The Crazy Canuck gunned the cruiser along a path marked previously with crime-scene tape. Next thing Barrett knew, pine trees were flashing by his window like a picket fence.

"Keep her coming, Cricket. Don't let up."

Jarold Pearson stood cursing at his Jeep. He had a rottweiler when he needed a hound. A hound could track the bitch in no time. But then—Jarold was no slouch at tracking himself.

It just took a little time.

"Easy, dog."

He would lead Rolly's dog to her. She would be running. Bleeding and scared. Scented with sick and scared. Exactly the kind of behavior and smell that triggered an aggressive response from the animal he had leashed in his hand.

"Find you first," the warden promised his quarry. "Then you get the dog."

A pair of tracks were easy to spot, in the soft earth beside his vehicle. He kneeled and drew a bead from that intial indicator to the bramble beyond. A vine of black-berries was trampled ten yards away where she entered the thicket.

"There you go." His smile was without mirth. "Come on, dog."

This bad boy was strong! Concerned about losing the leash, Jarold slipped its loop over his wrist and gave it a couple of tight wraps. Even so he had to lean back on the dog's leash to keep from being hauled off his feet. He broke into a jog. The dog fell in easily.

Jarold tossed aside his hat, loosened his tie. He was calmer now. He knew he could find her. He could tell that Laura Anne was literally tearing a path that led away from the lake and directly into the heart of the hammock. There were no exits in there. Jarold actually smiled. So he'd be hunting this morning. And without a limit!

A mirthless laugh boiled with anger.

"Come on, dog." He stepped up the pace. "Let's get us some meat."

Barrett and Cricket slid Session's cruiser through a cordon of yellow tape and practically into the shack that Jarold Pearson used to torture and kill Juanita Quiroga. Barrett spotted Jarold's Jeep and was out of the cruiser before it had fully stopped, barging into the shack's open door with a shotgun leveled.

"FDLE, get your fucking hands . . . !"

Moments later he came out cursing.

"No sign?" Cricket covered from the car.

"He was here. Goddamn it!" Barrett cursed. "LAURA ANNE?! LAURA ANNE!"

No reply. But then they heard that heavy, punctuated bark. Distantly. In the woods.

"Was that—?"

The dog again, the deep, throaty lust of a rottweiler.

"That's him!" Barrett was running like a fullback into the thicket. "He's taking her into the hammock!"

Laura Anne's lungs boiled. She paused, fighting to find air. Her head was splitting.

"Oh, God." She leaned heavily on a pine tree's slender pillar. "I don't care if I starve. Die of thirst. Just don't let this man take me."

God did not answer her prayer, and for a brief moment there was silence in the hammock. Then she heard it, the muffled challenge of the beast behind.

"He's . . . not a hound." She staggered into a palmetto barrens. "I'm . . . upwind . . . long as . . . he can't see me!"

She ran into the stunted palmettos, loping with lungs on fire, deeper and deeper into the hammock. But her strides became shorter. The hammer in her head would not quit.

"Oh, God!"

She fell on her knees and vomited.

Laura Anne cried for the first time. She had a concussion, she knew. And it would not let her run. She was going to have to find another way. Some other way to hide, or to fight.

The rottweiler's rough bark came again: *rope-rope. Rope-rope.* Like Morse code from the hammock.

He was closer. Which meant that Jarold Pearson was closer.

"I'm walkin' the Valley, Lord!" Laura Anne rose limping this time, looking for she knew not what, hoping for salvation in the unforgiving terrain ahead. The arrowhead that earlier had given her a shred of confidence seemed woefully inadequate now. Its serrated edge cut into her uncuffed hand.

* * *

Barrett and Cricket could see the fresh signs of Jarold's trail. They could hear the dog.

"Oh . . . Baby!"

Barrett could barely breathe, but he would not stop. Laura Anne would not stop. She wouldn't quit. Bear cursed himself for being in such lousy shape, for giving up his runs along the beach, his bouts with the heavy bag. He cursed himself for cigarettes, for beer—

He had to keep running, he had to keep running.

Barrett's legs felt like blocks of wood. The shotgun weighed like a log in his hand. The tendons over his shoulders burned into his neck like strands of heated wire.

He kept on running.

"Laura Anne . . . Laura Anne!"

Jarold Pearson could not tell whether he was gaining on his quarry, but her trail had begun to wander, had become more erratic. She had to be tired, bitch. Lick on the head and sick, she shouldn't be able to run at all.

The dog was pulling him along the path now, whining eagerly, sensing the game that was well afoot.

Then Jarold saw something, the slightest sway of mulberry from a limb ahead. It might be a squirrel, chasing. Or a bird.

"Come on, dog!"

He broke into a run, plummeted through a stand of palmetto and past a thin boundary of scrub oak to a stand of mature yellowheart pine.

There she was. There was the wife of the man he had hated for years, not forty feet away. Sprawled out like a sick puppy, those long legs spent, just waiting for him in a clearing that spread damply between the pines. She looked up. Those big eyes. Like a deer. And then she began to crawl, a handcuff clutched in one still-cuffed hand. And in the other hand—what was that? What was brandished there? What pitiful weapon?

Then he recognized the flint-hard point.

"My, my," he wheezed. "Kitty's done found a claw."

"Don't . . . you come . . . near me!"

Oh, this was good! He laughed. This was better than he had hoped.

She was crawling on elbows and knees now. Crawling to get away.

"Ain't you a sorry sight?"

He was surprised she had gotten this far. She could barely breathe. He wondered what she'd look like with that sweatshirt off. That glossy skin covered with puke and mud.

"Just keep your black ass where it is," he commanded. "It's just a little time, now. And it'll all be done."

But then to his amazement she pulled to her feet and began to run.

"Git her, dog!"

The rottweiler jerked Jarold like a toy across the short divide that separated him from the panting, helpless target beyond.

Laura Anne offered a labored scream.

Jarold shouted like a cowboy. He had her now! He had her! But then the dog lunged and Jarold felt the earth give way suddenly beneath his sure foot.

"The fuck?"

He was floundering waist-deep before he saw what she had done.

But it was too late.

"*Dog!* Dog, *back to me!*"

But the dog kept churning, churning. He was trying to swim. Not a bad thing to try. Either spread out and try to float, or, if you can, swim.

"*Bitch!*"

The leash was still wrapped tight around his hand. And

as the dog churned, Jarold was pulled after him. Farther into the mire. Farther.

"Dog!"

Jarold scrambled to retrieve the knife in his belt, the Boy Scout knife that had been so useful to him, so very useful, in so many situations before. But it took precious seconds to retrieve that tool from its pouch. Seconds more to fit a thumbnail now slick with filth into the indentation of steel that would allow him to open the blade. His nail slipped off that shallow flange. Slipped again.

"Bitch!"

Jarold used his teeth to open the jackknife.

"Fuck you!"

He pulled a well-honed blade across the nylon leash. The dog lurched inches ahead, as if trying to swim in a barrel of butter. His pink mouth filled now with mud. A snarl turned into a choke. And then the rottweiler's flat skull dipped into the bog. An angry howl strangled. He came up with a whimper. Once more, briefly, paws churning. Then down again. That sucking sound. Like a swig of cherry cola.

"Bitch! Wait 'til I get . . . hold of you!"

Jarold was chest-deep and sinking. He tried to turn around. Tried to backtrack.

"Shit!"

Up to his neck, now. Up to his neck in deep, deep shit.

"Gemme . . . gemme outta here. Bitch . . . ! Gemme out!"

She tossed the arrowhead aside.

"I will fear no evil . . ."

Laura Anne edged back to the boundary of the bog. A pine limb no thicker than her wrist stretched across the mire. Jarold saw it, too. A lifeline not three feet away. Just out of reach.

". . . for Thou art with me."

Laura Anne stretched on her belly to find a purchase on that slender tether.

". . . Thy rod . . . and Thy staff . . ."

"Cunt!" His chin mopped the liquid earth.

"Oh, *God!*"

She snatched the pole away.

Barrett came crashing through the scrub minutes later. He saw his wife ashen and covered with mud and blood, propped up beside the stump of a fallen yellowheart.

"Laura Anne!"

Her head jerked up. *"Quicksand!"*

Barrett skidded to a stop. He saw, now, what Laura Anne had used to disguise the bog.

It was straw. Years and years of pine straw had accumulated from countless sheddings of fat-hearted pine trees onto the hammock's damp floor. That straw floated now at the boundary of the quagmire, a gentle, golden camouflage. But Barrett could see as clearly as you could see ruts in a sand road where a man and a dog trailing into the sucking mud had cleared a path through a needle-thin veneer.

"Okay. I see. Just stay where you are, honey!"

She was too spent to acknowledge.

A bubble broke languidly from the bowels of the mire. It burst slowly, like bubblegum. *Plop!*

Barrett backed carefully away.

"I'll go around."

Laura Anne refused to spend that evening in the hospital, and the doctor at the ER, showing remarkable common sense, agreed.

"She should see somebody with experience in counseling victims of trauma," the young M.D. told Barrett. "The physical wounds aren't what we need to be concerned about so much as the inevitable confusion, anger, or fright that come afterward. I understand you're in law enforcement?"

"Yes," Barrett answered.

"So you will be required to undergo some counseling, won't you? In the aftermath of this situation?"

Barrett had not thought about that.

"I s'pose I will," he said.

"You should," the young woman directed. "And I would strongly advise that your wife see the same group of counselors. She needs to see someone who is used to helping victims of violent crime. I could give you the name of a local psychologist, but I can tell you that anyone who routinely helps cops get over the trauma of a shooting will be better suited than anyone here to help your wife overcome the aftermath of her kidnapping—and the fact that she was forced to take a man's life."

"But for now we can take her home?

"Mr. Barrett, home is the best place either one of you could be."

Epilogue

In the wake of Laura Anne's abduction, all charges of homicide against Linton Loyd were dropped. Laura Anne's statement was pivotal in attaining that result since she was able to report Jarold Pearson's unequivocal admission of responsibility for the deaths of Juanita Quiroga, Hezikiah Jackson, and Gary Loyd.

Once released, Loyd accepted his reversal of fortunes in his usual style, threatening the county and state with suits of harrassment, violation of civil rights, and false arrest, all of which actions were dropped when Roland Reed, to Barrett's great chagrin, agreed to forgo charging Linton with civil rights violations against the workers in his dummy-held company. Thurman Shaw reduced that promise to writing. Roland signed with his platinum-plated tool and within the hour the paterfamilias of the Loyd family walked free and clear from the courthouse to embrace a forest of waiting microphones and cameras. He cozened Stacy Kline and Channel 7 first.

"Except for the death wish of a sociopath and sheer luck, I would still be in jail for three counts of homicide. Three chances at the death penalty! This case ought to demonstrate to anyone concerned about justice in this county that the time is long come for us to find and elect a new sheriff. And then we need to give that entire office an enema and start over."

Linton's chutzpah was greatly diminished in effect when Elizabeth took her turn in front of reporters to announce that within the week she would file for a divorce from her husband.

"That's justice?" Barrett grunted. "Seems to me Linton got off cheap."

Cricket didn't see it that way.

"He's a pariah, Bear. You think his customers aren't gonna find somebody else to get their tractors and fertilizer from? You think anybody's gonna want to hunt on his lease?"

"Someone will," Barrett predicted. "Someone always will."

"I see in the *Herald* there's a service planned for Hezikiah Jackson. Another First Baptist Church."

Cricket Bonet eyed his partner. Bear did not reply.

"If you don't mind me asking, Bear—what was it about that old woman made you go to the newspaper office in the first place? How'd you ever get the idea to look for a history there?"

Barrett kept his eyes in his coffee.

"I dropped by to price some cards that would announce my run for sheriff. Pauline and I started talking about the case, about Hezikiah . . . Just luck, really."

Cricket didn't budge.

"Something you'd rather not share, Barrett, just tell me. But don't bullshit me."

"You're right." Barrett met his partner's eye. "It is personal. But it's not relevant. And I don't want to talk about it."

Cricket spread his freckled hands wide.

"No problem, pard. Now. How about Laura Anne? Is she getting over this thing?"

"Getting there."

The truth that Barrett did not amplify for his partner was that both he and Laura Anne were struggling to overcome the effects of her ordeal. The first day or two Laura Anne seemed to be doing fine. No obvious fears. Some restlessness but no reported nightmares or obsessions. But then one morning, Laura Anne came to the breakfast table looking sapped. Barrett recognized the signs—the bags under the eyes, the head dipped low over her coffee.

"Baby?" He took her hand over untouched cereal.

She was crying. "I've got the wearies," she said.

"Oh, Lord."

He pulled up a chair beside her.

"You got to remind yourself that you beat him, Laura Anne. You beat him. Hang on to that. You beat him. He's dead. He can't hurt you or me or any of us anymore."

"I know that," she sniffed. "That's not what's bothering me. I don't think. But I *do* keep thinking—"

"Go ahead."

"No, it's unfair. It really is. It's terribly unfair and simplistic and—everything else."

"You're allowed, Laura Anne. Go on."

She turned to him, eyes brown as coffee.

"Well, I just keep thinking—why did you have to tease that beast of a man? 'Grouper Head.' 'Fish Head.' All the things you used to say to taunt Jarold Pearson on that miserable bus. Why did you do that, Bear? You of all people?"

His throat ached.

"I was young."

"So was he." She turned away. "And I can't help thinking if you had just been decent to that man—even once— Jarold Pearson wouldn't have hit me, and tied me, and *humiliated* me—"

She cried, now. Open sobs.

"And taken me to that horrible, horrible place!"

Barrett's stomach tied into knots.

"I'm sorry, Laura Anne."

He reached to hold her. She tucked her arms into her housecoat and Barrett remained in misery as he watched the woman he loved cry tears to warm her coffee.

The FDLE offered to pay for a psychologist to help Laura Anne through the aftermath of her ordeal. She would not miss a day of school, so the first session was scheduled for a Friday afternoon, in Tallahassee. Barrett drove her. The celebrations of Christ's birth and all the trappings and demands of Christmas lay only days ahead, and Laura Anne seemed determined to put Jarold Pearson behind her in that space of time. The psychologist, an older woman from Fort Meyers, explained to Laura Anne that her timetable was unrealistic and that her quick-fix strategy was likely to backfire, but Laura Anne would have none of it.

"Slaves used to get whipped, lose their husbands, their children, and be back cutting cane or picking cotton the very next day. I have grandmamas and great grandmamas who have told me stories. Way you get over hurt is to work, what my people tell me. They did it. They bore it. If they could, I can."

Barrett watched, helpless and filled with guilt, as Laura Anne sanded the scars of her experience like a carpenter smoothing a fire-damaged cabinet. He would give anything to retract the boyhood cruelty that led to his wife's ordeal. But he could not afford to wallow in his own guilt; Laura Anne needed him, shamed him with her determination, and so Barrett displayed an outward mein of cheer and optimism. He spent a lot of time washing dishes and folding laundry. Made Laura Anne pots of coffee. Threw a lot of footballs to the boys. The Raineses would not go to Fort Walton this year. The top was pulled back tight on the Malibu. It had turned too cold for convertibles.

Barrett tried to approach the coming season of light with thanksgiving for his wife's survival and with gratitude for the twins and Thelma and family. Captain Altmiller gave him all the time he needed. And even after Barrett ran through his sick leave and vacation, Cricket Bonet worked double shifts to let his partner remain with his healing wife and their two untouched sons.

Cricket was surprised, therefore, when at a quarter to eight the morning of Christmas Eve, Barrett shouldered his beefy frame into the crowded hall carved out of the disco that was now the Live Oak field office for the Florida Department of Law Enforcement.

"The hell you doing here, partner?"

"Got a fax I want to send on FDLE letterhead," Barrett replied. "Wanted to make sure it got logged before the holidays."

"Who's it to?"

"FBI, with a cc to our people and the justice department," Barrett replied. "I've got statements from probably twenty workers who will testify that Linton Loyd has used extortion and intimidation to deny them jobs or fair wages. I've cited five civil rights violations that fall under federal jurisdiction."

"Linton will shit. Roland will shit."

"Roland needs to shit or get off the pot. We don't bust our ass finding criminals to make his life easy. He doesn't want to go after Linton—fine. Doesn't mean the feds can't."

"Merry Christmas." Cricket accepted the fax with a smile.

"When you getting off?"

"Noon," Cricket replied.

"We expect you at the house," Barrett said. "Boys are counting on it."

Barrett left his Viking companion to shut down the Live Oak field office. Laura Anne was waiting for him in the car.

"That didn't take long," she said.

"No." He pressed her hand.

They drove home, clearing first the crushed rock that was the field office's parking lot, turning right on Martin Luther King Jr.'s seldom-mentioned drive to shortly pass the old firehouse that was jerry-rigged to serve as offices for Live Oak's municipal police. They cattle-gapped over a set of railroad tracks that led past a train station no longer in use, rolled through a downtown hung poorly with lights and tinsel. Past the Dixie Grill. Then they swapped over to Highway 53. Only a minute or two more and they glided by the new brick homes marking the town's western limit. Then they were in open land, farmland, stretching in sections on either side.

Another hard freeze had wreathed the region in a blanket of frost. It clung now to kudzu and cattails with democratic tenacity and hung like lace on the grasses crowding the battered blacktop road. The fields rolling by were mostly fallowed for winter. A patch or two of winter rye glowed emerald green to contrast the brown defeat of other pasture. Circular bales of hay were stacked along fencelines like enormous rolls of tissue paper. Cattle grazed indolently.

There was no visible labor. There were dairies, certainly, where no holiday preempts work, where boys and fathers rise early year round. Cows have to be milked. But there was no sign of that labor. One or two chickenhouses recently unloaded could be seen. A few horses sipped water within sight of the road from a pond or tank. But Laura Anne and Bear saw not a single person at labor this close to Christmas. No crazed shoppers on this stretch of road. No traffic jams to confuse the season of reflection.

It took about a half hour to reach the Hal W. Adams Bridge. A single guard waved lazily from the weighing station. There were no tractor-trailer rigs stopped for inspection this morning, no produce from Pittsburg or Wal-Mart. But there was a styrofoam Santa Claus mounted in a plywood sleigh, his mittened hand raised in congregation with the solitary guard, his cargo exempt from the measure of idle scales.

Past that archaic checkpoint rose the bridge itself. Frost clung like a cake's icing to the bahaya that grassed the broadly shouldered approach. The cables suspending the bridge seemed to pull them onto its careful arc, high and taut and silver, and within seconds they were high over the Suwannee. They could see the slow, majestic turn of the river below, its dark water stained with iron and calcium and other minerals. They were almost exactly halfway over the bridge when Laura Anne pointed straight over the Impala's beige hood.

"Barrett. Look."

A deer straddled the road at the bridge's terminus. A magnificent Virginia whitetail. No other vehicle approached to hazard the buck. None behind. Barrett slowed his unmarked sedan to a crawl and stopped, finally, not ten steps away from the wild animal's unblinking gaze.

He had the notion that his soul was opened to inspection before those large, liquid eyes.

"You feel that?" he asked huskily.

"Oh, yes," she replied.

Barrett reached to press his palm to the car's horn.

Laura Anne stayed his hand with her own.

"Barrett?"

"Yes, Laura Anne?"

"Did you kill your father?"

So she knew. Someone, he realized then, would always know.

"Yes." He settled his hands to his lap. "I did."

She turned away from him.

"Will it ever quit feeling dirty?"

"If you didn't have a conscience, it wouldn't feel dirty at all. Still—you need to remind your better angels that there is a time to kill. You took Jarold's life because he forced you. You didn't seek to do it. You didn't want to do it, except in the moment when you *had* to make yourself. And that's what's hard, Laura Anne. That moment. Because, in the moment, you have to *want* to do it. And the wanting-to is what you remember. What makes you feel dirty."

"I see."

"But you had to do it, Laura Anne. For yourself. For your family. And so did I."

She sighed, then. A deep melancholy exhalation. The handsome buck tossed a widespread rack of antlers, eight points flashing white as ivory.

"Isn't he beautiful?" she asked languidly.

"Yes."

Probably only a second or two more passed. And then, abruptly, the deer wheeled and bounded once, twice, to clear a five-foot fence that bordered the road, and disappeared somewhere onto the land that clung like a lover's hand to the flanks of the river.

"And innocent," she murmured, turning back to face her husband. "The land is always innocent."

Barrett blinked hard.

"Yes."

He eased his unmarked sedan off the bridge and onto the waiting farm-to-market road. They rolled quietly through the sleepy little town of Mayo, past the renovated courthouse and a frost-white lawn to follow a road straight as string. A half hour due west. A ribbon of sky showed through the press of pines on either side. Barrett lowered his window; his nostrils flared with the fresh plunge of salt and sea wind.

Deacon Beach, straight ahead.

They were quiet all the way home.